THE SISTERS

ANNE LAMBTON

Coward, McCann & Geoghegan, Inc. New York

to Namet el-Hoss
with deep affection

THE SISTERS

Chapter One

The yacht *Maria,* of Lebanese registry, eighty meters long, lying low in the Atlantic swelled like a naval destroyer as it snored its way east toward Tangier, threw sheafs of brilliant sparkling water high over its sharp bow to rain back on beautifully kept teak decks.

Seated uneasily in the stern, not far from the edge of the deep mosaic-lined swimming pool, Jensen Blot watched the Lebanese master of the *Maria* as he sat in the noon sun, bald pate glistening, eyes shut tight, head thrown back, cadaverous unshaven cheeks soaking up sunshine.

It had been one hell of a yesterday for Blot, and even more for his wife, Elizabeth, now lying below in her stateroom with a twinge of nausea that everyone else thought to be mal de mer, but Jensen knew to be morning sickness. The doctor had seen no reason why Elizabeth, only in her third month of pregnancy, couldn't make the transatlantic jaunt from New York to Tangiers, even on one day's notice. Now that they were actually under way, her husband, Jensen, wasn't sure it had been a wise decision.

Wise decisions were Jensen Blot's stock-in-trade. As the youngest partner in the Wall Street brokerage that handled the private investments of the master of the *Maria,* Jensen was of course fairly familiar with the great man's portfolio, at least as it pertained to United States investments. That was the trouble. Jensen's familiarity was the reason he and Elizabeth weren't spending their usual calm, pleasant, relaxed weekend in East Hampton, among their friends and guests.

"You, there, Blot," the master of the *Maria* had sputtered in his heavily accented English only yesterday morning. He persisted in pronouncing Jensen's last name to rhyme with "dot," whereas, being a French name, it rhymed with "dough." Since he spoke French fluently, this was a calculated insult to Jensen Blot, or to his American education? Probably both.

"You I need this week, at my side, Blot. Pack a bag and your wife, too, if she's pretty."

The *Maria* crested through the growing swells, bursting them into sprays of hard diamonds that shattered back on the deck. The movement of the big craft—big enough to require thirty-five in crew—had already begun to give Jensen Blot a large touch of queasiness.

Watching the easy way the master of the *Maria* took this growing motion of the ship, Jensen envied him. It was not the first time for such envy. Over the years, handling the land deals, the money deals, the corporate proxy fights and all the rest of the portfolio's business, Blot had many an occasion to envy Kemal Kerem.

The Kerem name, the Kerem wealth, the Kerem way with women, the Kerem wives and mistresses, the Kerem wheeling and dealing—all this came back in a nauseating wave of memory as Blot sat there holding onto the arms of his chair and trying to keep his stomach calm. This yacht, the *Maria,* over eight hundred tons of sheer luxury, with nine-karat gold plumbing, a speed faster than most trans-

10

atlantic liners and a radio room that would put even one of the U.S. Navy's spy ships to shame . . . this yacht from which Kemal Kerem had staged so many surprise coups on the business communities of the Western world, had become a symbol of the man and what he stood for.

And yet, Jensen Blot thought as he eyed his host now in the brilliant sunshine, the bald bastard looks more like a cook in a diner.

"Ordinary" was hardly the word to describe the man whose closest friends called him "Kee." Of course, Blot reflected, he was seeing the man at his worst, unshaven face haggard with sleeplessness, hairy breasts pendulous and shivering in the rumbling thrust of the yacht beneath him.

Much better to see Kerem as he wanted to be seen, in one of the fifteen or twenty identical dark blue flannel suits he kept at various handy places around the world. Beirut, of course, and the islands he owned off Turkey. But also in his London hotel suite, his Manhattan apartment, the Paris flat of his actress mistress and one more at a Paris hotel in case of sudden complications. These plus a few shirts completed the worldwide wardrobe of the man rumored to be among the richest in the world, certainly in material possession, if nothing else.

Blot also knew that Kerem hated social events, even though his current wife adored them. So to the arsenal of blue flannel suits one white *smoking* and one blue had been added over the years, with Lebanese peasant economy.

For all his lack of sartorial distinction, Jensen Blot realized, all doors opened to Kerem. Customs officials rushed to stamp his passport, beautiful women laid intricate snares for him, reporters pressed close for rumors and tips, even the executives of his worldwide bank never knew where he would appear next to issue his orders, lop off heads, and hire a whole new staff for a branch office. He ran his Beirut-based merchant bank as, in some prior cen-

11

tury, a pirate chieftain ran his fleet of cutthroat corsairs.

And, finally, Blot thought, there was the current wife, Leslie.

If Kee Kerem were to die in his sleep this very night, Jensen mused as he watched him basking in the sun, his epitaph might dither on about banking coups and political schemes, but for any American—for any citizen of the world—his most impressive achievement was marrying Leslie French.

It wasn't that Leslie and her twin sister, Doe, were the highly publicized daughters of a socially prominent Texas family. Many women could claim that, including the Paley sisters or the female Kennedys. Nor was it that they both regularly made the best-dressed lists through their supposedly infallible fashion sense.

Talking about it between them as they hastily packed for this impromptu command crossing of the Atlantic, Jensen and Elizabeth had discussed whether the fabled Leslie Kerem would even be aboard.

"She won't," Elizabeth assured him. "She's at the French family compound near Dallas. Her son Robert fell off a horse and she—"

"That's silly, Lib," Jensen had cut in. "She was in Manhattan last night at the opening of the new Bernstein musical."

Elizabeth had delivered her ultimatum. "As far as I'm concerned if she's not on board, I'm swimming back to New York, pregnant or not. Who in God's name cares about that bald headed Lebanese? It's Leslie French I want to meet."

"Leslie Kerem."

"Leslie Miles," Elizabeth reminded him. "I still remember her maiden name after all these years. Who doesn't?"

It was a mark of how disciplined the *Maria*'s crew was that even now, three hours off Ambrose Channel, far beyond sight of land and moving eastward at a neat 20 knots, neither Jensen nor Elizabeth Blot had any idea if

12

Leslie was in fact aboard. The crew was German, from the captain and mate to the assistant steward in the dining room. Not only German, Jensen realized, but entirely gay.

Like anyone who made his living in New York, Jensen Blot had long ago given up the luxury of hating homosexuals. There were simply too many of them, and too many powerful ones among them, to allow for the doubtful privilege of baiting them or using derogatory names. It was obvious to Blot, however, that the crew was homosexual not because this in any way reflected some unknown side of Kee's notorious heterosexual drives, but rather because it shaped them into a cohesive mininavy with almost Marine Corps-like precision and discipline.

And, of course, there was no danger of one of them sampling any of the fabled favors of the glamorous and exciting Leslie Kerem.

That, however, was not the main problem that concerned the master of the *Maria* on this sudden dash across the Atlantic. Jensen Blot knew the very real problem Kerem was facing at the moment and it had nothing to do with his wife, Leslie. It had to do, in fact, with Jensen's own presence on board.

The *Maria* had been anchored the previous week off Bermuda, Blot knew, where a very confidential meeting had been taking place between Kee Kerem and the representatives of a major U.S. merchant bank. Kee had been trying to effect a merger that would slough off his unprofitable branch offices in South America and the Far East.

The other bank was in even deeper trouble than the Kerem network. The deal, between paupers, never got off the ground.

Jensen Blot knew enough about Kee Kerem to understand that he didn't really want to merge the bank. Quite the contrary. It gave him a sense of luxury that little else could match.

But Blot was also aware that for some time now Kee had

been selling bits and pieces of the Kerem empire. He had long ago flogged most of his hotel chain and his silver mines. The merger of the bank was yet another of these calculated sheddings of property for the purpose of— Of what?

Jensen Blot was one of the few people who knew the answer and was well paid by his firm to keep it confidential. For some time now Kee Kerem had been liquidating holdings and buying dollars.

It was as simple as that. No sophisticated international currency arbitrage. No complex multinational deals. Kerem had patiently been selling his holdings for pounds sterling, lire, Deutschemarks, franks, yen, and guilders and then converting every centime and pfennig into dollars.

True, the dollar had been a bargain, floating at or near its all-time low for some time now during this long summer of discontent when the American economy sank lower and lower as public confidence in the Presidency submerged almost out of sight. The President had been caught in almost every crime short of murder. He stood revealed as a cheat, a thief, and a conniver. Slowly the American system of justice ground exceedingly finer, moving inexorably toward his impeachment or resignation. Kerem was certain that before that moment came, the President would cut his losses, scoop up his pension, and escape like any common thief.

And the dollar, like a balloon from which a dead weight has suddenly been cut, would soar skyward to its rightful position among the major currencies of the world.

Kee Kerem, Blot mused, would then sell off every dollar he owned, sending the currency plummeting once more. In the space of perhaps twenty-four hours, he would cash in on his foresight, rake in the winnings, and let the dollar sink out of sight once again. The man he relied on to handle that savage rape of the dollar was Jensen Blot.

Like all gamblers, Jensen Blot knew, the master of the *Maria* thought himself psychic, a mind reader. As if to prove his power now, Kee opened his eyes and squinted through the noon sun at his broker.

"You, Blot," he called, "where is that wife of yours, eh? It's all right to keep a woman in bed all day, but not by herself."

Blot nodded, knowing that it was his thoughts of the coming dollar play that had stirred Kerem from his reverie. Like a lot of rich men who single-mindedly pursued profit, Kee liked to clothe his naked desire for money by pretending to be overly interested in sex, as if this were a socially more acceptable obsession. "I'll see if she's up," Blot agreed, getting to his feet.

He had been seated with Kee Kerem on the raised rear crescent of the deck directly over the stern of the *Maria,* the canvas roofing rolled back on its monel-metal framework to let sun pour down. Now he walked down a half flight of curving steps to the stern deck itself that surrounded the swimming pool.

Empty of water at the moment, the pool's bottom lay more than six feet below, rimmed by an intricate metal edge of nine-karat gold. Blot had been told that the bottom of the pool raised hydraulically to become a dance floor during parties. Otherwise it would have been too tempting to push guests into. A mural by the pool, in rich Mediterranean blues and bright reds, had been copied from an ancient mosaic.

It depicted a long piebald bull in full leap across an immense expanse of blue mosaic tile, with a small, red-clothed dancer somersaulting over the bull's arched back and, to one side, another wasp-waisted acrobat, naked except for a girdle, his powerful arms bound with leather straps, holding them aloft to catch the somersaulting comrade and keep him from danger.

Jensen Blot knew enough of the old bull-dancing mys-

15

tique to remember that those who agilely taunted the bull, using no weapon but their own daring and trickery, their own grace and strength, might live to vault the bull's back yet another day.

Those who were ugly, or coarse, or slow of foot might die in the arena, gored by the bull. The rest, that vast class of merely average performers, ended up sacrificed to the Magna Mater, their testicles torn off and eaten.

It said something for Kee Kerem, didn't it, Blot thought as he skirted the pool, that he had chosen as his symbol this most horrifying and, at the same time, most courageous symbol of antiquity. Always the gambler, it said, always ready for a flyer, a roll of the cosmic dice, winner take all . . . or lose it.

Thoughtfully, Jensen moved in under the canvas awning and opened one of the doors to the grand salon. It stood easily sixty feet long and only slightly less wide, beginning at the doors to the outer deck through which Blot had just come, a vast expanse of carpeted floor.

A full seven-foot concert grand piano stood to one side, memento of Kee's actress mistress, with easy chairs upholstered in soft tan leather and, at the far end, a wall of obviously bought-by-the-yard library books surrounding an onyx-and-gold fireplace.

Above this hung a painting of a small girl standing beside a pale blue chair, her head only a bit higher than the seat of the chair, a mysterious half smile of both pleasure and pain on her face, her flaxen blond hair swooping down in soft, thick curls that lay on her shoulders like down dropping cascades of white water.

Blot stopped to gaze at the painting. The face haunted him. Where had he seen that face?

Blot went through a door to one side of the bookshelf wall and continued walking along a corridor that seemed to run forever along the spine of the ship, almost out of sight in the far distance. Off this corridor lay the various other rooms of the *Maria* and at this hour of the day, he saw, most of the doors stood open as crew members vacuumed, swept-dusted, or otherwise cleaned the rooms.

Only two doors were tightly shut. That on the right he knew was his own stateroom because he had late yesterday taken the trouble to count its place along the corridor. Blot had that kind of mind. He already knew his room was the fourth door on the right, still closed. The other closed door was second on the left.

He pushed open the door to his stateroom and immediately inhaled the sickening smell of jasmine. It was Kerem's idea, apparently, to perfume the air-conditioning system that swept the entire ship so that each room stank of this abominable odor, constantly renewed and kept strong and cloying.

Still, Blot reflected as he stood in the doorway, one could put up with a lot to live in such a sumptuous room. It was a full thirty feet square with off-white walls and closet doors papered in a blue-green forget-me-not print that matched the spread on the huge kingsized bed. The window was at least six feet across, with white curtains edged in blue and green velvet. The chests and chairs were French, off-white and lined faintly in gold.

"Jess?" Elizabeth muttered.

"It's me, Lib. Time to get up. How's the stomach?"

Her soft blond curls were pasted to her forehead as she opened one eye. "Churning still."

"Mine, too. I think this godawful jasmine doesn't help. Come on deck for some fresh air and wear a bikini. Kerem wants to see your tits."

"Did he say so, the filthy old pot?"

Jensen moved to the dresser. "No. Where are those sickness pills your doctor gave you?"

"You can't take them, Jess. You're not pregnant."

"I'll chance it." He threw two pills in his mouth and moved into the bathroom to draw water from the gold tap.

"Any sign of Leslie French."

"Leslie Kerem. No."

She lay silently for a moment. "My breasts are starting to get too big for a bikini, Jess."

"God, the things women worry about."

He swallowed the sickness pills and instantly felt much worse. A fine dew of perspiration broke out on his forehead and the back of his neck. "Damned ship rolls like a rowboat." He watched her turn over and bury her face in the pillow again. "We're a fine pair," he observed. "No class, no way. Me seasick, you morning sick. And it's afternoon already."

"I'll be up," she mumbled, mouth pushed into the pillow. "Leave me alone now, darling."

"Okay. Don't be too long."

As he walked out into the corridor and turned to shut the stateroom door behind him, Jensen Blot saw a steward approaching with a tray on which a golden coffeepot and a porcelain cup and saucer stood. The man was blond, slim, tall and handsome in an almost stagy way, as homosexuals often were, Jensen noted. The very young man nodded politely to him as he passed by on his way toward the stern of the *Maria*.

Since this was the direction Blot had to go, he found himself trailing the lithe young man along the carpeted hall. The steward stopped at the closed door, knocked softly three times, then slowly swung the door open. He disappeared inside the room as Jensen Blot came abreast of the door.

Good Christ, he thought, there she is. That face.

And there, indeed, she was. The girl of the painting grown full and desirable, the flaxen-gold hair like wings spread out on either side of her as she lay back on the pillows of the tremendous bed, the huge eyes under their full eyebrows and long dark lashes, the rich, sensual mouth twisted into a faint smile of welcome for the good-looking

18

homosexual steward, her slender body and full breasts covered but not really hidden under a thin white voile night shift.

Leslie French.

Blot realized he had stopped dead in his tracks and was gawking like the lowliest autograph hound or film-star fan. As if to register his presence, her immense eyes shifted slightly past the face of the steward to fasten nearsightedly on Jensen Blot, trying to place him.

Leslie French.

Christ, Blot thought, we've never really met. She probably thinks I'm some sort of Peeping Tom. He smiled nervously. If he'd been wearing a hat, he'd have tipped it. And, still, he felt riveted to the spot, unable to move along.

A bit sleepily, yet with a sort of presence that only an actress or a great beauty has, she let her faint smile of welcome to the steward broaden into a false smile of full recognition for Blot. It surrounded him, the smile, it engulfed him in a wave of pure sexual beauty. It pulled him down and drew the breath from his lungs and left him gasping.

"Good morning," she said.

Leslie French, he thought. He watched the steward put down the tray and return to the door where, almost regretfully, he closed it in Blot's face.

Jensen Blot moved slowly along the corridor toward the grand salon and the outside deck, his legs shifting unsteadily as if in a dream. He was a married man and he guessed he loved Libby and she was to have their first child and it went smoothly between them, as always. But Leslie French. . . .

As he came out into the brilliant sunshine of the aft deck, he stared at the bald Lebanese who, with his help, would soon be staging a billion-dollar raid on the currency of the United States. He hated him. He hated Kee Kerem. And not out of patriotism or business envy. He hated him

19

because he had only to snap his fingers and all the languorous, flaxen-tressed pleasures of Leslie French were his.

He pictured this tall, cadaverous man fondling her body. Jensen Blot's stomach shifted alarmingly and he almost threw up.

Chapter Two

The sun was sinking behind Buckingham Palace, throwing the front courtyard into shadow. From where Brassington stood, on the deep balcony of the Drew penthouse, she could look across the corner of Green Park to the whirling auto traffic and the crowds that milled round the two guarded entrances, tourists hopefully waiting to catch a glimpse of a member of the British royal family.

On two separate occasions, she often recalled, in her capacity as lady's maid to the late Lady Wolverhampton, she had accompanied her mistress to Windsor Castle for Ascot race week. For two weeks she had slept under the royal roof, enjoying the gossip and privileges of the servants' hall. All this was rightfully hers, part of the many perquisites of waiting upon one of the famed beauties of the twenties. And Lady Wolverhampton had been a *real* lady.

Not that Brassington had anything against her present mistress, Mrs. Kemal Kerem. Being an American, she could hardly be a lady, but she was considerate, generous,

and very modern. Even a little too modern, in Brassington's view. Surely an American "lady" showed some modesty in front of her maid, but the way Mrs. Kerem and her
twin sister, Lady Drew, stripped to their panties and nothing else to waste hours of time trying on each other's
clothes drove Brassington nearly frantic.

It was all right, perhaps for *nouveau riche* women, Bras-
sington mused, or for longtime international celebrities.
But Madame Kerem and Lady Drew were quite different,
or should be. The Miles twins came from money, tons of
Texas ranching money that went back to the days when
Texas was an independent nation. And Madame's first
husband, Maurice French, had been of an even wealthier
Texas family whose fortune was based on oil.

Like a pair of teen-agers, she thought. One would simply never believe they were both over forty. They rushed
around the world, always shopping, dragging Brassington
and one of the ship's stewards with them to carry parcels.
Over the years they had bought hundreds of dresses that
had never even been on their backs. Not that they couldn't
ruddy well afford it, of course, but the waste!

Every time either woman heard of a new cosmetic, Brassington was sent to buy not a modest sample, but quantities
of the cream, or dozens of lipsticks, with the result that
their dressing tables were more like cosmetic counters. A
stateroom on board the *Maria* had recently been converted to hanging space for an ever-increasing wardrobe,
which they seemed to share jointly with no sense of whose
clothing belonged to whom. A whole stateroom!

If the newspapers were ever to get hold of that one.

Brassington disapproved of publicity. A real lady did
without it. But not these two. There was a constant struggle to keep pace with the mounds of newspaper clippings
that flooded into the mail each time her mistress appeared
in public. The job plain got on Brassington's nerves. Past-
ing up a scrapbook was not a job for a lady's maid.

No real lady, in Brassington's opinion ever gave interviews to the press. Not that her real mistress, Mrs. Kerem, did anything like that. But Lady Drew! Brassington sniffed with disapproval as she recalled the embarrassing half hour that had taken place only that morning, a half hour during which Lady Drew had blundered from one unfortunate remark into the next.

How would her husband, Sir Philip Drew, the eminent Shakespearean actor-director, feel when he read that Doe Drew regarded self-reliance as the most important thing for a woman? If he didn't fume, he'd surely have to laugh.

How, for that matter, did Brassington feel being asked to hand around coffee and biscuits—not the job of a lady's maid—while her mistress' sister took all the credit for their fabled dress sense. Brassington smiled bitterly now at the recollection. As often as not it was she who had to tell them which way around the dress was supposed to be worn.

Brassington came from a long line of highly paid superior domestic servants, bred to take their status from those who employed them. The deterioration of the British aristocracy had been a cruel blow to many of them. To Brassington the blow had been so crippling as to force her to accept employment with one American . . . and inherit her twin sister in the bargain.

But as her dear father, then in his thirty-fourth year as butler to the late Duke of Argyll, had pointed out: "One must move with the times."

So Brassington had crossed the Atlantic to take up her duties as personal maid to the lovely young wife of Governor Maurice French, firm in the conviction that within a year he would be suitably installed in a Cabinet post, if not in the Supreme Court. Her father, being a regular reader both of *Time* magazine and the racing news, had described the French rise to power as a dead cert.

Thus Brassington had taken the unprecedented step, and flown the Atlantic. It had been her first flight over the ocean, over anywhere, for that matter. At the time she never guessed that one day she would find herself taking transatlantic jets with the same regularity that she might once have taken the number 14 bus from Piccadilly to Harrods. And for the same trivialities.

Wherever Mrs. Kerem might find herself, her dry cleaning was now sent to London on the whimsical advice of Doe, her sister. Brassington's lopsided smile grew broader. How I'd like to see Her Majesty's face if I were to say, "You hop on the bus, dearie, and drop the cleaning off at Lilliman and Cox."

Not for the first time Brassington felt irritated at the way she was expected to wait on Lady Drew. But by now she had come to accept the plain fact that Mrs. Kerem was really two people, herself and Doe. Nothing anybody might do would alter the fact, now or ever.

It was odd the way the twins complemented one another, backed one another up, and made a tremendous impression when seen together. Yet apart, Doe was all nerves and chain-smoking, while her sister sat moodily flipping through a magazine or staring at herself in the mirror.

But they really did depend on one another, Brassington mused, not in the normal way of sisters or even twins, but in a special way quite different, quite apart from anything Brassington had ever experienced in her life.

She had herself been a bit close with her own sister, now married and recently a grandmother. But the links between Brassington and her sister were . . . well, normal. They wrote each other twice a year. Brassington might telephone when, as now, she was briefly in London, if only to get news of the family. But that was the limit of it.

Not so the two women who had once been Leslie and Doe Miles. The links between them were so strange and so strong that even to think of them now bothered Brassington in an oddly disturbing, almost scary way.

They had identical bodies, that lanky, rangy Texas look,

24

but much fuller through the bosom. Their faces, in a dim light, with the ash-blond hair and big violet eyes, also looked identical, but were not. Doe was very pretty in a conventional model-girl way. But there was a certain set to Leslie's eyes, a certain faint change in the mouth, that made the difference between prettiness and phenomenal beauty, Brassington felt.

She shook her head impatiently. It's all the traveling and spending money, she told herself briskly, as though it were a crime not to buy, buy, buy wherever you go. And they never eat a proper meal, Brassington added pragmatically.

But she would never have accepted the position had she known where it would end. Four months after Brassington had gone to work for Leslie French came the tragedy. The nightmare that Brassington had only witnessed on the television screen as she watched Governor French's motorcade drive through the crowd-packed streets of Caracas.

It had been bad enough to see it that way, thousands of miles away, on television. How much worse it must have been for her mistress, who had been attending the governors' convention with him and was behind her husband in the next open car. To this day, eight years later, her mistress had never once referred to that moment. A strange woman, full of unspoken pain.

Brassington had tried to blot the incident from her mind. She had pressed her lips in grim acceptance that her employer might well become increasingly withdrawn and therefore difficult to work for. Many months had passed silently by, with only Lady Drew and no one else beside her.

Quite unexpectedly Brassington had been asked to pack holiday clothes and get ready to travel. Almost overnight Mrs. French had regained her feverish interest in clothes. Doe had arranged for them to holiday aboard the *Maria*.

Brassington remembered well the first time she had followed the sisters up the gangplank, carrying Mrs. French's jewel case. On deck they had both been warmly greeted by a tall, ungainly bald man in a blue flannel suit, his face hidden behind dark glasses. At the time Brassington had felt they might have found someone more presentable to invite them on a cruise, but the change of scene would be good for her mistress.

Then, with neither due warning nor modesty, Mrs. French had married that appalling Lebanese.

The cabin in which Brassington was forced to rough it now became her room, her sole quarters. Even worse, she was now being paid in Swiss francs. Naturally, patriotism caused her to convert them month by month to pounds sterling. It was true that she got her copy of *The Tatler* and *Woman's Journal* regularly. And she had every comfort, of course. Her duties were strictly limited to caring for clothes. Yet, though it was contrary to her upbringing to think ill of any master of the house, try as she did she could find nothing to like in the master of the *Maria*.

It was not merely the flashy life-style that she found so disagreeable, though she did detest being cooped up with all those fancy Krauts and took most of her meals in her cabin for this reason. She could stand the sea, no fear of that. But what she did dislike was when the steward called her Mabel—which wasn't her name, anyway—and told her to get set for a big party in Monte Carlo. The next thing she would wake to find the *Maria* tied up in the Beirut yacht club, and she had to go surging into the gold souk with all those Lebanese pushing and pulling at her skirt.

Neither sister ventured there, but preferred to let Brassington pick up Bedouin jewelry and gold bracelets which they wore once only, then dropped into a dresser drawer and forgot.

There was, in Brassington's view, something very deliberate, almost nasty, in the way the sisters behaved toward their expensive jewelry, cosmetics, and clothing, almost a vicious glee in waste, in abandonment, in the destruction of all the material things they kept accumulating. When, as now, she allowed herself to brood about this thin edge of nastiness, Brassington found herself not only confused by her mistress and Lady Drew, but in a strange way almost . . . terrified.

She drew a long shuddery sigh and straightened up now to almost military attention. Time to stop all this self-pity!

On the plus end of the job, her friends could write to her anywhere in the world, simply by dropping a letter into the Kerem bank office. Like the diplomatic service, all of Kerem's mail came to him by private courier. And Brassington did think this showed some style.

Chapter Three

It's unbelievable, thought Walter. The man Blot
was a guest aboard the yacht, yet he just stood outside Mrs.
Kerem's bedroom door, gawking.

Walter's long fingers shook slightly as he tied back the
curtains that framed the picture window of Leslie Kerem's
cabin. Sun poured into the room, a luxury of golden light.
He wondered if he should speak to the mistress of the
Maria or wait for her to say something. Finally, moving at
a grave pace, he closed the door in the face of Jensen Blot
as he stood outside, staring.

Walter was new; he had joined the yacht in Bermuda.
Flown down by Kerem from New York, he was still being
put through his paces when Mrs. Kerem joined the yacht
in New York.

It wasn't exactly the kind of job Walter was used to, but
the chance of returning to Europe in the exotic company
of the woman he had adored since childhood was hard to
resist. Besides, it had been eight months since Walter had
acted in his last television commercial. He needed money.

"So you're Walter, our new steward?"

The voice from the bed was deep, the accent vaguely Texan, the tone resonant. In an instant it released all the long-stored-up power of a childhood memory. That she knew his name was incredible. But Walter had always known that his father had been most impressed with Governor French and his beautiful wife when he'd played host to them many years ago in Munich. Walter had been twelve at the time, young enough to ask Leslie French to sign her name on a photograph. Young enough to treasure the picture, even to kiss it fervidly in the privacy of his bedroom at night.

Walter spun round, catching his foot against a sofa set in the window recess. He was unaccustomed to clumsiness. It made him feel stupid. "Yes, Madame. Is there something I can do for you?"

Leslie Kerem lay in the center of a wide yellow bed, her pale blond hair spread out on her slightly rumpled pillow. Obviously she had spent the night alone. Walter realized the thought filled him with relief.

"Can you tell me who the hell that gawking man was?"

Her mouth curled in a friendly smile. Walter's heart thudded. He felt his throat contract. Finally, hating the sound of his German accent, he managed to say: "His name is Jensen Blot, Madame. He's in the forget-me-not cabin with his blond wife, Madame."

Leslie Kerem lowered her head. Walter stood rooted to the spot, waiting. Her left arm lay across the bed, her third finger circled with a wide gold wedding band of the old-fashioned kind that was currently in style. He noticed too, how slim and fine her fingers were, how gracefully she did everything, even now as she began to to eat her grapefruit.

"I'm sure," she murmured, "that Mrs. Raschid has done all the right things."

It was a statement without any particular feeling. Walter had the impression that Leslie Kerem wasn't the least interested in who else was traveling aboard the *Maria*. She seemed to him totally detached as she lay in the huge bed, and perfectly happy to be alone there.

She tilted her face up to Walter, causing her blond hair to fall back against the lemon pillow. "Would you please have them put a call through to my sister?" She nodded in the direction of the pale yellow telephone.

It took Walter two strides to reach the bedside, his shoes sinking into the deep pile carpet. He picked up the receiver, and speaking in German, as all crew members were instructed to do, he asked the radio room to call Lady Drew in London.

While he waited for the radio operator's reply, he forced himself to look away from the bed. With an effort of concentration, he observed that the pair of Chinese lacquered commodes that stood either side of the bed was near perfect. Walter knew, because his grandmother was especially fond of this overdecorated style. On the side where Walter was standing, a copy of *Cosmopolitan* and a pair of reading glasses lay next to the telephone.

"The operator estimates the call may take up to an hour, Madame. And he reports that we're heading for gale force nine."

"Good," said Leslie Kerem. "I love rough weather."

"Not everyone does, Madame."

"Next to riding, running along the tilting deck is simply the greatest. Did you ever notice, Walter, that it's always the bores who get seasick?"

To Walter's astonishment she grinned at the prospect.

"Yes, Madame."

Her violet eyes locked glances with him. Walter felt like a twelve-year-old again. Yet they were both adults now and with scarcely a dozen years' difference in age between them. She looked easily as young as he, both their bodies lithe and well trained. Only the glances were different. Walter found himself almost hypnotized by the look deep behind her eyes, a look almost of pain, but not necessarily

30

walked across the living room to the steaming bathroom door. Her nose wrinkled. Gales of strong-smelling pine scent were wafting through the flat.

"You sister is calling." Brassington looking straight in front of her to avoid the sight of a naked woman. The woman must have tipped at least half a bottle of essence into the bath, judging by the smell.

"Is she actually holding on or is it just that crackling business?"

"The latter, Madame."

"Okay. Go back and hold on. I'll get dry."

Brassington returned at a leisurely pace to the writing desk. From past experience she knew that a ship-to-shore call could take anything up to an hour before both parties were actually on the line and talking. Then, as often as not, the line would continue to emit a series of crackles and long intervals of humming before a nearly unrecognizable voice could be heard at the other end.

Such telephone calls were a ridiculous waste of time and money. Yet Mrs. Kerem persisted in trying to speak to her sister wherever she happened to be, and regardless of the time—every morning of her life, on waking. Of course, it wasn't Brassington's place to help either twin save money. Madame Kerem had it to spare, naturally, and so did Lady Drew, who probably made more through her dress designs and jeweled accessories than did her talented husband. Brassington adored Philip Drew in any of his plays, but what actor, even one who'd been knighted, could ever earn enough to compare with the ancestral wealth and go-getting enterprise of his wife?

Brassington looked at her watch and guessed the time aboard the *Maria* to be between eleven and twelve.

Doe Drew appeared at her side, reeking of pine. She had draped herself in a deep-purple bath towel, her corn-silk-blond hair piled on top of her head and secured by a couple of pins. She was without a trace of makeup, her

34

pain received. What was it? His heart was beating faster suddenly. The look of pain . . . of pain inflicted and . . . and enjoyed?

"That will be all, Walter. Thank you."

He walked slowly back down the long carpeted corridor in the direction of the galley. He realized that beneath the Kerem uniform—white cotton trousers, white shirt, and black belt—his muscles were tensed, as if to receive a blow. He longed to light a cigarette. But no crew members might smoke except within the confines of the mess and Walter was on call until after lunch had been served.

There must be some way around the rule, he was thinking. If he were regularly to see Leslie Kerem stretched out in bed each morning, asking him to perform minor chores that gave him a direct look at her softly rounded, tanned body, he would somehow have to find a way to sneak a calming smoke.

By the time he arrived in the galley, the chef was at work preparing a buffet lunch.

"How's Brünnhilde?" The stocky little chef, his left hand covered in shredded ham, winked at him.

"Telephoning her sister." Walter helped himself to a slice of ham. "Christ, I'd give anything for a cigarette."

Privately he cringed at how crude his countrymen could be. He hated the way they referred to Leslie Kerem with a bear-garden vulgarity to express how all of them felt about an attractive women. Naturally, with his actor's good looks, Walter was taken as one of them.

"What's all this about a gale force nine?"

"You get sick?" the chef asked.

"Hell, no." Walter lapsed into his newly acquired American. "But the man in the radio room said we were heading for a real storm."

"Can't happen soon enough. By this time tomorrow we'll be serving only cups of Bovril. Imagine"—the chef brandished his knife dangerously near Walter's left ear—

31

"during the bloody season I'm preparing Lebanese specialties for him, low-calorie dishes for Brünnhilde, German grub for the fucking captain, and Christ knows what when a fancy guest comes aboard. And to cap it all Mabel, the Brassing-Ass, only eats grilled sole and honey sandwiches. Honey sandwiches, imagine? I tell you, sweetie, you've got it made, handing the trays and the cocktails."

Walter made a disgusted face. It was only a matter of time before one of the German crew made the first pass at him. It would come from someone higher in rank than the chef, of course, but it had to happen.

A picture flickered through his mind of Leslie Kerem, naked on that immense yellow bed. Dear God, this voyage was not going to be any picnic, was it?

Chapter Four

The telephone pealed through the Drew house. Brassington, who had been enjoying the program on television, switched off the set before the room to answer it. But apparently she was mo slowly.

From the open bathroom door came the irate Lady Drew. "For God's sake, Brassington, an phone."

About to lift the receiver, Brassington allowed phone to ring once more. Somehow Mrs. Kere had to learn that she couldn't be treated like s nary cleaning woman. Brassington pursed her l long composing breath, and waited yet anothe before saying into the reciever in her grandest v Drew residence."

"We have a call from the ship *Maria*. Will hold the line?"

Brassington laid the receiver on its side.

hair dank from steam. Even so, Brassington had to admit that she was very nearly as beautiful as her employer.

"Anything happened?" Doe tucked the towel under her left armpit, reached for a cigarette, and lit it. She inhaled deeply.

Brassington cupped her hand over her left ear, the better to make out the sound of a human voice through the series of sharp noises.

"Nothing," she said, "just the usual noises. I can't even reconnect with the London operator, Madame."

"Shit." She continued to smoke.

Brassington looked steadfastly at the line of books above the writing desk. She detested vulgar Texas behavior. She especially detested this modern habit of crude language.

Both her employer and Lady Drew swore like troopers, but not the good round oaths Brassington had occasionally heard on the streets of London in her youth. Instead, the two women seemed to have an inexhaustible supply of monosyllabic Texas expletives, uncorked with neither feeling nor heat, but dropped idly as if almost devoid of meaning.

The minutes ticked away. Brassington leaned against the desk. Doe lit another cigarette. Then suddenly the operator said, "Speak now, please."

Lady drew stubbed out her half-smoked cigarette and grabbed the telephone. "Darling . . . how are you? How's it been?"

· Brassington tiptoed from the room, knowing full well that this nonconversation could run to thirty or forty minutes if nothing occurred to interrupt either sister.

As she reached the living room door, she heard Doe say, "I've just had one of the greatest baths ever, with this fantastic new muscle-relaxing oil of pine. I can't wait for you to try it, darling. It's almost better than a fuck." A giggle.

"No, but seriously, I'll give you a bath in it the first chance we get together."

35

Frowning deeply, Brassington turned back to close the door of the room behind her. As she did, she saw that Doe had dropped the towel. It had fallen about her hips, displaying her small, well-formed breasts in the light from the antique desk lamp. The globes glowed pinkly in the soft light. As she stood there, half naked, talking over thousands of miles of ocean to her sister, Lady Drew began to play with her left nipple, teasing it with the tip of her fingernail.

"If Kee won't rub you down with it, darling, I will," she was saying. "Or can we get the whole threesome together for jollies? Quite like old times, love?"

Brassington's frown deepened as she closed the door firmly on the scene.

Chapter Five

As soon as Leslie Kerem replaced the telephone receiver it rang again. Thinking that perhaps it might be her husband on the *Maria's* intercom, she answered in her strong contralto voice, the one that normally excited him. The voice of Mrs. Raschid, the secretary, at the end of the line, was low, soft, and at the same time not really warm.

"Oh, Elly, dear. . . ."

"Just to warn you that we have two guests aboard, a Mr. and Mrs. Jensen Blot. He's a Wall Street broker. Seems quite nice and young. . . ."

"You don't say." Leslie, remembering the gaping man at her bedroom door, laughed privately.

"His wife is called Elizabeth. Are you planning to be with us for lunch?"

"Of course," said Leslie. "What's the time?"

"Ten of one."

"Oh, turds. I'll get up at once."

Leslie replaced the receiver and swung her legs over the

bed. If there was one thing she disliked more than meeting strangers during the daytime, it was feeling that everyone was waiting for her to make the grand entrance.

She looked at the sea racing past the large square porthole, sending great splashes of spray against the glass. It would be quite windy on deck. That meant she could tie her hair in a turban.

Thinking about her hair made her suddenly realize that Brassington was in London with Doe. So for the next five days she was going to have to fend for her own hair.

If Elly Raschid had been a different sort, Leslie might have cajoled her into helping put up her hair. But while Brassington was definitely her servant, Elly definitely was not. She was paid directly by Kee Kerem, who had hired her. Their relationship was so close that it had come as a shock to Leslie to find that Kee had never taken Elly to bed in all the years she had served as his social secretary while a parade of wives and mistresses had filed in and out of Kee's life.

It wasn't that Elly was unattractive. Quite the contrary. The closely kept secret of her inviolability at Kee's hands was far simpler. He had reason to suspect she might be his illegitimate daughter. And Kee had a distaste for incest.

Leslie smiled maliciously. Maybe she should call Elly back and tell her not to expect her for lunch. Maybe not. It might be a good moment to catch Kee in a reasonable frame of mind.

She padded into the bathroom to take a shower, wondering as she let the water stream over her tan just what Doe had meant by muscle-relaxing pine oil. Leslie had always understood that one needed to keep one's muscles tensed in the fight against flab. Maybe she had got it wrong. Black could sound like white over that bloody awful radio-telephone connection.

She realized, as she toweled herself dry, that she had made a mistake in not flying directly to London with Doe.

Why spend a boring week being tossed like a cork across the Atlantic when she could be shopping or at the movies?

If only that poisonous French family lawyer hadn't made her feel like some kind of ex-call girl, and not Maurice's widow and darling Robert's mother. If it hadn't been for that hideous meeting in his office Leslie's judgment would have been more acute. What had he actually said?

It was something like, "Mrs. Kerem, you are a foreign national now, and anything the French trust allows you is by way of a courtesy gesture. You have no legal rights. The family must conserve its resources for the use of the future French generations, your son, Robert, among them. Who knows, one day you may find yourself the mother of the President." He had laughed inanely.

Leslie could find no reply for such an unbelievably tactless remark. She had left the office feeling miserable and humiliated. She shrank from the man's hand on her arm as he assured her that there was nothing personal, and that it was not *his* wish that her allowance be cut in half. Indeed, he had been the one who had advocated among the family that they treat Maurice's widow with the utmost generosity if only to keep her from doing the very kind of publicity-mad thing she had gone and done. But now that she'd done it . . . well!

God knew the Frenches had more money than the Shah of Iran, and from the same source, oil. The original founder of the clan had been one of Lafitte's pirate crew with an unpronounceable French name and a price on his head. He'd escaped a New Orleans jail for the wide-open plains of Texas and, just to help along his new identity, had started calling himself Maurice French. The man Leslie had married was actually Maurice French IV, but no Texas politician could ever hope to get elected governor unless he dropped the numeral.

Yet, nowadays, even the Frenches had to look into ways of conserving capital. The lawyer had an unpleasant way of slurring the word "conserving," running his tongue along his bottom lip, which sent a sick chill through Leslie as she remembered it, as if he were licking blood from his lip . . . not his own blood at that.

She had never liked this particular lawyer perhaps because she had sensed that he secretly cherished a "thing" for her. She knew, for example, that if she had allowed him to grovel before her and lick the sole of her shoe, she could have made a slave of him. He was that kind, that bullying kind, whose outward brusque nastiness was so like her own father's had been. Men like that exuded an air of not caring if women existed at all, except to be dominated and hurt.

But underneath a bully, she knew, lived someone who craved to be mounted, whipped, and ridden like a spirited stallion. She'd dominated many a horse in her time. Her Texas bully of a father had shown both girls the trick of it . . . and given himself away in the bargain.

Leslie sighed and tried to think of the practical affairs of the moment, getting dressed.

Off her cabin Leslie maintained a walk-in closet in which she kept clothes suitable for the time of year. They hung, as if they were in a shop, the trousers with appropriate shirts, the beach dresses with bikinis in shelves below. The evening dresses, with their coordinating shoes, hung with three fur wraps and four evening coats along the other wall.

Leslie never went into the second cabin, in which she kept the rest of her clothes, unless her sister Doe was with her. It was simply no fun sorting out things to wear on one's own.

She selected an ankle-length cotton jersey shift, a sort of long T-shirt, currently much in style in New York for beach weekends. It was utterly plain, a bright yellow that looked super in strong light, very flattering to her coloring. She shook her hair and decided after all to leave it

40

loose. Tonight, when she was dressing for dinner, she would fix it with heated curlers.

She slipped into a pretty pair of gold sandals. As she stood back to admire the effect, the telephone rang.

It would either be Kee, bawling her out for keeping him from his lunch, or Elly, always the tactful secretary, urging her gently to hurry. Spraying herself generously with Chanel 19, which she had selected as a good alternative to the Yves St. Laurent scent called Y, she left the cabin with the telephone still ringing.

Leslie Kerem moved carefully along the corridor, conscious that the yacht was beginning to roll. She enjoyed the sensation. It made her feel young, like being on a merry-go-round at a fair. Lord knew she needed something to cheer her up. She and Doe had their forty-third birthday only two weeks away—a day that would go uncelebrated—and her allowance had suddenly been sliced in half. What a good thing she had got that original settlement out of Maurice when Robert was born. She also supposed that Kee's settlement would be honored in the event they divorced. But you could never outguess foreign lawcourts.

Leslie Kerem sensed, before she saw, that the little group of people seated on the raised rear crescent of the deck were ill at ease. To be more precise, the two strangers looked strained and unhappy. One she recognized as the man who had stood outside her bedroom. The plump little blonde she assumed to be his wife.

"We've already met." She held out her hand to Jensen Blot, avoiding his gaze and smiling directly at his wife. Starting to gear up for her hostess role, Leslie said, "And you must be Elizabeth Blot." Then she let her smile widen.

Leslie had long ago realized that since she was in the public eye, if she made the effort to smile and speak to people, especially to rather ordinary people, and remember their names, it would have an almost electrifying effect on them. Unfortunately, she couldn't be bothered. It was

41

so *political.* Maurice had done it. She remembered a newspaper story that illustrated the point by telling about Lord Mountbatten as viceroy of India. He had placed a decoration on the chest of an Indian soldier, one of hundreds of terribly ordinary men so awarded. Two weeks later the same man had been awarded a second honor and the admiral had said, "I've already decorated you once this month. How many more deeds of bravery are you going to perform?"

It might do for Mountbatten, but Leslie Kerem simply didn't have the knack of it or the desire to learn how.

Leslie listened politely to Elizabeth, who was struggling to make conversation. Such a waste of time, Leslie thought. Long ago she had perfected the art of smiling and saying nothing. It didn't always work, of course, but she really didn't care if it did.

Walter, the criminally handsome steward, was suddenly at her side with a Bloody Mary on a small Georgian salver. She took the drink, smiled at him, and for a brief second their eyes met.

Behind his tall, slim handsomeness Leslie detected something familiar, a look she had seen before in her life. The tanned French lawyer had had it. So had her father. It was a kind of perilously balanced arrogance. Perhaps German men came by it naturally. What did they say about the Germans? They were even more obsequious as servants than they were nasty as masters?

"I'm starving. Let's eat." Her husband's voice cut in on her thoughts.

Leslie winced. Why was Kee always so deliberately crude? "A good idea, darling," she said, hoping she betrayed nothing of what she felt. Then she turned to Elizabeth, whom, for some reason, she had found very negative for all her attempts at conversation.

"We eat very simply at lunchtime," Leslie told her. "Just a buffet. My husband likes hot Lebanese dishes, all yogurt

42

and lamb and mint, whereas I prefer to eat a salad and save myself for the evening. I hope the arrangement suits both of you."

While she was talking to Elizabeth they had moved over to the buffet, where Elly's Raschid was acting hostess.

Leslie frowned, not because she disliked Elly's taking charge of the food, which frankly she was totally uninterested in, but because the outfit she was wearing was too chic. Why, wondered Leslie, didn't Doe and I buy denim gaucho pants? They looked fantastic and Elly's were exactly the right midcalf length that was bound to catch on for fall. She must see if Doe couldn't pick up some in London. Perhaps she could find them in one of those small shops that imported French merchandise. If not, she could simply design some and have one of her manufacturers run up a dozen or so pairs.

She eyed Elly's compact body, full-breasted, narrow-waisted, and her Lebanese face with its tanned skin and narrow nose, heavy-lidded eyes, and sensual mouth. She looked nothing like Kee, Leslie thought. Perhaps he had been fooled into accepting her as his own blood.

Leslie surveyed the buffet with total lack of interest. It was far too early for lunch. But that was Kee's peasant gut for you. Once they docked in Monte Carlo all that would change. Lunch would be at three o'clock, a proper civilized hour, and time for everyone to get properly dressed.

She found that the sight of Elly, looking cool and chic, was irritating. Everything about Elly was irritating, chiefly because she gave no cause for complaint, handled everything with efficiency and calm. Why, she was even explaining to this ordinary little American pair what was in today's specialty.

"It's Tunisian. But then, as I'm sure you know, all Eastern Mediterranean food originates from the Turkish cuisine. It looks rather unsocial in color, but don't be afraid to try it. It's called mloukhya."

43

Leslie's eyes traveled to her husband, who, seated in a cane chair, was shoveling up a dark brown-green shitlike soup, from which cubes of beef protruded. He was wiping his plate with a chunk of bread and talking Lebanese to Ali, his nephew, as he joined the party.

"I'm sorry to be late." Ali was always polite to Leslie. He kissed her cheek. She liked him. In a way they were allies, but Kee kept him tied to his side. Even through meals they discussed business and nothing but business. In Lebanese. The details of the vast Kerem empire of banking, brokerage, real estate speculation, and the mining of precious metals were utterly boring to Leslie, especially as she'd never bothered to learn a word of the Arabic dialect spoken in Lebanon.

"Help yourself, darling. I gather today's special is extra special." She looked away disgusted as Kee wiped a sour green trickle of slime from his chin. There was only one word to describe what the three Lebanese, Elly included, were tucking into with such relish. Obviously the chef had had diarrhea.

"It's a bit like your own Texas chili." Blot, Leslie realized, was making a brave effort at keeping the conversation going. But she was still annoyed at the gauche way he had earlier invaded her privacy and she saw no reason to help him along socially.

She was used to the effect she had on men, but she never felt confident in her power over them. Walter, the deliciously good-looking steward, if he wasn't as gay as the rest of the crew, would make an interesting toy for her on this trip, something she could open up and take apart for fun, even if it killed him. Jensen Blot was another story. He was clearly hands-off territory, for both business and social reasons, and just as clearly he was hypnotized by her.

She treated him to one of her half smiles, often very effective with uncertain males, especially ones who needed Kee's approval in business. At the same time she drifted

44

away from the group, seating herself beyond her husband, so that Kee had his back to her.

She toyed with the ham salad, picking at the meat and the lettuce, inwardly amused at the way the Blots fussily reseated themselves, so that now they were facing her again. Oh, God, she thought, I'm being an awful bitch. They are so terribly ordinary, but we're the only Americans here, aren't we?

Lunch, it seemed to Leslie, went on forever. The cheese, the fruit and chocolates flown in from Switzerland, were served at last with Turkish coffee, which to her tasted like sweetened mud. At each turn of the meal the Blots ate exactly what she ate, even joining her in having instant coffee. The thought of follow-my-leader for five days, meal after meal, was hair-raising.

"Kee, darling, let's run a movie tonight," Leslie called.

"Sure, baby." He used a fingernail to extract a piece of meat from his front tooth. Then he turned away from Leslie to continue his conversation with Ali, as always in Lebanese.

Leslie sat sipping the instant coffee. The hours she'd had to sit listening to this. Ali was a twenty-seven-year-old replica of her husband, except that his chest and biceps were firm, his hair luxuriant, his eyes sound and yet bulbous from eating the overspiced food. He had a firm, round chin, albeit right now it was covered with black stubble. Leslie saw no real reason why some girl mightn't fancy him, if only for the money he would one day inherit from his uncle.

Ali was now explaining something, using his hand to emphasize a point. From time to time he fingered the large solid-gold St. Christopher's medal that hung on a thick gold chain around his neck. Like most of the merchant class of Lebanon, the Kerem family were Christians, just a notch below the aristocratic Moslem families of their land. Ali was not only Kee's heir, but his active assistant and seldom far from his uncle's side. Like the older man, the making of money appeared to be the only thing that interested Ali, though he joined in the freewheeling social scene on occasion. Leslie imagined that he must make it with some of the many pretty girls who flocked onto the *Maria*'s decks when they entertained.

Ali's lack of sex life was a constant interest to both Leslie and her sister. Yet she supposed that one day he'd marry if only to provide the Kerems with an heir.

Watching the young man now as he continued explaining something to Kee, Leslie noticed that occasionally Ali's glance shifted to the only other person on the afterdeck who spoke Lebanese, his (possible?) cousin, Elly. Although she was ten years his senior, Elly might (possibly?) be fucking her attractive compatriot, Leslie mused. Such a liaison might account for a lot of things, including the fact that Kee religiously kept his hands off Elly. Leslie resolved that when Doe joined their party she would have to seduce Ali and see whether she could (possibly?) wreck this cheap little romance, thus thwarting any plans Kee might have for Ali siring a (possibly?) grandchild on Elly.

Leslie smiled to herself. She looked across to see how the Blots were making out. Jensen was mopping his forehead with a handkerchief while his wife looked strained and unhappy. The American side wasn't doing too well in the swelling sea. On an impulse, prompted chiefly by her own boredom, Leslie decided to break up the lunch party by taking herself back to her cabin for a siesta. She knew the Blots would gratefully follow her lead and bless her for it.

Once in her cabin she took off her beach shift and hung it on a hook on the door. In Brassington's temporary absence, someone would take it away, wash it, and press it. She was very hazy as to how the domestic side of the yacht operated, except to know that the laundry was excellent. She believed it was manned by Pakistanis.

46

Back in her cotton night shift now, she tried to relax, to sleep at least for an hour. Yet her mind kept revolving around money. How was she going to get her hands on more of it? God knows, Kee was always complaining and suggesting that *she* should hand over her precious few dollars to him.

His finances were a mystery to Leslie and she preferred it that way. But it was unnerving indeed to hear Kee Kerem plead poverty. All his funds were tied up in some secret deal which, Leslie believed, required the presence of Jensen Blot on board. Other than that she knew little and cared less.

But surely, if he were to go bankrupt, she would be in an untenable position. It was marginally acceptable to let this powerful and famous, but actively ungainly, man use her body when he had bought and paid for it handsomely. But it was quite another thing if Kee went bust.

Perhaps he might have looked more appetizing with hair. The bullethead gave him a stark, forbidding look, like a bloodthirsty Turkish mercenary. She had even suggested a hairpiece, but he had jeered at her. "This head, bald as an egg, got me where I am today," he had told her. "It's my trademark. And as for women—they adore it."

The bedroom door opened. Kee stood framed by the light that was constantly kept burning in the corridor. It glinted off his dome.

Lying on the bed, Leslie raised herself to a half-sitting position, taking her weight on her elbows. Since Kee was wearing only his bathrobe, she knew the purpose of his visit. It was as if, by thinking of it just now, she had willed him here.

She watched him as he silently crossed the cabin. He grunted heavily as he seated himself with care in the center of the small sofa. He looked bored and tired, she thought, and for a brief moment she wondered if perhaps he was only in her room because he had no better way of

47

passing the afternoon. But she knew Kee Kerem better than that.

He opened his bathrobe and showed her his already erect penis. She responded immediately by swinging out of bed and pulling off her shift as she crossed the cabin.

"Keep it on." His voice sounded thick with desire, choked with anticipation. Not for the first time Leslie wondered if it was really true that spicy food acted as an aphrodisiac.

His New York doctor had advised Kee to restrict his sexual activities to three times a week. This had happened soon after their marriage, or at least that was how he explained his infrequent visits to her bed. He had also told her that he had been warned to perform only in the seated position. This was thought to impose less strain on his arteries and heart.

So the small sofa in the window recess had become their couch of love. He lifted her shift and made a kissing sound with his thick lips. There were beads of sweat on his bald head.

Leslie straddled his bony thighs, as though riding a horse, sensing a sharp wave of pleasure as he entered her. She closed her eyes and thought only of riding a horse, a stallion she had mastered.

Neither one spoke. She felt herself climax long before he did, but gave no sign of it. On this occasion they satisfied each other quickly, and almost clinically. After a moment she opened her eyes and smiled slightly as she got to her feet and let her shift drop around her legs. He grunted, nodded, got up, and left the room. The only evidence that it all hadn't been a figment of her imagination was the dent in the sofa. Kee had gone. The whole episode had taken under ten minutes, and virtually in silence.

Leslie threw herself back into the bed feeling used and humiliated. She lay quite still, staring up at the ceiling, trying not to cry and not to succumb to the waves of self-pity that flooded over her. There was only one revenge.

48

She reached for the telephone and ordered tea, certain Walter would be the steward to deliver the order even though he was normally off duty during the siesta hour. He had to get used to being at her beck and call. Without Brassington as her body servant, Walter would have to do . . . and he did have one prime advantage over Brassington.

A few minutes later, when Walter arrived with the tea, she smiled coldly, not a welcoming smile at all, a chill smile of recognition and nothing more. Instantly atune to her mood, he frowned nervously. "Is something wrong, Madame?"

She could hear the cup rattle slightly in its saucer. His hand was shaking. Good. She sat up slowly, her legs over the edge of the bed. "Slippers," she ordered.

He knelt at her feet and searched under the bed for her slippers, found them at last, and started to fumble one onto her small, slender foot. She buried her fingers in his blond hair and pushed his head down until his lips touched her toes. They were locked that way for a long moment of utter silence. Then he kissed her toes once, twice. She patted his head.

Pushing herself forward to the edge of the bed, she straddled his head with her legs. Fingers still locked into his long, thick yellow hair, she pulled his head up until it nestled between her legs, his face out of sight. "Continue, she commanded.

It would only be a matter of moments, she knew, before he fully realized what he was being forced to do. If he continued doing it, Leslie knew, then he would continue doing whatever she ordered him to do, perhaps forever.

Chapter Six

The restaurant-discotheque Annabel's, one of the few surviving enterprises in an otherwise depressed London, was about to close for three weeks' summer holiday. Tonight was the final evening before Luigi and his staff got a much-needed break. Perhaps because of this there was a feeling of genuine gaiety throughout the place, among the staff at any rate.

Outside, in Berkeley Square, the night was unusually damp for this time of year. The tall girl with the long black hair sat in the cab's rear seat as the driver threaded his way cautiously through the traffic.

"There we are." The cab stopped at the curb. The tall girl paid and dashed quickly through the moist air down a flight of steps under a canopy and into Annabel's. There she gave Luigi the name of her dinner companion, a member of long standing.

"Mr. Butler's table? At once, Ma'moiselle." She followed Luigi through the bar lounge to a central sofa table, aware that many pairs of eyes followed her with interest. Having dressed well for the occasion, she took her time crossing the dimly lit room. She produced a brilliant smile as the middle-aged man at the table stood to greet her. She allowed him to peck her cheek.

It was a perfectly timed scene, staged by a professional. Judi was a model. When she managed to keep her weight down, as now, she knew exactly how to make everyone in the room stop talking and look at her. They had already been looking at her dinner companion.

She slithered effortlessly onto the plum-colored velvet sofa, ignoring her companion, and smiled into the head-waiter's eyes.

"I've had one hell of a day. I'm absolutely starving. You, Jim?"

Watching her companion for a reaction, she smiled sideways at him and waited. He took his time responding. Waiting could be said to sum up her relationship with Jim Butler. This was their third date in ten days, and Judi had nothing to report to her friends.

There hadn't been even one little grope in the back of the chauffeur-driven Mercedes 600 when he dropped her home. This diffidence was making her positively paranoid. It wasn't as though his divorce hadn't gone through. Nor that he was really all *that* old, fifty-three. Not too old to get it up if he wanted.

"A nice portion of caviar, Ma'moiselle? Make a good beginning to your holiday?"

Judi was aware of what fashionable London, beginning with the headwaiter, was making of her third appearance with the man many people thought one of the best financial brains in the country.

"Yes. You, darling?" This time Judi swiveled in her seat to give her financial wizard the full benefit of her cover-girl smile.

"Then steaks," he said, nodding in agreement. "They're not fattening either."

Judi examined Butler while he selected the wine. He

had a firm jaw, a rather tight mouth, but a few wrinkles around the eyes, which she found quite attractive. Not bad at all. And he was very rich indeed.

Butler ordered iced Stolichnaya vodka to accompany the caviar, and claret with their steaks.

"So you've had a hell of a day. That makes two of us," he grumbled.

Judi ran her hand through her long black hair. "Have you seen the fog? At this season? What wouldn't one give to be off on a really super holiday." She sighed, keeping it light, but treating him to another of her sideways smiles.

"Surely model girls *do* take holidays," he suggested.

"That's just *it*." Judi knew that her ploy was now in motion. Would it work? Fearful lest she say the wrong thing, she threw out her hands, palms upward, and shrugged her slender shoulders.

Butler was fiddling with the stem of his vodka glass. He looked irritably at the wine waiter, who rushed to refill the drink.

"You might just have a shot at hurrying up our caviar."

Jim Butler tossed back his second full glass of chilled vodka. "I had a rather unusual holiday invitation today. It could include a friend."

Judi sipped her vodka, clutching at the sofa with her left hand. Oh, God, don't let me balls things up, she prayed.

"What sort of an invitation?" As soon as she asked, the caviar arrived.

"Hang on a second. Let's get the food organized. Then I'll tell you all about it."

Judi sighed with relief. She had said the right thing for once. Thank you, God. And because it really did sound as though he were on the point of inviting her to go away, she decided to celebrate, forget her waistline, and have a really big helping of caviar.

She watched Butler eyeing the waiter with considerable

impatience, waiting for the man to leave their table. The suspense was killing. To calm herself Judi bit into a bit of toast she had thickly pasted with caviar.

"I had a telephone call from a Lebanese called Kerem. Know who I mean?"

Judi nodded, her mouth full. Did any attractive woman not know who Kee Kerem was?

"Kerem agrees with me. We have a society in which you almost have to apologize for being a success in business. Here in England we've promoted the idea that the way the workingman can prosper is to catch the rich speculators, carve up the proceeds, and Bob's your uncle."

Butler stopped eating as he emphasized his words. A speech, thought Judi, that he trots out whenever he can't come up with something a bit brighter to fill the gap in a business meeting. But why lumber me with it?

She treated him to another of her camera expressions, the one that registers mild surprise, combined with interest. "Now, thanks to lipgloss, my lips are always kissable." She completed the scene by broadening her smile to include her eyes. When she did it for television commercials, perhaps a bit more slowly, it was considered by professional critics to be one of her best reactions.

However, it did not dam the flow of Butler's words.

"What would it actually yield if you wrung the rich dry?" he was saying. "Not a packet of cigarettes for each man. That's how futile Labour's policy is. We have a choice; either we work harder and better, or by ironing flat the best we have in Britain, we all die together."

"I don't want to die," said Judi.

She switched to her special-appeal expression, the one that looked like a child who'd just had a sweet taken out of its dear little mouth. It was the one she used when a man refused to buy her the expensive present.

She kept her round eyes trained on Jim Butler. What

on earth was he *really* on about? Imagine, a lecture on economics in Annabel's. And what had it got to do with taking her on a holiday?

"Nor will you, my dear." This time it was Butler who gave meaning to the words with a hand-plant on Judi's thigh. His strong fingers pressed into her firm flesh.

"Kerem has asked me to join him on his yacht. We've a number of things to discuss. He suggested I bring a friend."

Judi covered her hand with his.

"As you already know, Kerem owns his own world-famous beauty. So you see, my dear, I'm asking you along to give me moral support, as it were."

"How absolutely super. You lovely man." Judi smiled for the first time that evening with genuine pleasure.

"We'll fly down to Cannes at the end of the week."

Judi nodded dumbly. At last it was really all happening. She hoped the support she was expected to supply wouldn't be too moral.

Chapter Seven

The drawing room of the *Maria* was a strange sight this evening. The immense ship lifted and fell with shuddering regularity as the Atlantic storm battered it with high waves and howling winds. Inside the drawing room, leather straps had been fastened across the bookshelves to keep the volumes from falling.

At a long rosewood table, polished to the brilliance of patent leather, Kee Kerem hunched forward over a sheaf of yellow papers torn from the telex machine. Ali sat beside him, making notes on the back of one of the discarded sheets. Across from them, eyes closed against the nausea in his gut, Jensen Blot sat braced upright, as if by his posture he could somehow compensate for the wild, irrational heaving and thrusting of the ship beneath his feet.

The poor man has nothing more to upchuck, Leslie Kerem thought. She had taken a seat diagonally across the room from the rosewood table where the buzz of the two Lebanese, speaking their native tongue, had become less of a distraction. She glanced at her watch and saw that it was after midnight, New York time. She watched Blot reach for the water carafe and pour himself a tiny drink, which he sipped slowly, experimentally.

"If you need any more Dramamine, Mr. Blot," she called to him, "don't hesi—"

"Quiet," her husband snapped. There was such concentrated force in his voice that, seated across from him, the American flinched.

Leslie glared at the bald, arrogant man who had so casually filthied her body this afternoon. Men. Self-important world-shakers. Tin gods. But she had taken care of that particular insult, taken care of it well.

A faint smile twisted up one corner of her lovely mouth as she remembered the look on Walter's handsome face. Men.

"Blot," Kee Kerem growled, rhyming the name, as usual, with "snot." "The Basel indicators are all good."

The American broker looked warily at him. From a few yards away, Leslie Kerem couldn't tell if the pain in Blot's face were from seasickness or the general nausea that her husband induced in people.

"Has gold crossed the baseline we set?" Blot asked.

"In Brussels, yes." Kerem shuffled telex sheets. "In Frankfurt, yes. But I never believe anything, Blot, till I get it from Basel. And there the price of gold has not quite crossed our line."

"There is such a thing," the American said, speaking slowly as if it cost a great deal for him to say anything at all, "as being too cautious. Nixon will resign. Even two hours' delay can cost millions."

Kerem's swarthy face broke into smiles. He dug his elbow in Ali's ribs. "There he goes, teaching his grandmother to suck."

"To suck eggs," Blot corrected him.

"Not *my* grandmother."

56

Kerem's vast shout of laughter filled the room. Then, without missing a beat: "Where's your wife, Blot? I've seen her so little she intrigues me. You have to watch out for me, my friend. I eat little blondes, bones and all." This time his laughter, and Ali's, combined to hurt Leslie's ears. She put down her copy of *Vogue* and got to her feet.

"It's late." She started to leave the room.

"It's early," Kee Kerem countered. "Come here."

"Good night," she said firmly, her hand on the door.

"Come here."

"Good night, Mr. Blot." She opened the door.

The American struggled to his feet. "Good night, Mrs. French."

The sudden silence in the room allowed Leslie to hear the howl of the Atlantic, like a famished beast seeking food. She watched the blood drain out of her husband's face. Then, smiling brilliantly, she left the room.

It was not the first time someone had called her by the name that was no longer hers. But each time the mistake was made it did something to Kee Kerem that was unpleasant to watch. He would have Blot's head on a platter for that, Leslie mused as she slipped into her stateroom and locked the door behind her.

She undressed quickly and drew on the plain cotton nightgown she normally wore. It reminded her that she had worn it this afternoon when her husband had once again dirtied her. But what a delicious revenge afterward.

She reached for the telephone, intending to have Walter bring her a nightcap cup of chocolate, then decided against it. She took two of the red capsules with a glass of water, turned off the lights, and was asleep within minutes.

Perhaps it was the violent motion of the ship, rocking her in its gigantic cradle. Perhaps it was the Seconal. The dream was a recurrent one. She and Doe were teen-agers. The flat Texas countryside stretched out around them for miles, sage green, a faint smudge of smoke on the horizon from the spreads of her mother's tenant ranchers who kept shorthorns.

She had always loved Ginger, not because the pony was small and faintly reddish beige, like a Palomino, but because Leslie had been there at her birth and had herself nursed the foal through colthood. A quarter horse, Ginger would never be anything more than what she was, a ladies' hunter, if that, a casual horse for a casual teen-ager, to be used like a bicycle or a small car. Ginger would never be bred or shown. That was never in the cards for a quarter horse. They were closer to being house pets on the big, rambling ranch with its great central hall.

Yes, Sam Houston had slept there, and so had Davy Crockett, regularly enough to have sired a bastard on one of the Mexican women. Doe had been the one to uncover this tidbit, which the two girls often giggled over.

The dream began very formally, as always, with Leslie carefully grooming Ginger for a ride. Doe's animal was a big bay mare. Both horses were docile, safer for girls who had just turned fourteen. Each saddled her own mount, something their father had always insisted upon. "The Mex stable boys don't exist for your convenience, Missy-ma'am," he had told them. "You decide to ride, you groom and saddle your own. *And* cool them out afterwards. *And* water them. I don't pay those shiftless greasers good money to wait on your wishes, Missy-ma'am."

Privately, the girls knew that their dashing father, the best horseman in the county, in fact the best in all of Texas, was not paying the stablehands. Their money came from the girls' mother. The vast estate was hers. The twins had never been told how big it was, but it included three counties of Texas, ranchlands, water holes, and all. The money was paid to her by tenants. When the bank sent a senior vice-president around, it was to discuss with their mother the administration of million-dollar trust funds.

Jared Miles—Captain Miles, as he liked to be called—was the best horseman in the state, but he hadn't a penny to his name.

The dream moved along at a leisurely pace, as if inflicting itself on her sleep like some all-engulfing sickness, some infection that would spread at its own speed, calmly, coolly, to every pore and fiber of her body.

It was Doe who spurred her horse from a canter to a gallop, her tiny buttocks rising and falling with great control over the scrap of leather that made up the English saddle both girls used. Leslie dug her heel into Ginger's side and the little horse surged forward, easily keeping pace with Doe's larger bay mare.

The old rail fence loomed ahead, as it always did in the dream, with perverse slowness, as if this were a film of the dream and the projectionist had slowed it down deliberately. In real life it had all happened too fast. But as her unconscious replayed the film now, every detail was cruelly clear.

The mare went over first, Doe's rear end rising tightly above the saddle. The bay's left hind hoof negligently touched—grazed, if that—the top rail of the fence. The rail began to shift, toppling, one end starting up into the air, the other end sinking, like a child's playground teeter-totter.

Ginger cleared the top of the fence and the upraised rail slammed into her belly with such force that she landed off balance, fell, rolled. Leslie leaped clear of the saddle. For a moment the sweaty beige skin loomed over her as if to crush her. Then Ginger's momentum stopped and she rolled back. Her right foreleg had snapped. Bone showed through the reddish-tan skin.

Leslie took the pony's head in her lap and patted her. Ginger's eyes rolled in pain. Doe, sizing up the situation, galloped off across the plain for help. It came with that

59

same insidious slowness, Captain Jared Miles, ever the cavalry officer, on his fiery black stallion. Slowly, at a canter. Slower.

Stopped.

Leslie looking up into the sun at him. Squinting, seeing the set of his jaw, the line of his mouth under the broad Stetson brim.

He dismounts. He stands over her, legs spread wide as if still clamped around his stallion, the bulge between his legs a swelling mound of khaki twill.

He slaps his calf with his brown leather crop. "Careless?" he asks in that tight, thin voice of his.

She cannot answer. He flicks her behind with his riding crop. "Careless again, Missy-ma'am?"

She shakes her head. She cannot speak. His beautifully regular teeth shine in the sun as he smiles. He shoves her away from the horse. She sprawls face down amid the sagebrush. Glancing over her shoulder, she sees him draw the immense Webley .45 revolver from its cavalry holster. Doe begins to whimper.

He places the gun against Ginger's right eye and pulls the trigger. The gun jumps in his hand. The sound is not loud out there in the vast expanse of open sky.

She can hear it echo far away off. She grabs the riding crop out of his hand and begans flailing away at him. She strikes at his boots, at the flare of his jodhpurs. She whips at his crotch and he twists the crop from her hands.

A moment later her riding jeans have been pulled down so brutally that the belt buckle leaves a bloody scratch down her belly. He rips off her panties and with his boot he rolls her over, buttocks naked to the sky.

He begins whipping slowly, one slash of the crop for each of the swelling white mounds. After four or five cuts of the crop, she moans in agony and twists over so that the next blow falls across her vulva. She screams, covers herself. The next blow—

60

Leslie Kerem sat up in bed. The motion of the *Maria* had gone wild, out of control, bucking like a horse in agony.

Groggy, she switched on the bedlamp, her breath surging in and out of her lungs like air in the bellows of the blacksmith's shop back home in Texas. She glanced at her bedside travel clock. Two in the morning.

The wounds. The black hole in Ginger's eye. The blood of her own body mingling with the blood of the pony.

The grenade arching through the air and falling into the open limousine ahead of her. The cries of "*Viva! Viva!*"

The flash of orange and the gigantic roar. The blast throwing her to the street.

"*Viva! Viva! Viva!*"

Chapter Eight

At eight thirty in the morning the shrill ring of the telephone cut through Brassington's thoughts as she sat at the kitchen table. She glanced at her wristwatch—a small round Swiss model on a half-inch gold strap, once the property of Lady Wolverhampton. Who on earth could be calling us at this hour? she wondered. She set down her half-full cup of coffee and went into the living room.

Lady Drew had said she did not wish to be disturbed until she rang, usually at noon. Brassington lifted the receiver a bit apprehensively.

The unmistakable voice of Sir Philip came over the wire, crisp consonants, sizzling sibilants, and all. He sounded angry as he said, "Let me speak to my wife, please."

"Lady Drew left instructions that she did not wish to be called until she rang. But, of course, Sir Philip, I shall awaken her immediately if you say so."

"I do."

Trouble. There was no mistaking the pent-up rage in

his voice. It was, however, none of Brassington's business. She would be glad to get back to the yacht. At least she had her own things around her there. And no telephone to answer.

She knocked on Doe's bedroom door. There was no sound from within. She knocked again quite loudly, then pushed open the door, her heart pounding slightly as the thought suddenly struck her that perhaps Lady Drew had returned late last night with her dinner companion. She did hope not. Not that Brassington had any illusions about her employer's twin sister. But it embarrassed her to know exactly what the two women were up to. She was bound to admit that Mrs. Kerem was much more reserved, and therefore in Brassington's view more ladylike, than Lady Drew, who seemed simply not to care.

"Ma'am," said Brassington into the darkened bedroom. "Sir Philip is on the telephone and insists that I wake you."

"Oh, Christ. What time is it?"

"Just half past eight."

"What's he want?"

"I couldn't say, Milady. He was most insistent."

The bedside light clicked on and Brassington saw that Doe was indeed alone in bed. "Shall I bring in a telephone?"

Doe scooped her long blond hair from her face. "And make some coffee too."

Brassington returned to the desk on which the telephone normally stood and said politely into the receiver, "I am plugging in a telephone in the bedroom now. One moment, please."

Her politeness was rewarded by a sour grunt of thanks. It was not Brassington's problem. She had no wish to become involved.

"Hello, darling," cooed Lady Drew into the receiver as Brassington connected and handed her the instrument.

Brassington left the room and was on the point of re-

63

turning to the kitchen when she remembered that the telephone she had originally answered had not been replaced in its cradle. As she lifted it to hang it up she distinctly heard Sir Philip's rich Shakespearean voice grunt something that sounded horribly like "loudmouthed American cunt."

Quietly, she hung up the telephone and went to the kitchen.

By the time Brassington had made fresh coffee the telephone call had come to an end. One look at Doe confirmed Brassington's notion that it had not been a happy early morning exchange of mutual good wishes between husband and wife. She was smoking and twisting her left index finger through a flaxen lock of hair, a sure sign something was seriously wrong.

"Could you bring me my telephone book? It's on the writing desk."

By the time Brassington found the slim black crocodile-skin book with gold corners and returned to the bedroom, Lady Drew was on her second cigarette. She asked Brassington the time, again.

"Quarter to nine."

"Let's try my lawyer at home. I might just catch him." She handed Brassington her telephone book and pointed to a number. A little resentfully Brassington dialed the number and waited while it rang.

"Give it to me," ordered Doe, "and please check out my black-linen pants suit. It might need pressing."

"Might need pressing," Brassington muttered under her breath. What did the woman take her to be? No matter the obstacles, she would do her job as lady's maid, and that included never putting a garment back into the wardrobe without having sponged and pressed it, ready to wear and looking as fresh as new.

Doe was saying into the telephone, "Garry, I've got to see you. Philip's being impossible. Yes, unbelievable. He

64

seems to think it's grounds for divorce merely because I say in print that I'm all for woman's lib and believe a girl should be self-reliant."

Brassington took the black Valentino linen outfit from the closet. It was not in her nature to eavesdrop, but the apartment was small. And I must admit, she thought, that for once I'm on Sir Philip's side. Not that actors are anything but barbarians, especially toward women.

"Why not come for lunch?" Lady Drew was saying, much to Brassington's annoyance. In the absence of the rest of the staff it would fall on her to serve whatever Doe decided to have sent in, more work that she was in no way paid for.

As soon as she finished speaking to her lawyer, Doe lit another cigarette and dialed the overseas operator.

"When are we supposed to be joining the *Maria*?"

"In two days' time, Milady. In Tangier. The Kerem bank has already sent round our airplane tickets."

Brassington would have liked to escape from the bedroom, but Lady Drew kept escalating demands as she waited for her call to go through. First she wanted Brassington to look through a whole pile of things, which she was then to take by taxi to a resale shop. Imagine, thought Brassington, someone in her position actually *selling* her old clothes. When the late Lady Wolverhampton was finished with her Worth models, Brassington was always asked to choose anything she considered suitable for herself. The rest were dispatched to aid the Red Cross sale, which was what a *real* lady did with her old things.

Now Brassington had the hateful task of taking a taxi loaded with old clothes to the Fulham Road and bargaining with that awful little woman, smelling of gin, in her shop. Even in the morning she smelled of gin. And furthermore, if Brassington did not come back with a large wad of cash, Doe was not above flying into a temper.

Imagine the shame of it! It wasn't cheap-jack enough

that this well-known designer recycled clothes with her own label through her own boutiques. That, Brassington supposed, was just good business. But to flog other designers' clothes, in used condition, at some down-at-the-heels hole in the wall whose alcoholic owner always haggled over price, was demeaning beyond all nightmares of wretchedness. These Americans! These rich Texans! What, Brassington wondered, was the world coming to? And, even worse, was she now supposed to serve as a parlormaid when this Garry person, the lawyer, arrived?

If Mrs. Kerem intended to send her ahead on many more of these visits to London, she would plainly refuse. These days good help was hard to come by. She left Lady Drew still holding on for her overseas call.

The porter helped Brassington take the suitcases to the waiting taxi. On being given the address, the man expressed some reluctance.

"I shall require you to wait," said Brassington with dignity.

"And I shall *require* you to pay for the privilege," replied the Cockney. It was the only thing he said on the entire trip. By the time Brassington had been to the Fulham Road, and returned with nearly three hundred pounds, Doe had just made contact with the yacht. In a loud voice, as if addressing the deaf, she was demanding to talk to her sister.

With a sweeping gesture she indicated that Brassington was to tidy up the bedroom. Amazing, thought the maid. I'm scarcely gone a half hour and she has succeeded in turning her room into a bargain-basement shop. She could only compare the bedroom with the disorganized mounds of clothes scattered around the resale shop.

There was in Brassington's view only one word to describe the woman who did such a thing: slut.

Lady Drew had discarded her black Valentino linen suit by tossing it onto the bed along with a print dress and a beige linen pants suit, the top of which lay under her feet as she sat in front of her dressing table. She played with the coiled telephone wire as she spoke.

"Darling, of course, I understand. But Kee has only liked Philip on the yacht to balance the numbers for mealtimes." While Doe listened, Brassington began to hang up the clothes so carelessly tossed on the bed. When those two started talking, there was no knowing when the conversation would end. It's a wonder to me, thought Brassington, tht Mr. Kerem hasn't put a stop to their chatter. Why, it must cost a fortune.

"Of course I'm considering *your* position." Lady Drew's voice rose. "Do you imagine I want to be put through all that publicity? But he's being impossible, really an incredibly awful little shit. Surely, even Kee won't want me to remain chained to a jumped-up actor who's making me miserable."

She cupped her hand over the telephone and snapped her fingers, indicating to Brassington that she wanted her cigarette lighted.

Brassington, who did not approve of ladies who smoked, handed her first the cigarette box, then snapped the catch on the Dunhll lighter. Doe drew a deep drag of smoke before speaking into the telephone again.

"Darling, I'll see you the day after tomorrow. We'll get it all worked out then. This line is hopeless, as always." She paused. "But, darling, you know I won't do anything stupid. I've the lawyer coming to lunch." She laughed cooingly, as if at a private and rather obscene joke.

Brassington had the last of the rejected outfits back into the closet and was moving in the direction of the bathroom when Lady Drew called her.

"Mrs. Kerem wants to know if you have bought enough of the new pine bath oil, and how many pairs of gaucho denims you managed to find in her size."

"Ten bottles of pine oil. Three pairs of denims." Brassington opened the bathroom and shuddered at the state of the room. Three damp bath towels lay crumpled on the floor. Half-smoked cigarettes stank up the pink onyx ashtray. The plug was still in the bathtub, which was filled with lukewarm green water. Disgusting.

Chapter Nine

No one had asked any questions, thank God. It had been assumed that the storm of yesterday and last night, which had kept so many guests in their stateroom, had also invalided Walter. This was not true, but it served as a convenient excuse in case he was asked why he had taken to his bunk most of the previous afternoon. No one could have known that he had lain awake the entire night, or perhaps dozed fitfully as the Atlantic tossed the *Maria* about.

The exaggerated motion of the ship had not kept him awake. His own shame had. Only now, the next morning, had he finally come to terms with the terrifying humiliation that had fallen on him as suddenly as a gigantic wave could crash down a ship, with that same devastating cruelty that seemed to have nothing to do with him as a person, but only as an object. He knew how the lowest street whore felt, used impersonally, as one wipes one's boots on a doormat, and impersonally filthied in the process with a kind of savage disdain.

She was the Devil, he told himself. All night his mind had raced around the image of her. She was everything evil. If only he had known, when he knelt before her yesterday in all sexual innocence, the degrading humiliation she had planned, he would never have kissed her foot, never agreed to even this symbol of domination.

But the facts were otherwise. And, in the long night of considering them, of watching them chase themselves around inside his overheated brain, one thing had become very clear. It had struck some deep and Germanic chord in Walter and he knew enough about himself to understand that he had neither the strength nor the will to do battle with it.

Each of us has our fate, he told himself now, to become either master or slave. This is the law of the world and the people in it.

And if one's will is to be subjugated to the mastery of a woman, he thought, there were worse fates than being in bondage to Leslie Kerem. Among the crew, Walter had noticed, there were many of these master-slave couplings. The way all of them lived it had not taken more than a day or two for Walter to notice who was in thrall to whom. Nor had the casual brutalities escaped his notice, although he had his own tiny bunk room. It lay just off the general crew's quarters and the things they inflicted on each other out of love or sport or in joke could hardly be overlooked.

His domination by Leslie Kerem had begun at the lowest possible level, an act of obscenity worthy of one of the leather-tough ex-SS refugees from the French Foreign Legion who did the hardest manual labor aboard the *Maria*. Even their cruel sexual thirsts, slaked in faraway lands by the blood of tortured, mutilated, and murdered prisoners, could conceive nothing more elegantly vicious than what

70

she had forced him to do. Nothing she could command of him now would drive her heel any deeper into his neck.

He got out of bed and made do with a washrag cleanup at his basin, not wanting to run the gauntlet of the crew's shower room with his own sexual ego so badly bruised.

He found himself wondering what her evil mind would devise for him now. If he were her master—what? Perhaps she would ignore him totally, a likely idea. It would be what he might do to her, were their roles reversed. If so, she would find him equally distant. Not by a word or a glance would he indicate that he'd ever seen her before. Two could play this lewd game. He dressed and reported to the galley.

The *Maria* was riding more steadily this morning. Walter's first errand was not destined to bring him into contact with the woman he had begun to think of as Her.

He struggled to the bridge, bearing the captain's breakfast, in itself a quite unnecessary chore, now that the storm had abated and the sea settled into a choppy aftermath. The *Maria* couldn't possibly be in the slightest danger anymore. The first mate would have been more than adequate on the bridge, and the captain could have enjoyed a sitdown meal. Yet the captain persisted in dramatizing the situation, as if it were a criminal offense that, owing to bad weather, the yacht would arrive behind schedule.

The chief radio operator, a martyr to seasickness, had gallantly remained through the storm, puking in the tiny radio room. Walter felt really sorry for the man as he took him a glass of hot water and milk of magnesia tablets. Yet, when Walter suggested that he'd do a lot better, now that the weather had calmed, to hand over the instruments to his Number Two, the man had flown off the handle and yelled at him to get out.

Nerves. Could one bald Lebanese turn a first-class German crew into irritable animals? Or had the storm merely unleashed the true Teutonic temperament? The crew were of two types, those who ate twice their normal ration with a bravado that nauseated Walter, and those who feebly groped their way through their responsibilities, terrified that the master of the *Maria* would come upon them in some distressing situation such as throwing up over the side.

Walter had not realized until this voyage the extent that people went to please this one individual.

Even Leslie Kerem.

And yet, what she had forced him to do was not an act of homage to her husband. She had used him, Walter, to revenge herself on an entire sex, of which her husband was the most recent and repellent example.

It was not until noon that Mrs. Kerem rang for her breakfast. Walter panicked for a moment, then shouldered the tray and left the galley.

When Walter entered her cabin the first thing he noticed were deep circles under her eyes, as though she'd slept badly. Blondes showed that sort of thing too clearly. She looked languid and sad, and scarcely said good morning, but her eyes followed his every movement.

"It's a beautiful day," he announced, pulling back the curtains. He stood waiting.

"Good," she replied, without a trace of enthusiasm.

She stretched out for the telephone. By her doing so, Walter regarded himself as dismissed. He left quickly.

He felt both dismissed and forgotten in a single gesture, which was very confusing to him. One part of him wanted very much to be forgotten. But another part craved her cruel attention again and yet again.

As he went about his duties, setting out the chairs on the sundeck, Walter decided what she had done to him yesterday would not be repeated. It had been almost an accident. Leslie Kerem was the kind of person who simply was unable to involve herself with anyone she regarded as lesser except as her servant.

72

If Walter had been a guest, he thought now, it would be quite different. He could look forward to more, much more, of the same. But, even though something *had* gone between them, an instant recognition of each other's desirability, it could never be a lasting appreciation of each other's beauty, both sexual and intellectual.

At that moment Elly appeared carrying her own breakfast tray. During this trip Walter had come to admire Mrs. Raschid as competent and kind. The first night he had carried her dinner to her in her room she had asked him if he were happy on board the *Maria.*

When he'd jokingly replied that his only complaint was that crew members were not allowed to smoke, she had asked him to sit down. Pulling out a packet of cigarettes, she had offered him one, lighting up herself and letting her dinner grow cold. It was a very human gesture.

Walter had heard that, after her husband had died, Kemal Kerem had offered her the job of running the *Maria.* Walter had talked to her as one exile to another, both far from home. "Life in Lebanon is difficult for a middle-aged woman without qualifications," she had explained without a trace of bitterness or regret. "You could call it a heaven-sent opportunity for me." She had sighed reminiscently.

"At the time Mr. Kerem was divorcing his first wife. Life was not easy for him. He was constantly being hounded by the Lebanese press. That was before he became as internationally known as he is now. And I suppose that I made life a little easier for him. Certainly, I could see to it that he was comfortable. Then he met Lyda Lambros." She had ended the conversation at that point.

That had been just a few days ago, Walter thought as he finished opening deck chairs under Elly's watchful gaze. But he had never found himself alone with her again until this moment.

"Mrs. Raschid," he said courteously. "Have you survived the storm in one piece?"

"As well as you," she reponded in a dry voice. "They tell me you took to your bed. But you don't seem the worse for wear."

Walter smiled embarrassedly. "But the sea's no longer rough," he said lamely.

Elly's smile was friendly, but a shade too knowing. "Quite," she responded. She looked away from Walter and added, "I am very glad you have fitted into our life so well. By now, too, you understand Mrs. Kerem, which is very important."

On that note she had begun to eat her breakfast. What the hell did she mean by that remark? Walter asked himself. He forced himself to listen to the instructions she was giving him concerning today's lunch.

"How are the Blots holding up?" she asked. "Do you think it would be tactful if I were to pay them a visit?"

"They were dressing when I collected their breakfast tray."

"Then I need not bother," Elly concluded crisply. She finished her breakfast as Walter began to sort out the bottles on the bar.

"Almost there. The Mediterranean." Walter turned at the sound of Leslie Kerem's unmistakably Texan voice, deep and resonant. "Today I get to work on my tan."

Walter fetched her a beach towel and laid it across a mattress, looking away as she pulled off her dress to reveal a tiny black bikini.

"I hope you won't be cold, Madame."

Leslie looked up at him as she settled herself on the mattress. "Are you always so thoughtful?"

"Always," Elly remarked. "He's a good German boy, our Walter."

"Efficient?" Leslie asked.

"Thorough," Elly added.

"And obedient," her employer finished. She smiled enigmatically at Elly, who nodded, picked up her tray, and went indoors.

74

"Did I say something wrong?" Leslie asked in an innocent voice.

"No, Madame." Walter continued to fuss with the bottles. "Mrs. Raschid is a woman of the world." He hesitated, then plunged on. "She perhaps understands that I am a more serious person with serious interests."

"And you're seriously *interested* in me?"

"Is it permitted?" Oh, Christ, thought Walter, I sound hideously German.

"No, it's not," said Leslie, laughing. "I am permitted to be interested in you. You are only permitted . . . to obey."

Walter sat on his haunches, the better to hold her attention. She wasn't making things easier for him, lying back next to naked, her enormous eyes screened by very dark glasses.

"Certain people are possessed of magnetic qualities," he told her. "They can receive and register impressions. You and I for example. It just happened, that first morning when I brought you your breakfast.

"But to you I am only a servant, a slave. Although the truth is this." He took a deep breath. "We have met before. My father entertained you and your late husband, Governor French, when you visited Germany. My father was mayor of Munich at the time."

Leslie raised herself on her elbows and looked at him.

"It's true," Walter continued. "Look, don't think I don't realize what you see behind every compliment. That you're wondering, right now, if the *real* purpose for my taking this job wasn't to write one of those porno pieces that seem to find their way into all the European magazines, complete with photographs."

"That's unfair," she said. "Your father . . . ?" Leslie Kerem rolled over onto her stomach and stared at him. "But that was years ago."

He waited, but nothing further came from her. Not a word, not a sign that he existed now on a new level for her.

Walter got to his feet and went behind the bar. So be it, his Germanic soul decided heavily. I have gambled and lost. I could perhaps have hoped for something far better than just to be used, a convenience, like an appliance of some kind. He began polishing glasses.

Suddenly there she was, draping herself on a barstool. "I'd like a vodka and tonic, Walter."

He muttered, "Yes, Madame," unable to control his fumbling fingers as he sliced the lime. To hell with you, Mrs. Kerem, he added silently. In the future it would be yes, Madame, no, Madame.

With the return of calm weather, the Blots emerged on deck, looking white and blotchy. Walter mixed them drinks. He then mixed a Bloody Mary to Mrs. Raschid's specific instructions for the master of the *Maria*, who appeared on deck briefly to partake of mounds of rice and green pepper stew. He then disappeared below, taking the unfortunate Blot with him.

Maybe, Walter thought, being an unimportant guest is even worse than being a servant. To spite Leslie Kerem, Walter was particularly courteous to Mrs. Blot, who huddled over her plate of cold cuts, still apparently feeling far from well and very far from hungry.

Walter avoided looking at Leslie as she gathered her belongings and went below. He had made up his mind that yesterday was an accident. He would put all thoughts of her out of his mind. And he'd quit the *Maria* just as soon as it reached Monte Carlo. On his way to his bunk, off the crew's mess, he passed the galley.

"What's all this coffee-in-the-cabin routine?" The chef dug Walter in the ribs. "She fancies you, you crafty young thing." He handed a tray to Walter. "*Mach schnell.*"

"I'm the one thing she does not fancy." Walter picked up the tray with the cup and made his way down the corridor. When he knocked and pushed open the cabin door he was surprised to see Leslie Kerem in bed. Clearly she had nothing on under the sheet.

76

"Your coffee, Madame," he said in a perfect butler's voice.

"Walter—" With her hand she indicated that she would like him to set the tray on the table. "What's all this about your father entertaining Maurice and me in Germany?"

Walter stood by her bed without speaking, looking across the room at the sea flying past the porthole. Finally he said. "It happened. But what of it?"

For some reason that Walter did not understand his remark upset her. "Please," she said. "Are we to be friends?"

Her change of mood was so stunning to Walter that he could find nothing to say. When she held out her hand to him, he took it in silence, allowing her to draw him down onto the bed. She pulled his hand with hers under the sheet, where she introduced him to her nakedness.

"You're beautiful—and wicked." A brief wave of shyness made him hold back. He looked at her, helplessly, while she fiddled with the button on his shirt.

Finally she said, "Take your clothes and leave them in the bathroom. And the door to the corridor—lock it."

When he returned she had pushed back the sheets, exposing most of her body.

She smiled up at him. "We *are* to be friends," she said then. "We will be everything there is to be, my little German slave."

She pulled him down on top of her, stroking his arms and body. "How long can you make it last?" she asked.

"What?" Walter's voice sounded choked.

"Never mind, just try. And the longer you can wait, the more of a friend I will be." She giggled as she fitted him into her. "Begin."

They were locked together now. It blotted out everything for Walter, even the sound of the engine and the sea, even her whimpering cries and small screams. Finally, when he rolled away from her and she turned toward him again, he thought she had the most exciting body he had ever known. Yet she seemed sad. Why? He couldn't be-

77

lieve that she hadn't enjoyed the encounter. He ran his fingers through her blond hair reflectively, wondering about her swift changes of mood and what caused them.

"For someone so beautiful you spend far too much time looking sad. That was a most beautiful experience."

She responded silently by snuggling against him.

Was she worried that perhaps her husband might suddenly walk into the room and discover them? As the thought struck Walter, he also remembered that he had forgotten to lock the door.

He was reluctant to leave her. Nonetheless prudence prompted him to swing his legs onto the floor. He went into the bathroom, first to dress, then to tip the undrunk coffee down the lavatory. Her soft smile obliterated for a moment the look of sadness. She blew him a kiss, closed her eyes, and snuggled into her pillows. He watched her for a moment and got a sudden glimpse of the fact that the master and the slave could exchange roles. Could and would.

"*Auf wiedersehen*," he said as he carried the tray from the room.

Chapter Ten

When the *Maria* tied up in Tangier Harbor at eight thirty in the morning, the sun was already blazing in the sky, casting sharp black sideways shadows, long and inky. Leslie pulled back the porthole curtains and judged that even at this hour it would be a hot day.

She tugged at both curtains, the better to see the activity on the jetty. A noisy, nasty North African port, she thought, but down in the casbah there was that gay American designer who made the greatest kaftans. An errand was a good enough excuse to get off the yacht for a day. The thought of getting onto dry land and moving around the shops perked her up. She almost ran across the cabin to telephone for her breakfast.

Doe would be arriving today. She could get to the bottom of all this ridiculous talk of divorce. To undergo all the unpleasant publicity for the sake of legalizing a separation from a harmless actor of some repute seemed pointless. It wasn't as though he cost Doe money.

Having a stage celebrity to balance the numbers at dinner was very convenient, especially in places like Monte Carlo, where all the social occasions tended to be a bit formal. Doe must be made to realize what a mistake she was making.

At that moment Walter appeared in the doorway with her breakfast.

He kicked the door shut with his heel and moved toward the sofa, setting the tray down on the glass-topped table.

He watched her closely, silently, as if reading her face for clues. What would it be today, master or slave? But today was too sunny, too filled with the freedom of being ashore and away from this prison ship. Today she could spend without once seeing that pinched, distracted look on her husband's face as he and Jensen Blot fussed and worried about their shabby hoard of dollars.

"Today," she told Walter now, "is free . . . utterly free!"

A broad grin broke out on the young steward's face. He hastily ran his fingers through straw-colored hair. "Can I be with you ashore?" he begged. "Your . . . chaperon?"

"Equerry?" she suggested.

"Companion?" he asked "Or bodyguard? Yes, that's the word. I'm to guard your body."

She smiled up at him. He was beautiful and grew more beautiful every day.

It was absolutely necessary for Leslie to personalize sex. Had she allowed herself to consider Walter a servant who slipped into her bedroom when nobody was looking, she would have found it degrading and sordid. But a fledgling actor, working his way back to Europe, a man from a good family, a personality soon to be discovered by the public—that was entirely different.

"What's the matter?" Leslie glanced up at Walter. He was standing in front of the sofa looking suddenly very unhappy.

80

"I have to give you a message. It's from, er, Mr. Kerem. He wants to see you in the dining salon."

Leslie buttoned herself into a ground-length pale-blue housecoat. "Is he alone?"

"Is he ever?" Walter grimaced. "He has Mr. Ali taking notes while he's barking instructions at that Mr. Blot. Mr. Blot still looks seasick to me. What if the Blots want to come shopping with us?"

"Put them in a taxi and send them off to look at mosques?"

"Are there such things in Tangier?" Walter asked. "I'd always understood it was a naughty kind of city. Barbara Hutton playing in her personal Garden of Allah with some fabulous admirer. But I want to walk through the casbah holding your hand, preventing anyone from touching you. I don't want Mr. and Mrs. Blot trailing along."

Leslie laughed happily. "You forget I'm the boss' wife."

"Unfortunately I'm never able to forget that."

Leslie ran a lipstick over her mouth and reached for a large pair of dark glasses. She hated having to walk into a room when she wasn't properly dressed. Not that any of the men would even notice her. Except Blot. He had a thing for her.

When she reached the dining room Kee was demolishing his second jar of yogurt with mint, dribbling it over his chin as he dictated a cable in Lebanese. He waved Leslie to his side, wiping his mouth with the back of his hand before planting a kiss on her cheek.

She smiled dutifully and caught Blot staring at her. God, she thought, he really does have a thing for me.

Kee switched his conversation into English. "Blot, are you man enough to take care of the ladies? Ali here won't be much help as an escort."

"You may count on me."

Leslie wished Blot would wipe that fatuous grin off his face. Whatever happened, she was not going to have her

81

day spoiled by being thrown in with him and his wife. At that moment Walter came into the salon and quietly poured her a cup of coffee. Leslie kept her eyes down, hoping Blot would stop staring at her.

"Well, baby." Kee was in one of his jovial moods. "Don't buy up the whole of the casbah. There are thirty-two developed countries on the point of bankruptcy. Don't make me the thirty-third." He guffawed at his own joke.

"And, by the way," he added suddenly, "I won't have your sister getting a divorce."

Leslie looked up startled. Were her telephone calls monitored? They looked at each other, dark glasses into dark glasses. Kee grinned broadly and patted her hand by way of farewell. "See you in Monte Carlo."

"You're leaving the ship?"

"Business in Brussels, then Basel." Kee turned his grin on Jensen Blot. "Before I forget it, Blot, you did a good job. I'll remember how good when I get to Basel, eh?" Again his thick laughter filled the salon.

Leslie tried to look disinterested. "Then everything's back to normal?"

"Normal?" her husband snapped.

"You're finished with this big business thing that's made you such a grouch this past week?"

"Almost finished," he said. "And once again—" His nostrils flared as he filled his lungs to bellow: "Victorious!"

His valet appeared on cue with the jacket to match his gray pants. A black briefcase which bore Kerem's initials in gold was in his other hand. Ali rose and followed his uncle up the stairway to the deck.

Leslie remained seated, saying to his back, "Have a good trip."

"Perhaps I should see him off?" Blot looked at Leslie for guidance.

"That would be nice. I won't come on deck. You never know when there's a photographer with a long-range lens lurking around."

82

As soon as Blot had left the salon, Leslie turned to Walter. "Does someone listen into my telephone calls?" she asked.

"I've no idea. It would be easy enough."

"Because he knew my sister was thinking of getting a divorce. And nobody else knows. I've told no one."

"Maybe her lawyer told your husband. Or Philip. Perhaps he called Mr. Kerem."

Leslie wasn't wholly convinced. She sensed from the way Kee had dropped the news into the conversation that it was designed to have her worried. Had he caught a look between her and Walter? Was her stateroom bugged? She felt her lips trembling as she smiled.

"When the opportunity comes up, see what you can learn from the radio operator," she ordered.

"He's not exactly my type. But I'll see what I can charm out of him."

Blot came back into the dining room and Leslie thought he looked about ten years younger, now that he wasn't being subjected to orders and scrutiny from her husband. She smiled radiantly at him in preparation for dismissing him with his seasick little wife for the day.

"I've been thinking, Mr. Blot. I am going to ask Elly to accompany you and Elizabeth on a sight-seeing tour of Tangier. Unless you would prefer to just have the car and driver on your own?"

"I'd hoped to have the honor of *your* company."

"I have a fitting, very boring. But we could perhaps arrange to meet later."

To Leslie's surprise, Walter spoke before being spoken to. "Mrs. Kerem, the driver of the car has a whole day's excursion arranged for Mr. and Mrs. Blot. If you remember, you asked me to do this."

Leslie's smile broadened. "We all feel you should see something of the beauties of Morocco. So, go off for the day and enjoy yourself."

From the expression on Blot's face, Leslie realized this

was about the last thing he wanted to do. She didn't care. She and Walter had them nicely cornered.

Elly came into the dining salon and looked briefly surprised to see Leslie sitting at the table so early in the day.

"I'm so glad to find you," she began. "Could you possibly go shopping with just the chauffeur and Walter? Mr. Kerem has left me with so many letters to get into the mail tonight."

"Of course, Elly. I'm only going to look at kaftans. And the Blots have been given their own car for the day. Is there something I can get for you?"

For a moment of utter silence, Elly's large, lustrous eyes flicked from Leslie to Walter and back again with a motion that spoke louder than any words. But, like even nonverbal messages, it was hard to read.

Elly seemed to be saying, "I see you have your gay squire at your side." But perhaps she already knew Walter's shameful secret, that he was the only hetero in the crew. In which case the dark Mediterranean look meant something else, deeper and more dangerous, along the lines of, "If I were Kerem I'd have you flayed." Or, perhaps, "Go to it, woman, he's gorgeous." Or, even more obscure, "Once Kerem has possessed you, what good is any other man?"

But she said none of these in words, only: "Not a thing," smiled, and left the salon.

Leslie dismissed Walter and devoted herself to the problem of what to wear. Something, she mused, not too eye-catching. She didn't want to be spotted with Walter, have the U.S. press, or, worse, those awful European scandal magazines, reporting her movements.

Tangier, she remembered, was always windy, even in summer, so she could with reason cover her pale blond hair, which helped to disguise who she was. She returned to her stateroom like an actress to her wardrobe.

Finally, after much deliberation, the discarding of several possible dresses, and the trying of different effects, Leslie left her cabin wearing a plain sleeveless white hand-stitched cotton frock that just covered her knees. Around it she buckled a thin black patent belt. She had slipped into black patent sandals.

The black-white combination she had decided on for Walter's sake. She did not want to cast him too openly in the role of bodyguard, although that was officially his reason for going with her. She felt that if she were to complement the clothes he was obliged to wear, they would set out together as a pair, both in white cotton with black belts. It made a *statement.*

Over her hair she flung a long-ended multiblue chiffon scarf, with Lanvin's signature much in evidence. Around her neck she twisted three ropes of lapis lazuli and gold beads, necklaces she had picked up last winter in Beirut, but until today had not felt in the mood for wearing.

Beneath her dress she had drenched her skin in Audace, slipping a purse-sized atomizer into her pochette—the latest model from Rome, bought in Bonwit Teller last week.

She took one last hesitant look at herself, then walked with long Texas strides along the corridor, up the stairs, through the heavily decorated main salon, and out onto the deck.

There stood Walter, looking to Leslie exactly as though he had just come from his quarters, where he had washed, shaved, and changed. In his hand was a pair of dark glasses.

"Madame," he said, grinning, "this is my first occasion as somebody's bodyguard. Am I supposed to ask the captain to issue me a revolver?"

Laughing, she almost forgot herself to the extent that she had to pull back her arm before slipping it through his. "We're only going to buy kaftans," Her last remark was flung out for the benefit of any of the crew who might possibly be listening.

Already Leslie felt freer. The cloying smell of the perfume in the ship's ventilation system no longer filled the air. The dockside smells of Tangier—oil, tar, salt, fish, and the haunting peppery scent of burning hashish—claimed her attention for a moment, making her forget the sickly-sweet smell of the *Maria* and her life aboard the ship. Today would be a wonderful day of freedom.

Walter walked first down the gangplank, half turning to help her. On the jetty stood a Cadillac and uniformed chauffeur. Beside the car waited two officials, who more than willingly had deserted their dull places in the customs shed to get a close-up look at Leslie.

The chauffeur held open the car door. Leslie got into the back with only a faint trace of a smile for the two officials. Walter waited for one of the men to examine their papers and put a stamp on their passports. He then got into the front of the limousine beside the chauffeur. The black car with its tinted glass windows bore the insignia of the Kerem bank.

Leslie sat in the back almost hidden from sight. Tangier had never especially appealed to her. She wondered how quickly she could hurry through the selection of kaftans. Good though they were, kaftans were not really why she had hurried off the yacht.

She hoped Walter had made the arrangements, and that there wouldn't be any hitch. It was not the first time she had been to a hotel bedroom, in more or less these circumstances, but it was indeed a "first" in Tangier.

The excuse they had planned together was that Madame needed a room in which to try on her selection of kaftans. If she were to return to the yacht, Walter had told the hotel, with clothes on approval, it made for complications with the customs.

It sounded a bit feeble. As her bodyguard, however, Walter should accompany her to the suite. Oh, God, she thought, it really would make a great story if the truth came out. Just the sort of things the gossip magazines doted on.

It didn't bother Leslie that Kee still had his eternal Greek mistress, Leda Lambros. But the unflagging interest of the gossip press in all this infuriated her. And the sheer power of the lies often took her breath away. She remembered even now a group of obviously faked photos in which she and Doe, naked, fondled and licked each other. And the cruelest part was that her lawyers refused to sue for fear of giving the photos even wider circulation. She frowned as the Cadillac edged its way deeper into Tangier traffic.

She recrossed her legs and fiddled nervously with her lapis beads. The car had slackened speed as they turned into the tiny narrow streets of old Tangier. They parked outside a high whitewashed wall, in the center of which stood a double brass-studded wooden door. Walter jumped out of the car and rang the big hand bell. The door was opened immediately by a young Arab boy. Walter turned back to help Leslie from the car. "No snoopers," he whispered.

The pudgy American owner of the kaftan boutique waited in the doorway to greet Leslie. He had dressed in a white burnoose and his feet were shod in gold Ali Baba slippers. He bowed, hands clasped. Behind him two very young Arab boys, wearing tight black pants and T-shirts, eyed Leslie.

"Darling, I'm honored." He waved her with mock dignity toward a bizarre interior quite like Aladdin's cave. "I thought you'd prefer to make your selection from my private salon. I can entertain you in the tradition of the Arabs with Turkish coffee and sweetmeats. Or we could all be good little Americans and have a vodka martini." His eyes creased with a smile.

"Let's be American," said Leslie, "and democratic, too. We'll include my bodyguard, Walter."

"A martini at this hour?" Walter asked, all his Germanic sense of righteousness showing.

"Why not, sweets?" the designer asked. "I'm into early drinking myself, aren't you?"

Walter frowned at him. "As Madame wishes, then." He turned to Leslie and stood waiting humbly as befitted a bodyguard who was also her slave.

Leslie giggled. "Goodness." She stood there enjoying the situation for a moment, strangely pleased that Walter had taken such a protective line toward her, and even more pleased that he had placed his fate in her hands.

"Perhaps not yet," she said at last.

The designer echoed her giggle girlishly, a sound that did not match his broad frame. His belly protruded even beneath the fall of his loose garment. He rolled his eyes.

The two young Arabs began holding up exquisitely embroidered dresses for Leslie as she sat back on a mount of soft cushions in what was called the private salon. The designer chattered with Walter, since the lovely and famous lady had indicated that he was to be part of the occasion.

Walter helped the American refold some of the kaftans. "Dear, aren't you clever with your hands?" the designer simpered.

"Come and work for me." He dug Walter in the ribs, who stared wide-eyed at Leslie, making her laugh. Seeing how matters stood, the American added: "Just joking, dolls. Well, here's to the three of us." He lifted his own colorless martini to them and took a swig of it.

Leslie, who normally took up to three hours to choose clothes, picked nine kaftans at random and had them boxed immediately. When the job was done they came to three large parcels.

Walter made out the check and handed it to Leslie to sign. The designer mopped his face with excitement.

By prearrangement, a cab had pulled up behind the black Cadillac. Walter and the boxes went on ahead to the hotel. "Lovely boy," the designer murmured. "So efficient. So . . . ah, masterful."

Behind her dark glasses, Leslie eyed him coolly, deliberately wasting time to make sure this overweight specimen hadn't tipped off the press. "Do you fancy Walter?" she asked in an offhand manner.

"I adore men who don't sweat."

She nodded gravely as if this were the most natural taste in the world. "I prefer a man like you," she said.

He reddened, caught in the act of sponging off his face again. "Naughty." He pouted. As she moved toward the outer door he scurried after her. "When you're finished with him. . . ." He let his voice die away on a note of interest and regret.

As she ducked into the cab, Leslie noted there were still no reporters. That was a lucky break, but from past experience she knew that the kaftan designer would eventually be unable to resist telephoning his best newspaper contact with full details of her purchase. This was precisely why she had picked out so many embroidered items. It would make a fashion story. The world could devour it and so miss the *real* Tangier story.

Leslie hurried through the empty lobby of the hotel. The time was midday and most of the holidaymakers were by the swimming pool or otherwise enjoying themselves. No one saw her except a desk clerk.

Walter pressed the button for the top floor. They had the elevator to themselves. Except for the twelve-year-old page, half hidden under boxes of kaftans, nobody saw them enter the presidential suite.

As soon as they were alone Leslie fell into his arms.

She knew that she was worrying probably quite unnecessarily. But Kee's remark haunted her. How could he *possibly* know that Doe was thinking about getting a divorce?

Worse, if Kee knew that much, how much more might he know about Leslie's own life? Walter's arms held her firmly as they embraced, but her mind had wandered far from the affairs of the moment. A lot of time and effort and money and lying had gone into creating this moment of aloneness for them. A lot of Leslie's fantasies had projected the things she would have Walter do in this secluded hotel suite. Now her thoughts were flying away from the "now" she had created into the misty area of uncertainty Kee's casual remark had produced.

Not that she and Doe had ever done anything of which they were ashamed. Their detested father had raised them that way. "Never explain. Let no one judge you but yourself." A facile motto, rich with snob ego, and not all that easy to enforce anymore.

The strain of not knowing quite what had gone wrong now engulfed Leslie. Rushing through the shopping, all the time wondering if some prying person was reporting back to an ever-interested press. She could feel the beginnings of headache.

"Darling, order lemon tea." Psychosomatic, the New York physician had called these headaches, but the pain which shot through the back of her neck in waves felt as if someone were turning a screwdriver along a nerve.

She opened her bag and took out three tablets. "Can I drink the water?"

"No. I'll order some mineral water." Walter had his back to her as he talked to room service. She eyed his broad shoulders and narrow hips.

"Order something for yourself." Leslie rubbed her neck to lift the pain. Why now, of all times, did she have to feel this wretched?

Walter hung up the telephone. "Lie down. You'll take your tablets and then I'll massage your neck."

"Why didn't you order something for yourself?"

"Bodyguards don't drink on duty." He kissed her very gently on her forehead. "Lie down."

His words trailed away, as he walked out of the bedroom

into the living room, closing the door so that when he arrived the waiter could not see her lying on the bed.

Leslie lay back on the bed and tried to relax. She knew these headaches. The codeine-based tablets helped a little. But somehow, with Walter's promise still in her mind, the pains had already begun to subside a little.

If he could do this for her, he was even more of a jewel than she'd dreamed. Leslie sighed, not unhappily, and looked forward to telling Doe all about it.

Chapter 11

Leda Lambros lay stretched across the long white sofa in her living room. Listening. Waiting for the ring of the front doorbell. The stage had been carefully set for an audience of one.

The plot of the drama: He would find her absorbed in her work as the curtain rose. She lay back now, listening to her latest album—Greek folk music with a guitar backing. The stereo could be made to crowd the apartment with sound but, turned down to a soft all-over low, it was a romantic backdrop for anyone as flamboyant as Leda, and she knew it.

Her long slim legs were encased in a pair of very fine skin-colored tights. Her gypsy-style skirt rode up around her thighs and a white cotton shirt revealed plenty of olive bosom.

Only the skin marked Leda Lambros as totally and forever Greek, that time-textured, somber cast that is less a color than a reflection of the deep, wine-dark sea. The rest of Leda could be any nationality. Her celebrated legs, as long as any Texas beauty's, had flashed and pranced through many a Molière comedy or Feydeau farce. Her uptilted breasts, full and yet still conical, gave her dancing a savage African tension. Her face, perhaps in its mobility, was at least Mediterranean, if not notably Greek. No one knew—and Leda never told—whether the short nose was hers alone or had had highly expert help from a deft surgeon.

Big gold earrings hung from her tiny ears. Around her narrow wrist coiled the first present Kerem had given her. Or, to be more exact, the first present Kerem had been asked to buy her. She regarded the gold bracelet, twisted into a snake and heavily studded with rubies, as a good-luck penny.

She was playing with a glass of ouzo, but clearly not drinking it. Her pose, the drink, and the music had been very carefully thought out. She sensed, rather than knew, that Kemal Kerem was very vulnerable at this moment. Now was *her* moment to strike, to lure him back, not as the lover returned, or as a rich provider. Her last two record albums had taken care of all foreseeable money worries. She could really afford to have whom she wished as a lover. This time she would have Kerem—for good. This time things would not go wrong.

After talking to Kerem yesterday, she had the impression that he was growing bored with his marriage. Certainly he was bored by all the nincompoops that surrounded him, and perhaps this included Leslie French.

An ideal moment to capture him.

Leda twisted restlessly on the sofa. The living room, which looked more like a greenhouse than a place where intelligent people lived and worked, annoyed her. But then the whole apartment here in Paris was not of her choosing. A furnished flat she used only a few months of the year.

The doorbell rang.

Suddenly she felt almost sick with fright. It was one of those moments of stark panic before she showed herself to an audience. She picked up the pad and pencil that lay on the table at her elbow, pretending to make notes. She heard his voice as he spoke to her maid. She judged the moment he must be in the doorway.

With a dramatic gesture she threw down the pad and pencil and ran across the white carpet in her stocking feet. She flung herself at Kerem as he stood, slightly self-consciously, with a small parcel in his hand.

"Darling, you look wonderful." She held him at arm's length. He in fact looked exactly as he had when she'd seen him last, three months ago in Zurich. But she continued in her throaty voice, "I've missed you. So much."

She led him to the sofa. With theatrical aplomb she tipped the glass of ouzo into the nearest rubber plant, saying, "It's a drink for peasants. But I become wholly peasant when I work. Now that you're here, we drink champagne."

Anna, the maid, came in on cue with champagne and a little dish of lamb on toothpick skewers.

"I made a luncheon reservation for us at Le Grand Vefour," Kerem said.

His smile was almost mechanical, as his first words had been mere protocol. As was often the case, his mind was elsewhere. The bitch hasn't been treating him well, Leda surmised. She knew more about Kerem than even his doctors. She knew, for instance, that he felt best when slightly overtaxed by sex. One orgasm too many might leave another man cross and unwilling. It gave Kerem renewed drive and an almost high-voltage spark. But Le Grand Vefour for lunch? Abysmal.

God, how bourgeois, Leda thought. If there was one thing she hated it was an overpriced tourist restaurant. But she smiled sweetly over the top of her wineglass.

"To us."

He still held the parcel and she was beginning to wonder if perhaps she'd been mistaken. Perhaps he hadn't brought her a present. As though reading her mind, he said, still in a lifeless tone: "To make up for my having been away from you for so long."

Leda tore off the paper and sprang the catch of the small black leather box. Set out on black velvet was a wide, exquisitely worked gold bracelet. It was the kind of luxury she found dull. Middle-aged good taste, but not for her. Nevertheless it was quite heavy. He would never have chosen anything so ordinary in the old days but, in sheer weight alone, this was worth quite a lot. Leslie French's filthy middle-class Texas taste must be contagious. Such typical Texan ostentation!

She fought off the fleeting pang of jealousy that always tended to make her say the wrong thing.

"Fasten it, darling." She offered Kerem her arm and the bracelet, because actual words of pleasure simply failed her.

They sat beside each other on the sofa. The pale Paris sun shone through the picture window. Leda's voice, singing in Greek, now filled the room from the stereo speakers.

"It's a big hit." She inclined her head toward the sophisticated sound equipment that ran along the opposite wall. "Very patriotic, just right for now—" She broke off because Kerem seemed not to be listening to her.

His glance ran over the apartment. She wondered if perhaps he was looking for signs that she had been entertaining someone else. Or was he preoccupied, worried about something else?

She began another approach. "I need your advice. About the apartment."

"What's wrong with it?" His question was defensive as he looked around the room again in a somewhat proprietary way. As though he still owned the place, Leda thought.

In fact, the deed of the apartment had been given to

her. It was as legal as his French lawyer could make it. After that ghastly blowup in Monte Carlo, a disastrous row that had raged for three days, this flat was a peace gift.

Leda deliberately turned her thoughts away, because she was once more about to remember it had been this row that had led to his marrying Leslie French. And whenever Leda allowed herself to think about Leslie she felt a flash of Greek temper.

"I've had a very interesting offer for this apartment," she said evenly, sipping her champagne.

Although 46 Avenue Bosquet was entirely hers to sell if she wished, she had no desire to sell it. But the thought was as good a way as any to get conversation going. Money was about the only channel that Kerem thoroughly enjoyed exploring in depth.

"Although the offer is very good, I need to know how you feel. If, for example, I accept the money, what do I buy? Not another apartment in Paris. That would seem stupid. Or maybe not so stupid? Darling, you're so clever—what should I do?"

"Nothing. Keep it. It's in one of the best districts."

Leda nodded. She was bored with owning such a sound and bourgeois apartment, as she was apt to explain to her more artistic and less successful friends. But the resale value of anything in this arrondissement, and especially something so well built, with dull respectable neighbors, underground garaging, and a liveried porter in place of the usual sleazy concierge, was an asset in any crisis.

"The world's so uncertain," she ventured then, letting a certain tremor creep into her voice.

Kerem was stuffing lamb bits into his mouth two at a time. "I'll take care of you."

It wasn't quite the answer she had hoped for. There was something on his mind. All her plans for brilliant conversation, followed by, or interspersed with, highly erotic antics on her bed, seemed to be receding.

He's not really tuned into me yet, she thought. So I suppose we'd better just go and eat. She drained her glass although she was still quite determined not to drink very much. Nor under any circumstances was she to flare up and lose her celebrated temper one more time.

She walked across the room for the bottle of champagne. It was a movement, like the preening slink of a cat, designed to attract attention. With her arm around his shoulder she remained standing.

"Darling, I must just find a pair of shoes. After all we don't want to look like the peasants we really are."

As she spoke she ran her firm, broad hand along his neck, kneading it, digging her fingers into his flesh.

His arm went around her thighs. "I've missed you."

"Naturally," she said with spirit. "You must miss me for a few more minutes while I dress."

She went into her bedroom where Anna had set out a pair of new black boots with high heels and a little black beret. This rather *apache* rig struck a new note in chic.

Leda examined the new bracelet more closely. It was top workmanship and very heavy, but dull, sane, uninspiring.

In the good old days, she thought, I'd have flung the thing out the window, whatever its cost. But now she fingered it reflectively. I'll just keep it. And sell it the first time he does something to annoy me.

She returned to the living room and moved dramatically to the doorway. Kerem struggled to his feet, leaving the best part of a glass of champagne. Together they went through the hall to the elevator.

As Leda swept through the glass lobby downstairs, she noticed that the porter, who normally dozed in his little glass case called an office, now stood by the door, chatting to the car-hire man who'd driven Kerem.

More tidbits in the newspapers, she thought. Well, all Paris knows he's mad about me.

She treated the chauffeur to one of her wide theatrical smiles as she settled into the back of the car.

It had been a fine warm day and was now reaching its

peak. Paris had still not entirely gone on vacation, but by the end of the week most good restaurants would be closed. Leda had yet to decide how she would spend the month of August. A fleeting resentment went through her that the man at her side was largely responsible for her unattached state.

They reached Le Grand Vefour to find the restaurant almost full. There was an intellectual table consisting of a famous writer, his publisher, his regular girlfriend, and another couple, perhaps American. Leda nodded to the writer, artist to artist.

A well-known French politician sat with two other men. Nearby, a rich American foursome, regular visitors who knew their way around Paris, chatted amiably among themselves.

Kerem, she noticed, bowed to the politician as he seated himself on the banquette beside her, explaining to the headwaiter that he preferred to sit beside Miss Lambros and look out across the courtyard. Thus they occupied two tables and had rather more protection from eavesdropping.

For the next few minutes the ritual of ordering took up their attention. One didn't just eat here, Leda thought, it was a total experience in middle-class gluttony. She found herself growing irritable under the petty details of the cook's promised expertise. Kerem took great pains with their order and the headwaiter assured Leda they would enjoy a memorable lunch.

To be followed by a memorable afternoon. Leda slid her hand into Kerem's and was rewarded by a firm response.

Because she knew that the famous writer and his publisher had trained their eyes on her, Leda began to tell a story. It was neither funny nor especially interesting. But she described the situations, making full use of her hands, tossing back her head to show her hair, mimicking the characters she was describing. Leda felt that all the other lunchers were more interested in what she was telling Kerem than in what they were eating. After all, what was an artist for but to bring a bit of excitement into their drab lives?

As Leda came to the dramatic climax she dropped both knife and fork in her plate and made a big circular gesture with both hands. At the same time she leaned forward, knowing that the intellectual table across the room was by now riveted by her performance. She whispered into Kerem's ear: "My new recordings plus your business acumen. What a merger."

Kerem polished his dark glasses on his napkin. "But why leave Paris? Why must you go back to Greece?"

"I feel dead, strangled in this superficial atmosphere." She waved her hand around the room, almost clipping the waiter on the ear as he removed their half-finished plates of whitebait. "Darling, you know you too must one day join me in Greece," she added.

She paused, having made her point, while they were both served large helpings of Beef Wellington, elaborate and cloyingly rich. The wine waiter filled their glasses with a claret as smooth as velvet.

She sipped her wine. It was the only really good part of the meal as far as she was concerned, but she watched Kerem tuck into his beef with relish.

The trouble is, she thought, you simply don't pick up the threads of any relationship just like that. Like fixing a drink and knowing it is going to help. It took time to tune back into each other's way of thinking, and so far she felt she had totally failed to get through to Kerem.

And yet she was determined to reestablish the complete head-to-toe intimacy they had always before enjoyed. It was not that she loved this preoccupied man for himself or for this money. It was something else about him that she craved, his power.

Perhaps later this afternoon, after she had brought him

to a first climax and then, cruelly, to a second one he had no dream of achieving without her, perhaps then she would begin to recharge the relationship between them until it crackled and sparked with sheer, thrilling power once again.

Chapter 12

The person-to-person call came through at 10 A.M. New York time, making it late afternoon in Tangier. The chubby, sweating American designer, who had placed the call as soon as Leslie had left his premises, had been lying on his bed all afternoon, waiting for the connection to go through.

He swung his short legs over the side of the bed. Whenever he made an important business call he felt the need to tackle it in the sitting position. With his back straight he could think more clearly, whereas when he gossiped or made a rendezvous he preferred to recline. Preferably naked. It was quite a sight.

He still wore his burnoose and he sat very straight, since the conversation he was about to have was very important indeed. It was almost as important as the first time he had leaked a romantic story concerning Barbara Hutton to his same contact on *Women's Wear Daily*.

"Roy, darling, the most interesting piece of news. No,

101

my dear, it has nothing to do with my harem of pretty boys. They just get younger and plumper.

"Leslie Kerem paid me a visit today. Yes! She bought nine kaftans. Nine, love. Have you any idea just how much that is? Each kaftan is upwards of two thousand dollars.

"Why are they so expensive? Darling, they're embroidered, stitch by stitch, with *real* gold thread and *real* pearls. They're copies of work that goes back hundred of years.

"What? Yes, of course, to my specifications. But, doll, they're genuine traditional Moroccan designs, all of them made in the old city of Fez.

"Fez, sweets. That's the old medieval capital.

"Her actual bill? Wouldn't that be rather unkind? I mean for you to publish the *actual* amount she spent? Wouldn't it be kinder, my dear, to say that it was between twenty and thirty thousand dollars?

"No, her sister wasn't with her.

"Nor the English maid."

"No, just one very pretty boy. She called him her body-guard."

At that point the designer giggled into the receiver and ran his hand through the long hair of the young Arab boy who stood by his side with a golden plate on which lay three neatly folded, scented damp towels.

"He was six foot two or three, with a marvelous head, a bit Germanic.

"No, she never introduced him. But she called him Walter. And she was quite willing for him to have drinkies with us. So he isn't a *real* servant, my dear. Just called one for appearance's sake. But gay, lover, or I miss my guess."

Chapter 13

After she had finished the tea, and as the headache tablets began to work, Walter slowly undressed her, removing each bit of clothing gently, as if her skin were raw, flayed with pain, and even this friction was too much to bear. Leslie lay on her stomach, head cradled in her crossed arms, and watched Walter strip.

Then he mounted her gently, his penis lying between her creamy buttocks as he bent over and began to knead the tight, hard muscles at the base of her neck and across her shoulders. He could feel his erection grow as he moved up and back, pressing here, sinking his fingers in there, slowly moving each muscle back and forth until it softened under his touch.

She had begun groaning softly at first with the relief of pain. Now her groans came more quickly and with the recklessness of pleasure. A sudden half shriek, half giggle escaped her.

"From behind," she almost shouted. "At once!"

Her buttocks rose under him like the unruly rump of a fine mare, twitching with lust, sleek with perspiration. He pulled back slightly.

"Now!" she commanded.

They had drawn the curtains in the presidential suite against the midday sun. By five o'clock the sun had moved and the room was almost dark.

Walter lay on his back, his eyes wide open, breathing carefully. He felt the least movement on his part might wake Leslie. Yet he was beginning to think that perhaps it was time for them to return to the *Maria*.

He was longing for a cigarette. He was also quite hungry. She moved in against him as she stirred in her sleep, imprisoning him with her arm. It would be impossible to slip out of bed without disturbing her.

Walter decided to give her a few more moments of peace before gently caressing her awake. Walter felt both protective and privileged, almost to the point of arrogance. And why not? The fabled Leslie Kerem had chosen him from among all the men in the world.

If only, thought Walter, people realized what she had been through. They wouldn't be so quick to condemn her for her marriage to Kerem. He tried to remember just exactly what she had said.

They—the French clan—had listened to everyone's telephone calls. They even eavesdropped on one another. A secretary would switch on a tape recorder so they actually had recordings of her conversations with everyone, even her own innocent little morning chats with her twin sister. So it was understandable that she'd panicked this morning when it seemed clear she was being eavesdropped upon again.

There were other things she had said, things which had thrown a whole new light on her relationship to the French family.

Walter had listened in dumb amazement to her story of

what had happened after Maurice French had been killed.

She hadn't actually described it. Well, after all, no one needed a description. The TV cameras had brought it into practically every living room on earth. But she had talked about herself, afterward, weeks and months after.

Everywhere she went she kept thinking she'd seen him. She would suddenly catch sight of the back of a man who for a moment looked like him. She'd hear a voice and turn, but it wasn't Maurice. These fleeting reprieves would come and go, leaving her increasingly more nervous, fearful of going out anywhere. And all the while, of course, the doctors pumped everything known to science into her, sedatives, tranquilizers, mood elevating drugs, everything.

The French family had been cold toward her, as if she had let the side down, as if in some mysterious way she had connived at his death. All they wanted of her now was a waxwork dummy of mourning, an aging lady in perpetual black.

The only man they'd thought sufficiently respectable for her to date was a roving Spanish ambassador, because he had a title, was widowed, and as dull as a pair of Texas boots. *They* would have allowed her to marry him with all their blessings. It was exchanging the immense family ranches and oil fields of Texas for the Catalonian wilds, an overseas prison, like Devil's Island.

Later Walter had made love to her again, very gently, whispering to her in German, because he was too emotional at that moment to translate his feelings into another language. Now, even later, it was time to leave.

He twisted around onto his side. She lay beside him, slim, tanned, with just the trace of a bikini mark across her buttocks. It was a difficult decision. Either he disturbed her by making love to her again, or he brought them both back to reality. As her clandestine lover and official bodyguard, he knew it was time for them to return to the yacht.

What, he wondered, did she *really* want?

It seemed to Walter that they'd spent an entire lifetime in this bed and run the gamut of emotions. Yet he didn't know if she wanted him to be serious. He was penniless, but his family went back five hundred years. Granduncles had always been at the Austro-Hungarian court. There would be a bit of family money, eventually, and property too. Meanwhile, there was the chance he'd make it in his own right. It was just that he was trying to break into movies and television at a very bad moment.

He ran his hand reflectively along her body. She stirred, rolled onto her back, and pulled him gently over her. All thoughts of returning to the yacht vanished.

She pulled at him with such sexual urgency that it almost hurt. Christ, he thought, I've never known anyone with so many sexual moods. The electricity flashed between, without either of them saying a single word. It was over almost before it had begun, and Walter felt a wave of shame as he rolled off her. He loathed the comparison, but that time, making love to Leslie had been very like making it with an inflatable plastic doll.

"That was fantastic," she had said. She stretched out, flexing her long Texas limbs in a way that was momentarily repellent to Walter. Could they program plastic dolls to do that?

"God, you're good in bed," she added as the final crusher.

He had got out of bed at once, hiding his hurt behind the necessity of getting them both organized and back to the yacht. Perhaps, he decided, she was suffering from remorse, regretting that she had taken him quite so completely into her confidence about the French family.

"I'm going to ask them to bring up the bill. Is there anything else you'd like?" he asked.

"Some mint tea. And two more of those blessed tablets."

He dressed and left the room. The anticlimax was com-

To fall for a woman who lived on painkillers? But it was her clinical attitude to sex that set his teeth on edge. He was a romantic and she wasn't.

He picked up the telephone and ordered her tea. For himself he ordered a beer with a double order of eggs and bacon. He then asked for the front desk and the bill.

Room service appeared almost immediately with the order. Walter gave the man a coin. With childish resentment he wondered if he ought to submit an expense account. He drew on his cigarette.

Leslie came into the room, dressed, fresh lipstick on her mouth, her scarf carefully tied over her champagne colored hair, big round dark glasss hiding most of her face. She looked quite like a magazine cover, not a real person.

"You don't have to wear those glasses. The waiter's gone."

Even Walter was a little amazed at the tone of his voice. He poured her tea and walked over to her. She had flopped onto the sofa. She accepted the cup and saucer in silence.

At that moment there was a knock on the door.

"It's the bill." Walter ushered in a man dressed in the conventional striped trousers and black jacket of those who worked at hotel management level. Without consulting Leslie, he examined the bill, made out a check, and handed it to her to sign.

"We'll be down in a minute." Walter spoke with quiet dismissal.

The man made a very formal little bow in Leslie's direction before leaving the suite, adding that it had been a great honor to have her patronage. Then he turned and left the suite.

"Honor, my foot!" Walter kicked at the Persian rug, eyeing Leslie and waiting for her reaction.

107

She eyed the beer and eggs. "You must eat, my darling."

"I'm not hungry." Walter was shocked at the juvenile note of petty pique in his voice.

"I've taxed you." She smiled at him. "You must be famished."

He shook his head.

"Please?"

"No."

"Please?"

"I'd only vomit it up," he said spitefully.

"Dear me."

"Yes, dear you."

"Walter, please. No problems."

She held out her hand and he pulled her to her feet.

He would have liked to pull her against him. He needed somehow to reestablish the intimacy of the afternoon. But this clearly was not what the lady wanted. She wanted him to stoke up on food so that he could keep up his strength . . . and service her yet another time . . . and another.

Chapter 14

Her own fame as a performer and her liaison with Kerem had squarely placed Leda Lambros in the jet-set goldfish bowl. Now she made every effort to act with restraint, a quality that in no way came naturally to her. She no longer danced barefoot in discotheques or sang in her throaty voice with unknown groups. She even rationed her public outings with her young-man-of-the-moment on the grounds that to be known to indulge as a regular diet did not enhance her public image.

In her effort to project glamour rather than wild unrestrained sex she had made two private rules.

The first was to cut down her drinking. It loosened her tongue, and as often as not she was simply not responsible for what she hurled at the heads of those who irritated her. It was also, she thought, beginning to show on her face, although, unlike many of her contemporaries, she fully understood the lure of slightly jaded looks. The power she wielded by making no pretense of disguising her considerable sexual experience was at times remarkable.

Young men were hers for the taking. Even in her worst moments there was always a boy willing to listen while she poured her problems into his ear as they lay in bed. But to confide in young men was, she had finally discovered, imprudent. On two or three occasions she had met with situations that came very near to blackmail.

So she had been forced to cut down on young love, as on alcohol. Those few occasions when she consciously reviewed her life usually brought a crooked smile to her lips. Fame was everything, of course. And to maintain it one gave up everything. Of course.

But there were some bright facets to the jewel of fame, and Leda Lambros took care to cultivate them. She had been very lucky with films and directors. She had now done five straight cinema successes in a row, two rather moody love stories, a murder mystery, a wildly funny farce and a wartime adventure film. She was, as the movie producers put it, "bankable." On her name alone, a producer could get his film financed by any bank. But not only her professional successes pleased Leda. Everything else had gone quite well, too. She had been seen frequently with the correct political group of expatriate Greeks in Paris. She had refrained from too harshly harassing the existing Greek government when being calmly interviewed on television. And it had all reflected excellently on her publicity, her record sales, and her social life.

That was the damnable part. Underneath, she resented the success of her new image.

Bourgeois, she thought bitterly. I'm as bloody bourgeois as the rest of the inhabitants of this odious Paris apartment block. She despised herself for knuckling under, toeing the line. She even despised herself now for trying to get Kerem back.

She walked restlessly to the end of the room and scowled at the Sacré Coeur, which rose above the rooftops, domed and beautiful, but not much help to an atheist like herself.

What in God's name had she done to turn Kerem off?

She tried to remember exactly what they had discussed over lunch. It was difficult, since all she could recall was his sullen resistance to every topic she had introduced. They had eaten well. Not drunk too much. She'd kept off the subject of his wife.

In fact, in her opinion she'd been all that any man could possibly desire for the afternoon. But Kerem had dropped her on the doorstep. Like some aging relation he had planted a kiss on her cheek and driven off. Left her, Leda Lambros, the object of millions of young men's masturbation and dreams, standing on the steps of her apartment block to spend the afternoon quietly waiting for his return.

She rampaged back into the room and reached for the telephone. She dialed the bedside number of the young guitarist currently in her favor. But as the telephone rang she realized that in all probability the boy would be sitting at one of the sidewalk cafés. She had, after all, given him his marching orders. For a moment the nasty little fear came to her that perhaps he was killing time elsewhere.

No, she thought. That wasn't likely. Not that she totally believed the boy's passionate assurances that he'd never known anyone like her before. He was, after all, English, and everyone knew how immoral they were. But perhaps the lure of a holiday alone with her in Lugano, after she'd introduced him to a Swiss bank in Zurich, would tether him safely to her side.

Even so, she regretted telling him that Kerem was just a friend, like pretending to have a cold in order to avoid doing something. By her peasant assessment, as like as not you ended up with a really bad cold.

Now it really seemed that Kerem was just a friend.

She replaced the receiver and dialed Karamanlis on a number very few people were privileged to possess. A secretary, a Greek expatriate like herself, answered, and explained that he was in a meeting.

Leda curbed her disappointment, and lapsing into

Greek, tried to learn if Karamanlis would be at the home of her Greek friends that evening. She dropped into the girl's ear the not altogether unexciting information that she would be bringing Kemal Kerem tonight.

Let the gossip spread. It could only be to her advantage.

She replaced the receiver and realized that she had three hours to kill before Kerem was due back to collect her. What a pity the young guitarist wasn't answering his phone. She dialed his number again. There was still no reply.

She wandered into the kitchen and brewed herself a very strong cup of coffee. She'd paste up her scrapbook. It was always so reassuring to reread flattering notices. And within her professional world her recent work had been a huge success.

She worked away at the kitchen table, trying not to dwell too much on what had gone wrong between her and Kerem. It had been his idea to come to Paris. He had wanted to see her. That was what she couldn't understand. If he hadn't wanted to revive the affair, then why was he here?

The afternoon dragged. She bathed, then dressed quickly because that was her habit. And still she waited. By the time he eventually rang the bell, she was tired and cross from doing nothing.

Kerem had changed. There were no wrinkles in his blue flannel suit. He was shaved and sweet-smelling. His bald pate positively gleamed. He also carried a large bunch of red roses. The sentiment they represented mollified Leda, but the dreary sameness of hothouse-grown blooms was depressing.

She fussed around the kitchen trying to find a suitable vase. When she returned to the living room he was sitting on the edge of the sofa, looking bald and middle-aged. He glanced up and smiled.

"You look very chic, darling."

Leda winced. The word "chic" was irrevocably associated in her mind with Leslie French.

112

"You look quite the tycoon yourself. Care for a drink?"

Kerem moved to the bar. "In the old days men fixed girls' drinks."

Leda stood back and allowed him to put ice into two tall glasses, she watched him pour scotch from a bottle and add the water. At least he remembered how she drank her whiskey. Or did Leslie like it the same way?

She took a furious swig from the glass in her hand, determined not to let her idiotic imagination ruin the evening for both of them.

"Greek friends of mine are giving a small party. I'd promised to go before I knew you were coming to Paris. But of course you're welcome. It's up to you."

She knew she'd made it sound totally ordinary, but she was a little put out when he frowned and replied, "Once and for all, Leda, don't involve me in your politics. I have my own trouble with Lebanese politics."

"Pooh! There *are* no Lebanese politics," she scoffed.

"It only seems that way from the outside, to a Greek like you, perhaps. But the Lebanese take politics very seriously. They kill for their politics. Sometimes are killed. One day they may even destroy themselves in a civil war. So don't talk about things you know nothing of."

"Why did you desert me after lunch?" she struck back suddenly.

"Business."

The word had a faintly derisive sound to it on his lips. When she repeated it, the sound was more of a curse. "Business! Always and forever business."

He nodded. "And very successful this time. The Americans will probably wonder what happened to their dollar. They expect it to up value and keep rising." He grinned for a moment, all teeth.

"You're just another profiteer, then," she taunted, "a political profiteer."

"Is that worse my dear, than being a political opportunist like you?"

She took a deep breath, the kind of pull-in that she took before stepping onto a stage, and, sweeping across the room toward him, she said: "Darling. The nicest evening of all would be to spend it quietly here with you." And to back up her outrageous theatrical shift, she slipped her arm around his waist, rubbing her cheek against his.

His solid frame relaxed very slightly, so she pressed her advantage. "You cannot imagine how often I look out across Paris and bless you for providing me with this apartment." They were now facing the Tour Eiffel and the river, a section of the city that was part high-rise modern buildings, but mostly the old boulevards, with buildings old enough to have weather-stained rooftops.

"I'm glad you're happy."

Happy. Leda instinctively felt that he resented her successful survival after the blaze of disagreeable publicity that had sprung from his sudden marriage to Leslie French. Could he really be vulnerable? Had he honestly discovered something other than money? She pulled her lips back into a wide smile to hide her vicious feelings.

"I thought we'd dine in my hotel suite."

"You and caviar. I can't think of anything nicer."

Leda went to her bedroom to fetch a green silk scarf, hand-painted in ethnic Greek designs. She regarded it as a luck penny. Her gypsy instincts told her that once they had made up their quarrel, in bed, the stilted conversation would end. They'd be able to tune into each other as they'd done in the old days.

They drove in silence down the Avenue Bosquet. There seemed very little traffic, Leda thought. The city had emptied since lunchtime. Holidays. She squeezed Kerem's hand hard, intending to hurt him.

In the lobby of the hotel there was a group of quiet Americans, the kind that came to Europe every year. They were loading a big Cadillac with luggage. Hell, thought Leda, everybody is leaving. Except me.

114

Her resentment vanished when a schoolgirl approached her, pen and autograph book in hand. The girl had broken away from a couple that might have been Dutch or Swiss. They apologized in French with a trace of thickness. Leda beamed at the whole family, delighted to have been recognized, reveling in the fact that she was keeping Kerem hanging around by the door of the elevator.

"I'm so sorry, darling." She apologized in French for the benefit of the bellhop.

If Kerem had any thoughts that their little dinner *à deux* in the Kerem hotel suite was to be clandestine, Leda would soon put that right. If nothing else she would see to it that the news reached the *Maria* before he did. And see what that did to his happy marriage.

The bar in the suite had been set out on an occasional table. Whiskey, vodka, ice, and even a bottle of champagne in a bucket.

"Stick to scotch?" asked Kerem.

Leda shook her head. "Get them to send up some real Russian vodka. And caviar."

She smiled back at Kerem, thinking that the hotel might be the height of discretion as far as favored clients were concerned, but this public reunion was too irresistible not to gossip about. Room service, if no one else, would know she was back in his bed.

"Sweetheart, do take off your jacket and tie. And relax."

Leda fiddled with the dial on the bedside radio, and was gratified by the sound of her own voice which filled the suite. She scuffed up the sheets, shook out her hair, and returned to the sitting room to coincide with the waiter bringing the caviar and vodka. Beaming with pleasure, she said in French, "What a perfect way to celebrate."

The waiter left, but not without momentarily catching her eye. Good, she thought, he got my message. The news will be all over Paris by morning. She felt sure some ambitious lad would have the brains to telephone the news to

115

the *Nice Matin*. As the happy-making thought struck her, she wondered if dear Leslie read French.

Leda made a mental note to telephone the social editor of the Paris *Herald Tribune* at the first opportunity. Maybe while Kerem was under the shower.

"You're looking very pleased with yourself," he observed, coming to sit beside her.

"It's having you back. My love." She twined her arm around his neck and pulled him across her. She kissed him first with a passion that was more loathing than any other emotion. Then, gradually, she felt the waves of spite drain away as waves of pure erotic pleasure came in their place.

"Let's go next door." She shook herself free.

"No, here." He pulled up her dress and pulled her on top of him for another of his seated pleasures.

Chapter 15

Doe Drew draped herself elegantly across one of the circular sofas that curved on either side of the fireplace and fitted beneath the paneled library wall. Every time she returned to the *Maria* she found herself inwardly envying her sister. The yacht possessed all the grandeur of an English stately home. The pictures on the walls were priceless. Any museum in the world would have jumped at the chance to own them.

And all of this *might* have been hers.

Doe sipped her vodka and tonic reflectively. She shared, and had always shared with her sister, all her secrets and her plans since girlhood. Except one.

If Leslie had known that her twin sister had already started an affair with Kemel Kerem, would she have made such a play for him?

It was a question that often came to Doe when at night she lay sleepless and worried as to where her life was going. If she had said to Leslie, when they had set off for that fatal summer cruise, that she intended to divorce her actor and marry Kee, Leslie wouldn't so much as have fluttered an eyelid. But she hadn't told her sister anything of the kind. Kee had never been marriage material in her eyes. Certainly not. She far preferred her title. But to snare him as a rich and powerful lover, she had dreamed many a lofty scheme with Leslie as the respectable widow, the ideal chaperone.

God, what a switch had taken place!

She lit a cigarette. It helped her think. She was faced with the problem of Philip wanting a divorce. He'd pay her a nice enough sum to get out but it wasn't big money. No actor had really big money. And what would she do with more money? This required a great deal of thinking out.

It might very well have a damaging effect on her design business. A woman who couldn't stay married to the dashing Sir Philip Drew might not be considered the best person from whom to buy a sexy, man-attracting dress. Perhaps she ought to play down her artistic side and play up what a fantastic businesswoman she was. Financial-genius type. Decisions. Changes. And Leslie had none of these problems.

It was always so easy for Leslie, thought Doe. She has always had unlimited money, a fantastic life. Even the use of the bank's cars and jets. She does as she likes while I merely cope.

It had always been that way since the time they were girls. Leslie was subtly prettier, shyer, helpless, worthy of sympathy. There was something in her violet eyes, something in the lush, vulnerable curve of her mouth, that made men want to help Leslie with anything she needed.

Of course, it had been fantastic bad luck about Maurice, Doe remembered. The man would have carried both Leslie and Doe to political heights, no question of it. Bad luck on Leslie, but bad luck for herself too.

But Leslie was always to land on her feet; she was like a

sleek white Persian cat, cuddly and lovable and with ninety-nine goddamned lives! Leslie got through it all unscratched.

Doe ran slim manicured fingers along her leg. She was wearing a new cotton pajama suit in fine green lawn. It was almost see-through and very flattering. She had changed the moment she arrived aboard the yacht, leaving Brassington to struggle with her mounds of luggage. She had half expected to find her sister waiting at the airport. When she found only a hired car and chauffeur she had presumed Leslie would be aboard the yacht. But no sign of her anywhere. No message. It was very odd.

She picked up a copy of a new publication on the Swiss economy. It had been translated from German and well reviewed in the Sunday newspapers.

Doe had reached a decision. Now that she was on the point of making a new life away from Philip and his dreary stage friends who did nothing but drink and play backgammon, she would turn financial wizard.

In her new role of being a brilliant businesswoman as well as beautiful and creative, she needed to be seen reading intelligent literature on economics. Or at least she had to hold the right kind of books in her hand. The trouble about being with Leslie was that you simply never knew where the next long-lens camera was hidden. Or which member of the staff had signed on for the job in order to write an in-depth scandal piece about the fabled Leslie Kerem.

There was a potential porno feature in every stranger's smile. And both girls knew it.

The trouble, too, was that no matter what charades Doe played in the company of her twin, everyone focused on Leslie, almost literally. Doe could be, and was, one half of a business brain. Doe could play financial intellectual till she turned blue in the face. But journalists always ignored her when Leslie was on hand.

119

Doe sighed unhappily. With all the tension the world put on them, it was a wonder the sisters still loved each other so dearly. But we do, Doe reminded herself, we bloody well do.

She got up and began to pace uneasily around the salon, helping herself to a cigarette from the heavy modern silver-and-gold box. Beside the cigarette box was a signed photograph of the late Sir Winston Churchill. Odd, the mixture of people Kee regarded as friends. She wondered idly who would be their guests this August, and just why Leslie had seemed so keen on her joining the party without Philip.

Doe drifted over to the piano, lifted the top up, and ran her fingers along the keyboard. If she had been in Leslie's shoes she'd have had the monstrous thing overboard. A Steinway concert grand on a yacht? Only a ghastly tart like Leda Lambros would have insisted on it.

She wondered where Leda was now. For a while she'd dropped right out of the news, but Doe vaguely remembered seeing something about her in a recent gossip column. She couldn't quite remember what. In any case it didn't matter; her longtime affair with Kee was finished for good.

Doe looked at her slim gold wristwatch. It was ten after six and not a sign of anybody. She walked back to the tray of liquor and topped up her drink with straight vodka. She always felt uneasy when alone. She never quite knew what to do next.

Neither of us has much repose, Doe thought. Most Texans don't. We're both at ease only with each other. Or on horseback. And no wonder, Doe thought. That terrible scene in Caracas, for example. That tragedy played before the television cameras of the world.

Doe shook off the troubling remembrance. What in Christ's name had happened to everybody this evening? Kee? Leslie? And weren't there some other guests, too? Americans?

Could something dreadful have happened? Doe didn't really know Tangier, but it did have a rather sleazy reputation. Of course Leslie always went everywhere with a bodyguard and a chauffeur. Even so, with the catastrophic pitch violence had reached these days. . . .

She lit another cigarette, opened the Swiss economics book, and found herself unable to concentrate.

She heard Leslie before she saw her, running across the teak deck. Next minute they were hugging each other and talking at the same moment. "Darling. Darling, how marvelous." Leslie scooped her blond hair from her eyes.

"You look magnificent. Really marvelous," Doe said with truth. There was a radiance about her sister that she hadn't seen in years. "Where were you? I was going out of my mind thinking something had happened."

"Shopping. You'll die when you see the kaftans I've bought."

Doe followed her sister's gaze to the tall blond man hovering in the background, mammoth packages under his arms.

"Walter, give everything to Brassington. I'll fix my own drink." When Leslie turned back, Doe again saw the shining brightness of her sister's large eyes. So often of recent times they had held only sadness. Not now.

Something quite out of the ordinary had happened, Doe thought. It took more than a shopping spree, however successful, to put that kind of expression into her sister's eyes. She had met someone. Doe watched Leslie pour herself a drink and sit beside her on the sofa.

There had been famously beautiful sisters before, Doe thought, but Leslie and I are almost identical. From the back or the side, we match to the millimeter. It's only in the face people can sometimes tell us apart. But inside the head, she knew, she and her twin were vastly different women.

"I look awful," Leslie said, smoothing her white cotton dress as she sat with care. "If you don't mind, darling, I'm not going to bother to change tonight. There's only this American couple, bush league, but here for Kee's business, wouldn't you know." She grimaced.

"The blond god . . . the one with the parcels?"

"The new steward." Leslie buried her face in her glass as she replied.

"Madame Kerem." The captain of the *Maria* stood in the door of the salon. He bowed and clicked his heels as he turned to Doe. "Lady Drew." The two women nodded to him.

"I am ready to put to sea," he announced.

"Fine. Thank you, Captain."

Doe watched her sister as she casually dismissed the captain, scarcely bothering to lift her head. To think all this had fallen, like a ripe plum into Leslie's mouth, and she didn't even take the trouble to appreciate it. She took not the slightest interest in the running of the yacht. Doe fingered her new book on finance reflectively, thinking it was time that her sister took more interest in the outside world again. After all, she couldn't expect to remain a world beauty for the rest of her life. Although Doe had to admit that she had never seen her sister looking better.

A tall, weedy man with a woman several inches shorter than he advanced into the room.

"There you are." Leslie smiled as she introduced Doe to the Blots, adding that they were the only two guests until the yacht reached Monte Carlo. "Did you enjoy Tangier?"

Doe found herself wondering what an ordinary-looking man like Blot could possibly be contributing to warrant his presence on the *Maria*. To her he looked like any one of millions of Americans who commuted daily in and out of New York. She watched him fix drinks for himself and his wife. She's pregnant, thought Doe. It's not that her figure's bad. She has that blousy look we all get just before it actually begins to show.

She hoped someone had seen fit to tell the girl that she

must on no account let Kee know. He was positively paranoid on the subject of pregnant women.

It was some Lebanese thing. He'd married several times
before he'd met Leslie, always to Lebanese women of well-
to-do Christian families. Not one of them had borne him a
child, let alone a son. They'd gone through countless preg-
nancies, but in every case the end had come with the bitter
finality of miscarriage or stillbirths. The Kerem women
had always been swollen with promise, but the Kerem
genes were seeds of death.

Which accounted, Doe surmised, for Kee's ridiculous attraction to his dullard nephew, Ali. The youth was a surro-
gate son, the heir Kee would never have. And it also accounted for his hatred of pregnant women, their swelling
bellies mocking his fondest hopes.

Doe smiled condescendingly in the direction of the girl.
"That's a nice print, cheerful. I'll be so glad when they
come back into fashion. I really enjoy wearing mixed colors."

Leslie gave her sister a sharp look. Had she been too
rude? Hell, why not? The idea of having to suffer them
through meal after meal until they reached the South of
France was awful. If Doe had known, she'd have gone directly to Monte Carlo and treated herself to a few days in
the Hôtel de Paris.

She looked up to see the blond god. What was his
name—Walter? He handed her a freshly mixed vodka and
tonic. "How very nice. Thank you."

What a pity he's not a guest, Doe thought.

Jensen Blot followed his wife, Elizabeth, along the jas-
mine-smelling corridor to their stateroom. Despite the
cool air conditioning, he felt sweat break out on his forehead and neck. He knew, from the way Libby strode
ahead, that she was as angry as he was. The moment they
were shut into their luxury cabin, she'd start. Well, the

123

doctor had warned him that pregnant women tended to be temperamental. But not plain impossible, surely?

It seemed to Jensen that Lib and he had been snapping and sniping at each other ever since they'd come aboard the *Maria*. That awful Atlantic crossing, with the yacht pitching like a piece of driftwood, had been bad enough. But the inconsiderate demands of Kerem had made it all worse. Twice Jensen had been summoned from bed around three in the morning. Another night, the only one during which he and Libby had felt well enough to make it together, the goddamned phone had gone almost immediately afterward and Jensen had had to grab a bathrobe and report to Kerem.

Watching Libby's back, he realized it had been unwise to bring her on this trip. He could accept any situation, or so he prided himself. He could handle the Kerem financial transactions calmly and well. Kerem could yell all he liked, but he needed him, Jensen Blot, and that was that. But Libby was something else.

He watched Libby's flower-print back, feeling himself drawing back involuntarily. He didn't want a scene and that was what he'd get the moment he was alone with her.

Guiltily, he realized he was comparing his wife to Leslie Kerem. He rubbed his hands down the sides of his denims. She hardly spoke. That was what he found so beautiful. His mind swam as he thought of Leslie's wide violet eyes. It seemed to Jensen that she had bored holes into his brain. That perfect face that had been turned to him throughout dinner. What had she said?

"Tomorrow we'll all sunbathe?"

He reached forward to open their cabin door for Elizabeth. Then he turned as soon as they were inside, to bolt the door and avoid looking his wife in the face. Perhaps now that Libby had him possessively locked in their cabin she might calm down.

When at last he turned to where she lay stretched out on

124

their bed, all he saw was the offensive print dress that seemed to be at the root of tonight's troubles. She was, he realized, on the point of tears, and he felt guilty when he felt that, instead of being sympathetic, he resented her anger.

"I don't care what anybody thinks," she said then. "I don't even care if the office fires you. We're getting off this yacht as soon as it reaches Monte Carlo. Sooner, if we can." Turning her face into the pillow, she sobbed. "I've never had a more miserable evening in my life."

Jensen knew that this was the moment to patch everything up. In the past whenever Libby had appealed in this way to him, he knew how to set things right. But tonight he remained leaning against the cabin door. He couldn't bring himself to cross to the bed. The idea of touching her was beyond him. Was this how marriages ended?

He went into the bathroom, washed his hands, and splashed on some of the after-shave he'd bought that day in Tangier. The face that looked back at him from the mirror was reassuring. The sun and sea air had brought a tan to his cheeks. In his new Cardin shirt, also bought today, he felt equal to anybody. He took two tranquilizers from the bottle, filled a glass with water, and went back to his wife's bedside.

She turned and pushed herself up on the pillows. Her hair was disheveled and puffy bags had formed under her eyes. She'd been crying, he realized. He tried to look at her, suppressing his feelings as he held out the tablets and glass. She swallowed one.

"One knocks me out." She dropped the second pill on the floor. Then she stood up to slip out of her dress.

"Don't just stand there, Jess. Come to bed."

"Later. I'm going to get some air."

"What do you mean, *air?*" Her voice rose as did her body. Her swollen breasts surged up and out as she removed her bra. He looked away suddenly.

"Take a turn on deck," he explained lamely.

"Then I'll come with you." She had begun to remove her panties, but stopped. Standing in the middle of the room, she looked dumpy, small, bursting with too much flesh.

Jensen shook his head. "Lib, you need sleep. I'll only be a few minutes."

She rushed at him, pulling at the lapels of his new sports shirt. "Is that why I need a tranquilizer? So that you can slip away to her? You're staying here." With sudden strength, she ripped at his shirt with her nails. He winced.

"Don't be silly." He half threw, half carried her back to the bed and got her under the sheets. Furious over his ruined shirt, feeling trapped now, he realized that even if he returned to the salon Leslie would probably be on her way to bed.

If only he'd made this trip on his own! He stood with his back to her while with his right hand he examined the tear in his shirt. It had been an expensive shirt and, because Elizabeth had been with him, she had allowed him to buy only three. Now one was ruined. That meant he was in the ignominious situation of having to ask for daily laundering of his shirts, since he had no intention of wearing any of the other shirts he had packed for the trip. He had seen how Doe had destroyed his wife with one remark. He noted too how Ali, their first morning at sea, had superciliously looked over his wardrobe.

Jensen learned fast. He could appreciate that the jet set dressed, talked, and lived in a wholly new pattern with a language of their own. The style of their dress alternated between freshly laundered poor-boy clothes to nearly homosexual extravagance of color and texture. They ate different things. They drank in a slow relaxed tempo. They did mostly speak English, but it wasn't the same language that he and Libby spoke. Come to think of it a lot of the time they hardly spoke at all.

126

It wasn't as if Jensen Blot were that much of a country bumpkin. In his own New York set of friends and business buddies he was considered quite acceptable as to dress and conversation. And, now that a child was on the way, Libby would be fully accepted by the other wives. Conform to the norm, Jensen thought. Don't stand out in a crowd. That was the motto among the overwhelmingly Anglo-Saxon Protestant crowd who still, despite inroads by other ethnic groups, controlled Manhattan's financial establishment. Lawyers, brokers, bankers, they all conformed to the featureless norm of their elders in the business world.

Even Kerem conformed, Jensen realized. His blue flannel suits, for instance. His conversation, totally about business. Even this somber Lebanese conformed to the Anglo-Saxon norm when it came to making money.

Thinking about money had made Jensen calmer now. Christ, I'm getting to be exactly like that Lebanese bastard, he thought. He turned back to the bed. Elizabeth had grown drowsy and was almost asleep after her outburst. He planted a kiss on her puffy cheek, tiptoed into the bathroom, examined the scratch on his chest. He dabbed it with peroxide, then applied more after-shave lotion. Walking very softly and carefully back into the cabin, he pulled out another Cardin shirt, put it on, and made for the door.

With the door firmly shut on his sleeping wife, he breathed again, pushing his shirttails down into his denims. At the far end of the long corridor a shaft of light shone from an open door. He calculated that it was the door opposite Leslie Kerem's cabin. He heard laughter. The sister? The twins were very alike and very different. Yet, outwardly they seemed like exact copies, struck from the same golden mold. It was only in their behavior, really, that they differed so sharply. Leslie had a calm magnificent smile that grew and spread across her face, whereas her

127

sister, Jensen thought, was too brittle, too sharp. She had been the direct cause of Elizabeth going off the deep end, with that quite unnecessary remark about her dress.

Jensen felt a pang of guilt. He had failed to spring to his wife's defense.

When he reached the open cabin door, he paused. There they sat, the pair of them, on a wide double bed, looking at the scrapbook. Leslie had changed into a pink fluffy toweling robe, tied tightly at the waist. She appeared like a kid on her way to beddy-bye. Doe, who sat facing the door, was still in her pajama suit. She looked up suddenly as Jensen appeared.

"You wanted something?" Her voice was cold, impersonal.

"The door was open. I thought maybe. . . ." Jensen faltered, his eyes on Leslie, who seemed neither to hear nor indeed to register his presence. "I thought maybe you all might like a breath of air. On deck," he ended lamely.

"No. No, thank you."

Lady Drew, it seemed, spoke for them both. Why didn't Leslie ever look up?

"Good night, then." He spoke louder, but still she did not move.

Doe inclined her head in what seemed to him a well-practiced regal nod, a gesture she no doubt used when dismissing lesser persons from her presence. As he turned to go he took one last look at Leslie, who sat staring fixedly at a photograph, beautiful as ever. To Jensen it suddenly seemed that, although there were indeed two of them, the personality was one.

As he made his way along the spine of the ship, he saw at the far end of the corridor the blond steward, a tray in his hand. It explained the open door. The sisters had ordered a bedtime snack. But it did not explain Doe's total coldness.

On the aft deck all the chairs and cushions, the bar, ev-

128

erything had been dismantled. It was a cool starlit night. The captain of the *Maria* must have reduced her speed, since she cut through the glasslike sea with only a soothing swish. Little flecks of white appeared on the waves cut by the ship's wash. A half-moon sent a shuddering path of light across the ocean. They had some time ago sailed through the Straits of Gibraltar and were now in the calmer Mediterranean, somewhere, he felt, off Málaga. Jensen leaned his elbows on the ship's rail. The air was damp and salty.

The situation could be explained in a single word—money. He had been educated to appreciate its importance and to be both skillful and adroit at making it, not only for his clients. He had, considering his age and American taxation, managed to accrue what was a reasonable amount for a man not long past thirty. Elizabeth's father had been quite impressed by what he had managed to invest. But all of it, Jensen realized, would scarcely enable him to take someone like Leslie Kerem for a week's holiday. There was money . . . and there was immense wealth. They were vastly different things.

The rhythmic swish of the Mediterranean, the gentle movement of the deck beneath his feet, the cool breeze on his face, after a hot, humid, harassing day with Elizabeth, now came as balm. He was beginning to get the message. To own a yacht was to be master of your own domain. No wonder someone like Kerem spent most of his time aboard the *Maria*. He left hurriedly, only to return at once to the yacht. And to Leslie Kerem.

Try as he might, Jensen simply could not explain her sudden change. Throughout dinner she had been all attention to him. Then the whole party had moved into the salon, where the chairs had been arranged to face a screen that dropped from the picture molding. With one of the crew members as projectionist, they had watched a movie that was still in first-run theaters in New York.

129

The movie had been funny. He had watched Leslie laugh. Everyone had seemed to enjoy himself. Then, when the lights went up, Doe must have said something else to upset Elizabeth.

That, thought Jensen, is the real problem here. Libby isn't trying to fit in. She's simply not up to this style of living. Each time she says something it sounds banal and wrong. And whatever she'd said after the movie, Doe had snapped her head off. There had even been further reference to the print dress. That had blown it. Libby had dragged him off to bed.

Too bad. If it had gone otherwise he might now be with Leslie. Or would he? That bitch, Lady Drew, seemed to have a very queer effect on everybody, including her sister and his wife.

He turned to see Ali coming toward him, a black cashmere pulled over his shirt against the night air, a cigar stuck in his mouth. He looked incredibly like his Uncle Kee.

"The Turks seem to be making maneuvers against Cyprus, if you can believe the overseas service of the BBC. They're in for a bloodbath one of these days soon." Ali leaned his elbows along the rail. "It strikes me we'll be spending the whole summer tied up in Monte Carlo. I wouldn't venture any farther east."

Jensen shifted his mind from his own problems and his fantasy dreams of Leslie Kerem. "Will there be war in the Middle East?"

"I devoutly hope not. Lebanon is riddled with fedayeen guerrillas. The Israelis may bomb us all just to get at the Palestinian terrorists."

"Arab politics are hopelessly complicated," Jensen said. "I don't pretend to understand them. But Cyprus I understand. Will this Cyprus thing affect your uncle?" He wished dearly that Ali had not found him, but now that he

130

had done so, at least he might serve some purpose and put himself in the picture as far as financial implications stood.

"Hell, no!" Ali surprised Jensen by laughing.

"What's so funny?"

"I'll let you in on a family secret. Not that it's any secret since every newspaper carries the news of it as regularly as they carry the horoscope. My uncle still sees his Greek girl-friend. And she's a Greek political nut-case." He beat his thigh and laughed again.

"There's the old boy off on a sex weekend in lovely Leda's bed, to find he's walked into Freedom for Greece Week." He cracked up again, unable to continue speaking.

Jensen knew he was about to act naïvely. But he needed to know. He waited patiently for Ali to stop amusing himself, wondering at the same time if the nephew had had too many drinks or something. He had never seen him in such a boyish mood.

"This Leda," Jensen began cautiously. "Does Mrs. Kerem know?"

Ali shrugged. "Leslie has a fortune to squander on clothes. She gets another fortune if they divorce. If she knows, or doesn't know, or pretends not to know, what's the difference?" He grinned.

Jensen felt his cheeks grow warm. Even though the nephew was surely right, he resented hearing such thoughts spoken aloud about Leslie Kerem. No one, not even a nephew, had the right to that much arrogance. "Look here," he began abruptly.

"How different," Ali cut in at the same time, "is your charming wife. She's a real woman, that one. You're a lucky man."

Jensen stopped suddenly and stared almost open-mouthed at the young Lebanese. "Uh, yes," he responded lamely. "Of course."

Both men were silent for a moment. Then Ali indicated

131

the bow of the *Maria* with a gesture of his thumb. "Why don't we check the radio room?" he suggested. "There may be some news about how the market reacted to the Turkish maneuvers."

Of course, thought Jensen as he followed him below. Never let us forget our real god. Money.

Chapter 16

"What about that?" Leslie fell back on the pillows, laughing. "He just stands gawking at me. Did you notice him at dinner and right through the movie?"

"Come on, Pussycat. You know you can't survive without an audience."

Leslie sat up, and leaning forward, the photograph still in her hand, flung her arms around her sister's neck. "You don't know how much I miss you. When you're not around I feel half dead. Nobody to giggle with."

There was a knock on the open door.

"May I enter?"

Leslie, still with her arms around her sister, looked over her shoulder to see Walter standing in the doorway. Briefly their eyes met, and she realized that for some reason he was annoyed to find her embracing her sister. He held a tray in his hand, their bedtime snack.

"Oh, Walter!" She disengaged herself from her sister's

arms, at the same time tugging to pull her open bathrobe together again.

Doe took charge of the situation. "Bring the table here." She pointed to the side of the bed. Her voice was impersonal and, to Leslie's slight embarrassment, she ordered Walter to move the table with care and to place the yellow roses on her dressing table, explaining as he did so that her sister always bought them for her cabin each time the yacht docked.

It was perfectly true. Three dozen fresh yellow roses were always purchased for Doe's cabin. The cabin had been specially decorated for her. Since Leslie's marriage nobody had been allowed to occupy her sister's room except Doe.

Such domestic details were, however, nothing to Leslie. She found it quite funny to hear her sister handling Walter as though he were indeed just another crew member. I've got to put her in the picture, she decided. It wasn't fair to Walter.

"Thank you, Walter." She smiled warmly at him.

"Shall I pour your tea?"

"No, thank you. That will be all," Doe chipped in. Her regal tones were so cool they froze the atmosphere.

Once Walter had left, Doe turned on Leslie. "Of all the familiar, arrogant—"

"He's not really that way at all," Leslie interrupted.

There was a momentary pause. "You aren't—" Doe stopped and fell totally silent as she eyed her twin sister with the glance of an interrogating officer. "Even you," she said then, her voice colder by far than it had been for Walter, "even you, the proprietor of the world's most aching cunt, haven't yet taken to bedding down with servants, have you?"

The embarrassed smile on Leslie's face faded away. "That's an ugly way to talk to your sister who loves you." Her full lower lip began to push out mulishly.

134

"Pout," Doe snapped. "It's your only weapon." She took her sister by the shoulders. "Swear to me, Leslie. Swear you haven't touched that steward."

"Walter's not a real steward."

"Swear."

"Either you let me explain," Leslie said, "or I'll just go back to my room, Doe. You can't bully me."

"Then explain, goddamnit."

"He's from a well-to-do family," Leslie began. "His father knew Maurice. We all met years ago when Maurice and I toured Germany. He's an actor, filling in with this job, and we're damned lucky to have him," she finished in a burst of non sequitur.

"And?"

"And what?"

"And he's fucking you," Doe suggested.

Leslie was silent for a moment. "Why do you assume that?"

"All right," Doe countered with mock charity, "then he's gay, like the rest of the crew. Am I expected to believe that, too?"

Pensively, Leslie folded her arms behind her head and lay back on the pillows again. Doe recognized this as a sign that something rather lengthy in the way of a girlish confession was now forthcoming. She was right.

"Doe," her sister began at last, "you simply have no idea what it's like being married to Kee. He's an animal, that we both know. He's a gross animal, as the whole world can see. But he's really at his worst when he fucks. First of all, his New York quacks have told him he has to sit up during the act. This puts the whole burden on me of getting him into me. He stomps into my room the minute his cock's up, sits down on the sofa, and exposes himself. I'm supposed to strip like a whore and impale myself for his pleasure, like a girl he's dandling on his skinny lap. It's grotesque. It's insulting, it demeans the whole sex act, Doe. It demeans our marriage. He's simply using me as a sort of animated glove into which he masturbates."

"And you get nothing from it," Doe cut in tartly.

"Rarely. I'm too consumed with shame most of the time. I do my best to make believe it isn't happening, but of course it is. Kee is the sort of man that can put a girl entirely off fucking, you know. He's the sort of man who can put you off all men. So you can see why I need someone like Walter."

"My dear," Doe said, her voice warming up a bit, "you've just described most of the marriages in the world, mine included. Men are all animals, darling, and well you know it. Even your precious Walter."

"No, he's different. For one thing he obeys me."

Doe smiled lopsidedly, almost a leer. "Obedience training, eh? How the German male loves it! Do you whip him?"

"Nothing like that."

"Get to it, Pussycat, or you'll lose him." Doe sat for a long while without speaking. "So that's where it's at. You're revenging yourself on Kee with that blond Adonis. Does the steward understand why you're doing it?"

"Of course not. He loves me madly."

"And will do anything you command." Doe's voice started to rise on an upward shriek of laughter.

"Forever and ever," Leslie added joyously.

The sisters hugged each other as they laughed uproariously. "But, Doe," Leslie went on in a suddenly serious vein, "you know what's mine is yours."

"Surely Walter can't love us both madly."

"I'll simply order him to obey you."

"He won't like that." Doe thought for a moment. "Or, wait a moment—I'm wrong. He'll adore the humiliation. Will you watch us?"

"If you say so."

"Lovely. When I get through with Herr Walter, he'll never be the same again."

136

"Don't ruin the poor boy," Leslie said. "He's got a sweet mouth and good hands for massage."

"And no doubt a lovely, long tongue," Doe added. "Is there any way we can delay arriving in Monte Carlo a few days? I wouldn't want Kee bursting in on us and firing the dear boy."

Leslie frowned as she thought. "There's that deserted beach on the lee side of one of the smaller Balearics. You remember, darling? We could swim nude there last year and not worry about *paparazzi* with long-lens cameras."

Doe jumped up off the bed and picked up the telephone. "Give me the captain." She waited, tapping her foot impatiently. "Lady Drew here. Do you recall that tiny Balearic we anchored off of last year this time?" A pause. "That's the one. Madame Kerem and I would like to moor off that beach again tomorrow. Perhaps we might stay a day or two. Yes. Quite." She hung up.

As she turned back to Leslie, her sister had lighted a cigarette and was handing it to her. Doe smiled broadly and took a quick puff.

"You darling," she said. "Now, look, we're both in mortal danger with this Kraut slave of ours. If Kee finds out he'll divorce you without a cent. You know that."

"He can't. The contract won't let him."

"But surely there's a morals clause in it somewhere," Doe suggested.

Leslie blinked. "Perhaps. But that cuts two ways. And with that Greek tart of his, he's in no position to play injured husband."

Doe inhaled smoke deeply, then kissed Leslie on the mouth.

"You utter darling," she said.

Chapter 17

Leda Lambros held court in the minuscule VIP lounge at Orly Airport. The time was 11 A.M. and the two young air hostesses were dispensing *café filtre* and drinks to the group of journalists and photographers who had crowded their way into the tiny room.

A glass of champagne in her hand, she was extolling the virtues of Greek democracy. With dynamic patriotism and flashing eyes she talked at length about the restoration of the free vote, liberty of the press, and her longing to be reunited with her mother, once the corrupt colonels had fallen from power. But she did not allow the excitement of the moment to eclipse her private rapprochement with Kerem.

This tasty morsel of international gossip was confirmed to all those present. Leda could afford a touch of exaggeration. In her purse was a substantial check, signed by Kerem. She had the freedom to use his bank's executive jet at whim.

These benefits had been bestowed most liberally as a result of Kerem's wonderful discovery that he did not drop dead of a heart attack when engaged in sexual dalliance on his back, his front, his side, standing, reclining, or otherwise arranging himself.

This medical discovery was not the reason Leda preferred to give the press. It was typical of Leda Lambros in this matter, as in all others, that she wove two and often three distinctly different threads of her life into an event. Her mercenary relationship with Kerem was thus linked to her highly volatile political life. And it was also typical of Leda that she had mastered the hidden, often cruel truth of publicity. To be successful, publicity has to hurt . . . someone.

Finally, it was completely typical of Leda that she really didn't give a damn who got hurt, including herself.

The night of love with Kerem had been anything but a lyrical experience for Leda. She'd been forced to use every brothel trick she'd ever heard of to keep the old man going. But now that she had him back, he bored her. And he snored in his sleep. Even so, she still felt sufficiently vindictive toward him and toward his wife not to let him guess that all she really wanted from him was the notoriety of being his mistress.

She chivvied the air hostesses into serving more drinks, then urged the press to toast her country's about-to-be-restored freedom. And another toast to her new happiness. She dropped her eyes for one brief, demure moment for the benefit of the photographers.

An airport executive appeared at the door to escort her by the Kerem bank's car to the very steps of the aircraft. In a flurry of hand kissing she left the room. A good morning's work. She was on her way home. This meant a great deal to her. But it meant even more to be returning in triumph, as successful actress and entertainment personality in her own right, with the satisfaction of knowing that by

139

tomorrow morning the entire world would read of her revived romance. That was pleasing and gratifying to the ego even if it made Kerem angry enough never to see her again.

It was a true Greek revenge. She dearly hoped the press clipping agencies would not fail to deliver sacks of cuttings when the *Maria* docked in Monte Carlo. Leslie Kerem would spend a tearful August being harassed by reporters.

She allowed the chief steward to fasten her safety belt. Flashing him a smile of warm appreciation, she accepted his offer of a glass of champagne. The first-class area was deserted except for an elderly couple and two businessmen.

"I wonder," she murmured throatily into the steward's ear, "if you could do me a small favor. In the tourist section sits my young guitarist. He's British and traveling alone. Since there are seats free would you allow him to come and sit with me?"

Another thread had been woven into Leda Lambros' complicated intrigue. And there were more that still lay hidden.

Chapter 18

The *Maria* lay at anchor about half a mile off this deserted stretch of coast, a beach beyond reach of any tourist without a large boat. Protected by steep cliffs that fell to either side of this sandy cove, it was an ideal place to water ski or sunbathe and picnic in private. And because of this it had become a favorite port of call for the wealthy, whose only danger lay in finding another equally well-heeled boatload there before them.

Today the *Maria* and her party held a monopoly.

The gangway had been lowered. The powerful motor-boat had been dropped into the calm waters with a crew member behind her wheel and one in her stern. Waiting, Walter noted with envy, since he was obliged to wait on deck, that the men in the boat were smoking discreetly, hiding their cigarettes in the palms of their hands.

Elizabeth and Jensen Blot were also waiting on deck. Walter hoped that he had done the right thing in suggesting they wait up there for the sisters to arrive. The rapidity with which Mrs. Blot got seasick was still fresh in Walter's mind. He did not relish having to clean up after her, and there was just sufficient swell to bring this reaction about if she remained too long in the speedboat.

Although it was only ten o'clock in the morning, there was real heat in the sun, August heat that by midday would make them all crave shade. Walter scanned the beach. Not a tree, not even a big rock. Wisely, he had loaded into the boat a large beach parasol, along with the picnic hampers, towels, and beach mattresses. Ought he to fetch a second umbrella? He consulted his watch.

Leslie Kerem and her sister had already kept everyone waiting a full half hour. There was still no sign of them. Walter called over the rail to the sailor at the wheel, telling him that he was fetching another parasol. The man nodded and continued to smoke.

When Walter returned from the aft deck, Jensen Blot asked him if he knew what had happened. Walter, struggling to lower the umbrella into the boat, shrugged noncommittally and descended the gangway for perhaps the fifth time.

He was beginning to feel the heat and he wished the sisters would make their appearance so that the picnic could get itself onshore before the temperature rose even higher.

If he was feeling the heat, the Blots were thoroughly uncomfortable. They kept whispering to each other. Walter felt like telling them to peel off their clothes, relax, and enjoy the sun. Well, perhaps not. It might produce sunstroke. They were, when all was said and done, guests and could dress as they pleased. He was obliged to remain in his cotton shirt and pants until such a time as Leslie Kerem ordered him to be dressed differently. Optimistic that this might happen, Walter was wearing his best pair of white swimming trunks under his pants.

Beyond setting up and serving lunch, he would be ex-

142

pected to wade ashore with the water-ski and sky-ski equipment. He just hoped that some vital item like a bottle opener hadn't been omitted from the booze hamper. Or that Lady Drew wouldn't dream up some odd demand that would send him hurrying back to the yacht.

Walter was forming a positive dislike for Doe. Apart from finding her cold and dictatorial, he was all too aware of her influence on his lovely Leslie.

It seemed to Walter that Leslie had completely changed from yesterday afternoon in the hotel suite. He was beginning to wonder if the whole affair had not been one gigantic fantasy.

Then he recalled her cool sexual behavior at the very end when, having used him like a common street whore, she had—what was the American phrase?—kissed him off with a few insincere words of praise as a stud.

There was a certain underlying coldness in the twin sisters, Walter realized. He felt his groin, in its athletic supporter, stir with longing. For what? For yet another of these chilling Texas Amazons to dominate him? Why should the prospect be so sexually arousing? Surely he didn't really want to be slave to both of them.

One hour and twenty-five minutes later, the object of his affection came laughing onto the deck. She was dressed in a dark red bikini, so close to a G-string that it embarrassed and annoyed Walter. God knew what it did to Jensen Blot, or his wife for that matter. Doe, also nearly naked, wore a flimsy voile throwover to disguise the fact that her skin was white and short of sun.

"How on earth are you going to swim ashore?" Taking command of the party, Doe swept Elizabeth with a patronizing glance, indicating that she take off her sundress and not keep everyone waiting.

Funny, thought Walter, considering how long the pair of you have kept *us* waiting. Brassington appeared on deck just as Walter was about to descend again to the speedboat.

143

"Madame's suntan creams," she said crisply, dumping a very large and heavy Moroccan shopping basket into Walter's arms.

As soon as Walter was aboard the boat the crewman cast off and sped her toward the shore, cutting the engine just short of the beach and skillfully allowing the shallow-draft hull to nose into the sand without grounding.

Leslie and Doe immediately dived into the shallow water, making for the shore, leaving Elizabeth to follow in their wake. Blot turned to Walter and, in true democratic style, offered to give him a hand by carrying some of the packages.

Walter decided to accept the offer. He pulled off his shirt and pants and began the first of four wading trips to bring ashore the rest of the gear.

"Get'm to ski and soon as you can," the German behind the wheel said. "We don't want to be stuck in this *verdamte* cove all day."

With the last hamper on his shoulder, Walter nodded, thinking somewhat uncharitably that all this loading and unloading would eat up most of his day.

Leslie had not so much as glanced in his direction.

By the time he staggered onto the beach, the Blots, Doe, and Leslie were all stretched out on towel-covered mattresses.

"Drinkies," called Doe as Walter put the hamper in the shade of the second parasol.

Cow, thought Walter. You'll get your damned Bloody Mary when I feel good and ready to fix it. He turned around to see that she was repeating her demand and waving her hand to indicate that they wanted four drinks.

Leslie, thought Walter, had a great knack of switching off, ignoring everybody and anything that didn't please her. She was doing just that at the moment. He took his time fixing their drinks, carried four Bloody Marys across the sand on a green plastic tray.

144

In the distance, beyond the anchored *Maria,* an even larger yacht steamed slowly past, headed for Monte Carlo, perhaps. Doe stared at it. "Ugly great thing," she murmured. "It's the Onassis tub. They probably hate us for taking their beach." She giggled mischievously. Then she decided that Jensen Blot should be the first of the party to sky-ski. She was explaining to the unfortunate man how to operate the release on the jacket, in which he stood with some reluctance.

"Any fool can get it right," said Doe. "Surely you'll manage. You merely walk down the sand as the boat gathers speed. Then you will feel yourself being lifted off your feet. This should occur on about the fourth stride. From then on all you have to do is float and soar upward. Into the blissful atmosphere, where all is quiet." Giggling to Leslie, she added, "And all is forgiven."

Walter watched Blot's face go gray. Then he saw that Elizabeth Blot looked even grayer. It wasn't fair of Doe to torment these people so unmercifully. She was a bloody tyrant, used to bossing people around, and Jensen Blot was no exception. He swallowed once and nodded.

Let him play the fool or the martyr, Walter thought. He's a grown man and it's his own business. But why torture his wife this way?

"Mr. Blot," Doe continued, "while you are floating you will come to realize that the faster the boat speeds the higher you rise. When she slacks off, you drop. And when you come to finally make your drop, you release your umbilical cord, thus." She pulled to demonstrate. "This is when you begin to drop. *Voilà,* snap." She pulled the tiny catch, rather like a zip fastener. "You float gently down into the water."

Jensen Blot looked as though he could do with a second Bloody Mary, and it went through Walter's mind that perhaps he should volunteer to double back to the bar before the man became airborne.

"There's just one final point." Lady Drew was coming to the end of her lesson in sky skiing. "Do not cut loose over land, unless you were a paratrooper. Only professionals know how to land without breaking their legs."

Jensen Blot was harnessed up. Doe signaled to the boatman and Jensen began to walk toward the sea. Suddenly his stride became that of a moonman. Up he floated, like a god, not walking on the water, but above it, and out to sea. Within minutes he was a dot on the horizon.

Walter went back to the bar and fixed Elizabeth a very strong drink without asking her. He thrust it in her shaking hands. The poor girl was quivering. She shot him a frightened smile.

Doe meanwhile had turned her attention to the suntan, rubbing a dark jellylike substance into her limbs and chatting to her sister's back.

The lovely Leslie Kerem lay supine, oblivious of everything. If Blot had hoped to impress her, she hadn't noticed. She was beyond them all now.

Even me, Walter thought bitterly.

Chapter 19

Both sisters were sprawled across Leslie's bed, smelling of tanning jelly, still in their bikinis, when Walter came into the cabin with a bottle of champagne they had ordered.

"Why only two glasses?" Leslie looked up at him from her reclining position. She had turned down the lamps on either side of her big double bed so that the room was almost half dark.

"Walter, I want you to say hello to my sister. Politely."

She saw Walter hesitate. Running her hand through her pale blond hair, she went on: "I know all about the rules of this ship. But, Walter, we're different. This is my sister. Now get a glass from the bathroom if it presents less of a problem than walking back to the galley."

While he was out of the room Leslie rolled across the bed to where her almost equally naked sister lay. "Is the ice broken now?"

"I know what I'm doing." There was an unmistakable note of steel in Doe's voice which Leslie could not fail to notice. "Germans dote on groveling."

Walter came slowly back into the bedroom and occupied himself with opening the champagne. When the cork flew off with a pop Leslie giggled childishly as the champagne bubbled out of the top of the bottle. She and Doe had drunk wine all through dinner and were quite high now.

"It brings good luck." Leslie reached for the neck of the bottle, dabbed her fingers in the white foam, and transferred some behind her sister's ears, her own, and finally behind both of Walter's ears.

Walter's face was grave as he poured out three glasses of champagne. He moved slowly and very deliberately, handed Doe her glass, then served Leslie, still keeping his distance. He picked up the glass he'd taken from the bathroom and held it high by way of a toast.

"What do we drink to?" Leslie laughed. "To us?"

Walter met her gaze. He was still standing formally, the steward in his uniform. Very slowly he raised the glass to his lips. Leslie decided she was moving him along too slowly.

"Sit on the bed beside me." She patted the cover, which had been turned down for sleeping. "Pretend we're back together in that hotel suite in Tangier."

She saw him visibly wince and continued.

"Walter, it's all right. My sister Doe knows *all* about me. We share *everything*."

She hoped by now he would begin to get the drift of the situation, realize that he was expected to do more than relax.

"I'd like Walter to tell us something about his acting career. Some of the parts he's played." Doe had stretched herself across the bed to lie beside her sister. The supercilious tone that she normally employed had gone. Her flaxen hair was tossed back and her great violet eyes shone in

148

the dark. "Come on, Walter, I've heard such great accounts of you. My sister says you're marvelous."

He turned his head away. Leslie put her hand on his thigh to keep him seated on the bed.

In addition to the ever-present odor of jasmine the room smelled of sunbaked bodies, the mingled scent of expensive tanning gel and even more expensive sweat. Leslie could see Walter's nostrils flutter as the combined scent of two virtually naked women hit him. The top of his tongue came out to moisten his dry lips. Then he took a gulp of cooling champagne.

Only champagne never cools, Leslie reminded herself. The poor boy is ours.

How odd, she thought, never imagining that Walter would be so correct. He really was embarrassed. She ran her hand up his thigh while sipping champagne and urging him to drink. All the time she could feel his muscles tense in his leg. His head was deliberately turned from her. It seemed the moment for extreme measures.

She finished her drink, set it on the bedside table, and pulled Walter toward her. She pressed him down against her, mouth on his lips. Only then did she feel him respond to her, slowly and unwillingly at first.

Leslie pulled Walter down with her across the bed, reaching at the same time for her sister's hand.

"Sometimes it's absolutely marvelous to share," she whispered into his ear, nibbling the lobe as she spoke. "Doe and I love to share." Doe rolled over and switched off one of the two lamps.

In the half dark Walter sat up and reached for his glass. "Fill all the glasses again." Leslie was beginning to feel that he had finally realized the game they were playing.

Walter filled the bathroom tumbler with wine. Rolling onto his stomach, he leaned across the bed offering his glass first to Doe, who drank and passed it on to Leslie, who drained the glass.

"I'm getting high." She giggled. "Walter, do you think you'd better sneak back to the bar for another bottle?" What Walter really thought she was not to know. He stood up, straightened his clothing, and left the room.

"I don't think threesomes are his thing," said Doe in a thoughtful tone of voice, "but our mission is to educate that young man. Even if we have to kill him in the process."

"But he is such a love. I'm sure we could persuade him. . . ." Leslie was beginning to feel that the cabin was spinning around her. At first she welcomed the sensation. She had a wild desire to clutch at her sister and Walter and spin with them. Yet Walter was gone and Doe was making her cruel plans. Why couldn't they all be children together on this big bed?

She sat up in the middle of the bed and began to cry. Why did simply nobody love her? Not even her sister or Walter.

At that point Walter reappeared with two bottles of champagne.

A second bottle of champagne was opened, and quite solemnly the three of them sat on the bed drinking. "All my plans have fallen apart," Leslie whimpered, drinking deeply. "Neither of you really love me. All that's going to happen is that we're going to get very drunk."

Slowly she pulled off her skimpy bikini top and G-string. "Take off your clothes," she told Walter. Even in the dim light she could see his hesitation. "Walter," she repeated, "take off your clothes."

"That's an order," Doe added in her steeliest voice. She got to her feet, standing on the bed. "Here's another. Undress me."

Walter choked slightly as he finished the last of his champagne. "But you're already—"

"Strip me."

He shrugged, reached over, and pulled off her G-string.

He stared for a moment at the curly blond mound of hair, absolutely identical to Leslie's. He stroked the furry pubis. "Nice Kitty."

Doe had removed her bra as she stood over Walter on the huge bed. "My sister doesn't think we love her. Take off your clothes and show us how much you love her, Walter."

He fumbled with his belt buckle. After a moment he managed to remove most of his clothes except for jockey-type underpants through which his penis was already making a wild bulge. Leslie watched all this fumbling with a certain sense of detachment. Perhaps they did love her, perhaps not. She reached out for Walter's jockey shorts and pulled them off.

"Yes," Doe commented. "I see what you mean."

Chapter 20

At London's Heathrow Airport Judi stood beside Jim Butler while he checked their baggage. She had nervous cramps in the pit of her stomach, which happened every time she went anywhere. It wasn't that flying frightened her. The feeling was more subtle: Once airborne there was no turning back.

The man behind the check-in desk was suggesting they might prefer to sit in the private Air France lounge. Or was Madame planning on buying some duty-free perfume?

"Do you need anything?"

Judi, discouraged by the lack of warmth in Jim's voice, shook her head. In any case she'd only brought ten pounds with her, judging that in the company they would be keeping everything would be free. Or else he would bankroll her in the event they went to the casino.

It wasn't at all clear to Judi whether they'd immediately board the yacht or not. Apparently Kerem was coming down from Paris to meet them on the Riviera while the *Maria* was arriving from somewhere else.

They had driven to London airport in silence, Jim having explained the moment she was seated beside him in the Rolls that he had a report to read and send back with the chauffeur. Mr. Efficiency.

The drive to Heathrow had seemed endless, and Judi had curled in her corner, miserable. It was all very well for her mother to ooh and ah over her holidaying in such illustrious company. That's what a mum was for, to celebrate her children's social triumphs. But as far as Judi could see the whole thing might turn out utterly ghastly.

For starters, she'd panicked about what to pack. She'd wasted an entire morning in Biba and come away with a too-tight bikini and a long candy-striped beach dress that made her look wide across the hips. Then, in a moment of utter despair, she had tipped most of her possessions into a battered suitcase, plonking her Carmen rollers on top. Now she simply didn't know what she had—or what she'd forgotten.

As soon as they reached the VIP lounge, Jim Butler made a grab for the *Financial Times* on the cocktail table. He asked if he might keep the paper, telling the steward who brought them glasses of champagne that he'd left his copy in the back of his car.

Judi paid no attention whatsoever to her traveling companion's problems; she had enough problems of her own.

When she'd dressed that morning she'd thought she looked really nice, in her denim trouser suit and pale pink shirt. Now she felt scruffy and wrong. Without even knowing why, Jim in holiday clothes still looked formidable. His gray flannel trousers were too well pressed. His navy blazer screamed Savile Row. In place of a tie he had tied a scarf inside his shirt, but hiding it in a way Judi felt was horribly middle-aged. Why didn't he let it fluff out?

Their flight was called. Along with the rest of the first-

153

class passengers they trooped off. Judi glanced around her at some of the wives of well-to-do travelers and decided she looked better than all of them put together.

Well, why not? Looking good was her business. The only specialty she had. She already knew from the few straight photographers and film directors she had screwed that she left something to be desired in bed. "You've no proper interest in it," her mum had explained. "I was the same way, luv, till I hit me changes. Now, good Lord, I can't get enough of it."

Judi wondered if her lack of sexual enthusiasm would bother Jim. Probably not. He'd probably feel too inadequate with a really torrid sexpot and had opted, instead, for one of your guaranteed super-cool Brit birdies who looked like a million and fucked like a farthing. Judi grinned and tried to hide it.

More champagne was served in flight, together with a full lunch that Judi ate greedily. She'd been far too nervous to face anything at breakfast. She turned to Jim, who was absorbed in the stock market figures and nibbling absentmindedly at a cheese biscuit.

Fine holiday we're in for, she thought moodily, all business and no fun. To cheer herself up she flashed her eyes in the direction of one of the young male cabin staff. He responded by filling her glass with champagne before tactfully drifting out of her reach.

One hour and thirty minutes later the aircraft flew in over the choppy Mediterranean and taxied across the tarmac at Nice Airport. The sea, a deep blue, sparkled in the afternoon sun. As soon as they walked out of the aircraft the heat came up to meet them. Judi pulled off her denim jacket, feeling self-conscious about her white arms. Briefcase in hand, Jim seemed oblivious to the heat. He had taken over Judi's passport, and as they stepped into the airport an official came up to them, took both passports, and got them out of the terminal before the rest of the passengers.

A uniformed chauffeur took Jim's briefcase and led the way to a waiting black Mercedes 600 with the Kerem bank's insignia on it. To Judi's amazement Jim appeared to speak perfect French. It seemed, at any rate, perfect to her, since her few sentences of stumbling schoolgirl French were only for dire emergencies or when she was not getting her own way.

But she more or less understood what was said. And she'd been quick to note that the Kerem bank official was functioning as a porter, collecting their luggage and bringing it to the yacht later. How about that for living in style? She thought how much her mother would relish this little tidbit, and wondered how she would be able to send her a telegram telling her of her safe arrival.

The big Mercedes was air-conditioned, which enabled Judi to slip into her denim jacket, and so feel up to the big-league aura again. As the car headed east out of the airport along the Corniche, Jim settled back in his corner and reached for her hand.

"You do speak French?" he demanded.

"A bit." She felt another wave of inadequacy and panic come over her.

"Not that it's necessary with the Kerem party. That's one of the problems with their marriage. She doesn't really talk to people—in any language." Thinking this quite a good idea herself, Judi squeezed his hand by way of reply.

"Mind if I smoke?"

Judi did. But now didn't seem quite the moment to stand between Jim Butler and a Monte Cristo medium blend cigar. He continued to run over the guest list now for her benefit.

"Kerem's man at the airport told me that he'd flown in on the Paris flight an hour ahead of us. The chauffeur

155

confirms that both Leslie—you know, Mrs. Kerem—and her sister, Lady Drew, are already on board. The yacht was delayed a day for some reason, but it got in just a few minutes ago."

And the two bints brown as berries with all the money in the world to buy the right gear, thought Judi miserably. Imagine me trying to look right next to that lot! She tuned back into what Jim was saying.

". . . the usual people that turn up for a night or two. And the ever-present Kerem nephew, Ali. Personally, I'll be glad when we up anchor and head for Beirut."

They were through the old fishing port of Nice, and had cut neatly back on the coast road that began to twist and wind along the bottom of sheer cliffs.

"Imagine how this place must have been before it got overdeveloped," Jim muttered. "Crowded as hell now."

"It's still pretty nice." Judi had been watching the scenery fly by and playing one of her favorite games, buying a house. She'd seen several villas she'd quite fancied. Two or three that had remained long enough in her vision for her to imagine them painted a different color with her mum installed as housekeeper.

As they neared the Principality of Monaco the traffic began to build up until, entering Monte Carlo itself, they nosed slowly through the street that led to the harbor. Big-city traffic kept them inching along between the glassy high-rise buildings that clustered over the hillside.

It was the first time that Judi had ever been to Monte Carlo but she would rather have died than admit it to Jim Butler. Therefore she was delighted at their snail's progress through the old streets, her eyes darting in all directions to take in landmarks and spot the *right* shops.

Finally the chauffeur swung the Mercedes sharply around a corner, and below them lay the harbor.

"There she is," said Jim, pointing to what to Judi looked more like a naval vessel than a private yacht. He couldn't

156

be meaning the big one that lay up in the harbor, could he? It had to be one of the others, although they too seemed enormous to Judi. Her only experience with yachting had been with two fellows and another girl last summer in Cowes. Cooking in the galley, no privacy in bed, minding the bloody decks, and freezing to death sailing around the Isle of Wight had been her introduction to the sea. She had vowed never to let herself in for such a holiday again.

This, of course, was quite different.

The car pulled up at a wide gangplank. To the side, and just on deck, stood a sailor dressed in white, who looked ready to pipe aboard at least a full admiral.

As Judi and Jim Butler were helped from the car a young man in blue jeans and a sleeveless white vest came on deck. Judi's first impression was one of black matted hair and dark glasses that hid an elusive face. The gold chain dangling round his neck was the only thing she fancied about this dark young man . . . at first.

Ali Kerem introduced himself and explained that his uncle was on a call to New York.

"Let me show you around." He took Jim Butler by the elbow, his eyes on Judi. She wondered if she could possibly bring herself to find him attractive. One day he would inherit his uncle's fortune according to the gossip columns.

Ali led the way to the aft deck. The swimming pool had been filled and Judi looked down at the glistening mosaic in stunned silence. There were chairs and mattresses on which to sunbathe. A bar seemed overloaded with bottles. It was hot, and Judi longed to remove her jacket. Ali pushed open a door and immediately they were in scented, delicious coolness.

While Judi was absorbing the size of the room, Ali was saying: "This is just an all-purpose area. We meet here for drinks before dinner. No prying photographers." He grinned at Judi as they moved on. "Here's where we eat.

My uncle thought that as we'd all been traveling in the morning, we'd dine early, around nine, and go to the casino if any of us have the energy."

"That won't be me," Jim grunted. "In one night at the Salle Privée I can be sure to meet at least ten shits I've been successfully avoiding in the City all year."

"You sound like my Uncle Kee."

Judi realized that indeed Ali was talking for her benefit when he added: "It makes a bit of a break for the ladies to go ashore for a couple of hours. There's quite a good disco."

The little party led by Ali moved into the long carpeted corridor. "We've put you two in the pink stateroom. I see by your shirt the color suits you."

This time Ali grinned at Judi, who made one of her patented little pouting expressions with her pretty mouth. She meant to indicate that she liked him and would like to go to the disco. She had the feeling the message was received.

Jim was already deep in a currency discussion with Ali. He was irritating when his mind returned this way to business, but as she stepped into their cabin all irritation was swept aside.

The walls looked like fabric, but they were painted in such a way as to give them a textured look. The color was a very soft rose pink, and the curtains, as well as the bedspread, were a mixture of large soft shades of rose print. A French-style bureau stood against one wall and on it a bowl of pink roses.

Heaven, she thought. Pure bliss, the kind of room I mean to have when I settle down.

"It's not got much," Ali apologized, as he opened another door to show a second room, smaller, also decorated in rose with a single bed, a modern desk, and a line of closet doors.

"I'll chase up your baggage. See you later, then." This time Judi noted he did not look in her direction, but fixed

158

Jim with his full attention, adding: "My uncle is looking forward to seeing you. The fatted calf is being slaughtered in your honor."

Judi resisted the impulse to bounce on the bed. That would be asking for trouble. How grand to be given a dressing room, too. If only Jim could be persuaded to use it. She watched him examine the light switches and open the bathroom door. Speaking with his back to her, he said, "Good. It has a proper bath and shower. I'm old-fashioned."

You can say that again, she thought. Their luggage appeared, carried by two crew members. Behind the men, a dark attractive woman in her early forties introduced herself as Kerem's private secretary, Elly Raschid. She wanted to know if they had everything they needed. Would they please ring for anything they might need. Dinner at nine. Informal.

Just before she left the cabin she turned to Judi to ask if she would care to have the temporary services of Mrs. Kerem's personal maid to unpack or press anything?

Christ, thought Judi, as she thought of her gear, screwed up into little balls, heatable hair curlers lying on top of everything. She smiled back at the elegant woman and said that if she found that anything needed pressing she would ring.

It worked. The woman smiled once more, the kind that covered any feelings she might have. "Her name is Brassington," she said and quietly closed the door as she left.

"Well, it all seems satisfactory." Jim seemed genuinely pleased with the setting. "I suggest we unpack, take a bath, and a bit of a siesta."

Judi bent over her suitcase, pulling out bits and pieces of clothing. Item by item she grew more depressed. What the hell do I wear tonight?

Jim was in a light beige cotton dressing gown. "Who's first for the bath?"

"You go." It gave Judi more time to organize an outfit at

159

least a quarter way suitable for grand company. Besides, once he got into bed and if she, too, soaked for ages in the bath it was just possible that he might drop off to sleep before she got in bed beside him.

The bathroom was like something in a television commercial for luxurious soap. Judi splashed in quantities of rose-geranium bath salts, one of her favorite scents and no doubt selected to go with the suite. She had always heard that the Lebanese, or at least a few of them, were very rich. But she had no idea that they moved in a setting out of the *Arabian Nights*.

When she went back into the cabin she found Jim propped up in bed, glasses on his nose, reading a report. "Come get in beside me," he suggested.

She held her big fluffy pink bath towel against herself. She had forgotten to borrow her mother's dressing gown, which meant she'd be dashing about the stateroom in a succession of damp towels.

"Forgive me, love, if I do just a little work?" He kissed the top of her head as she lay beside him. "As of this evening our holiday will start." He patted her gently. "How long do you need to dress?"

"About an hour." Judi turned her back to him and fell asleep almost immediately. What seemed like hours later she woke to hear Jim out of bed and noisily switching on lights.

"About time we got dressed." He retreated into his dressing room and shut the door.

The bed was soft and warm, the room cooled by air conditioning. Judi felt she could have lain there forever. She picked up the telephone and asked for a vodka and tonic. When it arrived a few minutes later it was brought by one of the most handsome men she had ever seen. His appearance was a bit disconcerting. She hadn't anticipated a sun-god with her drink and had twisted her hair around heated rollers to receive him. But he was in and out of the room so fast Judi decided she'd imagined him.

160

Frowning, she began to pull together an outfit. Dressing to please the older generation had never been one of Judi's accomplishments. In these awe-inspiring surroundings she felt positively hysterical as she ferreted through her meager belongings. She had one long skirt, which was a red that went with nothing else. Even Judi realized she couldn't possibly climb into a pair of jeans. She had no choice but to pair up a skirt with the pick of her Indian cotton embroidered shirts.

Jim came from his dressing room as she was winding a wide brown belt around her slim waist. He stopped in his tracks, saying, "Is that the only dress you've got?"

Judi had swallowed a Valium with her vodka and was by now beyond responding to criticism. "I think it's great." And to endorse her statement she wound three ropes of brown wooden beads around her neck, adding to the bizarre effect.

In white trousers and yet another dark blue jacket, Jim looked as square and dull as the rest of his generation. He had lit another cigar, a habit Judi was beginning to find just the slightest bit sick-making.

They made their way down the long corridor of the yacht and moved in silence up the flight of steps that led to the all-purpose room described by Ali. As Judi walked ahead of Jim into the room the same panic gripped her as it did before she stepped onto the catwalk in her first number of an important dress show. As always, panic mingled with daring and a determination to shine.

Ali came forward at once to meet her and introduce her to the assembled company. "My uncle," he said. Judi was feeling so tense that she could hardly focus as she looked for the first time into the cold eyes of Kee Kerem. A shock swept over her as his soft, almost mauve lips brushed the back of her hand. He was much taller than she had imagined and totally bald. It seemed to Judi that there must be some mistake. No woman could fancy him, far less a world-famous beauty like Leslie French.

Judi pulled away, relieved that Kerem now turned his full attention to Jim Butler. Like called to like across the Anglo-Arab abyss. Judi allowed Ali to lead her toward a lady spread elegantly across one of the sofas. She was dressed in white and wore a great deal of heavy gold jewelry.

"Lady Drew."

Doe inclined her head in Judi's direction with a movement that combined acknowledgment and dismissal in one gesture.

"Elizabeth and Jensen Blot."

The young American wrung Judi by the hand, said something about how glad he was to meet her.

For some reason, as she shook hands with the wife, Judi had the distinct feeling that the American woman was sighing with relief. Why? At having someone closer to her age on hand? Judi wondered why Elizabeth Blot was so pleased to meet her.

She got no chance to talk, however, as the ubiquitous Ali guided her toward the bar. His fingers seemed to play a bit with the smooth flesh of Judi's arm.

"Now let me give you a drink."

Judi was glad of Ali, but as she turned to accept the drink her eyes met those of the young barman, the man who'd brought a vodka and tonic to her room. Now that's what I'd like for my holiday, she thought, and immediately began to wonder how she might arrange a private meeting.

Across the room Kerem and Jim were complimenting each other. As Jim caught Judi's yes, they both moved in her direction. She had become the center of all eyes, a situation which normally made her respond at least with a smile. But as Kerem advanced toward her she felt a wave of nausea.

The handsome barman moved forward with a small silver tray on which were slices of white cheese.

Kerem's paw dipped into the dish for several slivers of

162

cheese, popping them first into Judi's mouth, then into his own with alternating speed. The goat cheese stuck in her throat. For one horrible moment she felt she was going to be sick.

"Eat. You're too skinny." Kerem fondled her behind without wiping his fingers and reached for more cheese. This time Judi managed to avoid having it thrust down her throat, but was treated to the equally unhappy sight of cheese being shoveled into Kerem's own mouth.

He placed his hands squarely on her arms, imprisoning her as he continued to talk to Jim. "These oil prices, Jim. We are all affected. And if America's strategy fails?"

"My problem is my beautiful girlfriend. Too little time to appreciate her."

Kerem laughed, cut short in his more serious train of thought. He bellowed to Ali to find out what had happened to Leslie.

"One of these days she'll find the yacht has sailed without her." The silence after this remark was broken only by Doe's small, tart sniff.

Kerem removed his hands and waved them, scowling. "Jim, your country no longer can influence the course of world politics." With a handsweep that only just missed Judi's ear he continued to thunder: "Why do you think I asked you to vacation with me? If you cling much longer to England, you'll have nothing to offer in a boardroom bargain. Quit England now and we'll make music together."

"You know the English philosophy. Every right implies a responsibility, every opportunity an obligation, every possession a duty. That's how we muddle through."

"Sell out, buy a yacht. Join the world of displaced millionaires."

Judi was glad of Jim's arm. It brought her back to normal. She felt his tenseness through his fingers as he replied. "A little more persuasion and you'll have me convinced."

163

"You persuade him what's good for him," Kerem rapped at Judi.

"I like living in England."

"You won't like it this coming winter, dear girl. Strikes, power cuts, and food shortages." At the mention of the word "food" Kerem was once more reminded that his wife had yet to appear. He bawled at Ali in Lebanese. The young man promptly left the room, and Judi felt once more a disagreeable sense of strain as though everyone, including Jim, were frightened of this man.

Perhaps sensing it himself, and wanting to be out of the limelight while he wheedled Jim, Kerem took Jim's arm and walked to the far end of the room. Judi had the not-unpleasant and not unfamiliar feeling, once again, of having all eyes focused on her. In fact, she saw, Doe and the American couple were watching her rather closely.

"Are you someone I know?" Elizabeth Blot said at last. "I feel I've seen you before."

"In the adverts, luv," Judi explained. "I model."

This seemed to end the conversation just as it might have been starting. Judi drifted toward the good-looking barman.

"May I have another drink?"

He nodded, turned away, and began mixing a vodka and tonic. Judi stood by, playing her little-girl role and wondering just how best to broach the subject of a meeting. When he turned back to hand her her drink she said, "I want to do some shopping." She paused and looked up at him. "But my French is ghastly. I was wondering—do you ever squire guests around for shopping?"

The most amazing change went through him. He flinched and the sudden contraction spilled the drink he was handing Judi. She saw that after the abrupt burst of near-terror in his face he got himself under control as he wiped the bar dry.

"Pardon me, Ma'moiselle."

She gave him her we're-old-chums smile. "Did I strike a nerve, luv?" she murmured discreetly. Instead of replying he fixed another drink and handed it to her. "Thank you," she said. "Now, about a shopping trip. . . ."

His eyes looked back into hers without expression. "I'm sure something can be arranged, Ma'moiselle. Excuse me." His glance went past her.

Judi turned to see Leslie Kerem glide into the room. The wide smile took in everyone without actually focusing on anyone until she reached her sister. Doe moved her white skirt just slightly to indicate that she would like Leslie to sit beside her.

The good-looking barman was bending over, handing her a drink. Even Jim, Judi noticed, had stopped listening to Kerem and was smiling stupidly in Leslie's direction.

Christ, true royalty, thought Judi with a mixture of jealousy and admiration. She stood in the corner sipping her drink. For once in her life nobody in the room was looking at her.

Chapter 21

Brassington did not—repeat emphatically, did *not*—ever wait on table. There was no combination of circumstances, no matter how dire or disastrous, no bizarre combination of emergencies that could possibly get a lady's maid like Brassington to serve anything more than a cup of tea. And the lady was likely to hear about it for several weeks thereafter.

Oh, it was perfectly fine for her to serve an entire meal to her lady in the privacy of her lady's bedchamber, or if she were alone in her flat. But to do the sort of thing the staff of the *Maria* did, serve a damned big multicourse dinner to an entire assemblage in full fig, was something Brassington considered quite beyond the pale.

However, the unsuitability of waiting on table did not preclude Brassington's spying on table.

She did this tonight, watching from a distant doorway as the meal progressed. Not out of vulgar curiosity. Certainly not. Nor had her motives anything to do with the more common of reasons, wanting to watch the rich at their feed, so to speak. Brassington had watched far richer, when it came to that.

No, she told herself as she occasionally peeked past the slightly open doorway, it's simply that Madame wasn't really up to par tonight. She'd been in bed most of the day since they'd docked at Monte Carlo. Not even Brassington had been allowed in, even to straighten out and brush her wardrobe. Only Lady Drew had been allowed to visit her sister. Oh, yes, and that good-looking young steward, Walter.

Aside from that, Madame Kerem had been in utter seclusion and Brassington was quite worried. It wasn't that she feared for Madame's health. Walter had brought endless lashings of toast and pâté and tea all through the day. Anyone with an appetite like that wasn't at death's door.

No, something else bothered Brassington. Something, to use her own phrase, was afoot.

She hadn't the vaguest idea what it was. But something had changed in the atmosphere aboard the *Maria* since her last time on the yacht. Between the time she'd flown from New York to London to stand by at Doe's beck and call, and today, when she'd rejoined the ship in Monte Carlo—a length of time extending, oh, say, a bit more than a week—something had changed about Madame French. Madame Kerem.

Was it the arrival at more or less the same time of the British financier and his model-girlfriend? Brassington wondered. But she knew both of them, Jim Butler by name and Judi by face. She knew them to be perfectly ordinary celebrities, nothing dark or different about them. Nothing *special*. And certainly not of the stellar magnitude of Madame.

Perhaps it was the fact that her mistress was used to liv-

167

ing aboard the largest yacht in the harbor. And this week the even larger Onassis vessel was in port, putting her nose out of joint. Was that it?

It wasn't until Madame had rung for her to help her dress for dinner tonight that Brassington had had a chance to assess for herself, close up, that in fact deep-seated changes were taking place.

There was a certain languid quality to Madame's movements. And the stateroom! Brassington had grown used to the utter filthy sty Doe made of her bedroom, her bathroom, and, indeed, any area she inhabited. But Madame was quite different from her twin. Careless, of course, but neatly careless. A stray Kleenex might find its way onto the floor now and then, Brassington recalled with some satisfaction, but her lady was simply not the sluttish pig her sister was.

And yet how to explain the state of her quarters this evening? Bed so mucked up Brassington had called for a complete change of linen. Bathroom awash in small, damp, smelly towels. A man's underpants in the tub, soaking wet. They looked too small to belong to that Lebanese she had married, but obviously they were his, Brassington concluded.

Strange.

And her mistress' manner had been even stranger, as though she simply hadn't the energy even to dry herself after a bath, even to slip on clothes, even to do her face or let Brassington do her hair. Languid? Well, yes. But a better word might have been *sapped*.

Brassington smiled faintly as she thought of the word. Sapped in both senses, eh? Sapped as if hit on the top of the head with a cosh, what the Yanks called a blackjack. And sapped as if drained, sapped of all energy, juiceless as an orange sucked dry.

Across the expanse of floor the waiters hovered about the long table, swiftly removing and replacing plates and

168

glasses as the meal progressed at a stately pace from smoked sturgeon with caviar through a veal marengo and spinach soufflé to a whip of pineapple into which the chef had mixed tiny flecks of preserved ginger.

The wines had gone from white progressively darker until everyone was now struggling with a heavy Lebanese liquid so dark it could have been used as ink. Not red ink. Purple ink, and tasting of piñon nuts.

Brassington knew the wine, in which a sickening dessert sugariness struggled with a nutty flavor, quite like very bad sherry, to cloy the palate after even one sip. Kerem tossed it off in gulps and called for more.

There had been only one moment during the meal which Brassington had quite enjoyed. The conversation had been entirely masculine, dominated by Kerem, who allowed Jim Butler to say a few words, and now and then let Ali and the American fellow, Mr. Blot, pipe up with a few corroborating facts.

Brassington had left her observation post untended quite often during the early part of the dinner because watching and listening had grown so crashingly dull. Imagine what it must be like, she thought, for Madame? Or for that dimwitted British bird, Judi, whose head could probably be used to strain noodles, in a pinch.

Speaking of the mounting Cyprus crisis and its future international effects, Kerem had gone off on a summary of how the Americans would totally misread the events.

"The Greek colonels and generals will topple, of course," he told the British financier. "The only thing holding them up is cash from Kissinger. The man generally tends to misread most situations because his mind is tied to the status quo."

"He likes the status quo," Butler put in. "The status quo had been good to Kissinger. Under what other status quo would he have risen so far so fast, I ask you?"

"So far," Kerem pointed out, "he's kept away from the

Lebanese. He knows they're too realistic to believe his line of compromise diplomacy."

"What line *do* you follow in Beirut, old man?"

"A line we learned from the British. It's called 'muddling through.' I suppose it's Kissinger's line, too, come to think of it."

From the other end of the table Leslie Kerem sat with a dreamy half smile on her face. It changed to a tiny frown as her sister spoke.

"Poor Kissinger," Doe said. "He really seems to lack an economic philosophical basis from which to shape a new political evolution. No fulcrum."

Lady Drew had trotted out the sentence as though she were repeating a lesson learned in a foreign language. She had first, Brassington knew, repaired her lipstick and the rouge on her cheeks, then checked that every eyelash was well mascaraed and just as in place as when she had left her cabin. This whole repair thing had made her slightly miscue her observation, so that it hung in the air. The moment of silence grew more awkward.

"Which boyfriend taught you that?" Kerem was chewing on a toothpick. "My dear, with a body like yours don't try to think about economics." He patted her thigh and laughed lewdly.

This time the silence was even longer, more awkward, and now suffused with hostility.

Brassington's smile turned up the corners of her thin mouth in a perfect half-moon of sheer joy. Good for Baldy! If no one else saw through Doe, he did.

As if to cut off any further opportunities for her sister to make a fool of herself, Madame Kerem rose slowly, a bit unsteadily, to her feet. As she swayed, the nice young blond steward rushed over to steady her by holding her arm. She gave him a dead, sightless look, as if he were a wall she had leaned against.

170

"You'll have to excuse us," Leslie Kerem announced to the room at large.

Kerem scowled at his empty wineglass. "You're not coming to the casino, then?"

"Afraid not, darling," his wife said in her Texas voice, but so indistinctly that Brassington could only tell what she was saying by a form of lip-reading from across the long room.

In the following silence Kerem got to his feet and, excluding the twins from his glance and his words, he announced to the English financier: "Jim, I believe you and I must show the rest of the ladies Monte Carlo."

He came around the table, brushing past his sister-in-law as if she were an inconveniently placed floorlamp, and took Jim's arm. "This way, then," he commanded, leading everyone out of the room.

Or not quite everyone, Brassington saw. The tableau that remained was frozen into its space as if glued to the floor, the two sisters, watching each other with lowered eyes, and the nice young steward, Walter.

Brassington let the door close and hurried along the corridor to her own cabin, where she busied herself with a few of Madame Kerem's clothes that she had managed to take from her stateroom just before dinner. They were just crumpled a bit and in need of sponging and ironing.

Through her open porthole she could hear the dinner party coming down the gangplank and getting into cars, which roared off along the quai toward the casino in town. Silence fell. The ship seemed deserted. There were no sounds except the faint lapping of water against the side of the *Maria*. Not even the noises from the galley could be heard. It was as if everyone had left to enjoy the sights and sounds of Monte Carlo.

Brassington sniffed. She felt sure most of the crew had gone off to gamble away their wages or sell whatever drugs they'd picked up in Tangier, or do their other little illegal errands. Brassington had no interest in Monte Carlo, never had had, for that matter. And as for the crew, with the possible exception of that new young man with the blonde hair, they were all a bunch of ruffians and worse, pederasts, thieves—the dregs of society.

She sniffed again, feeling virtuous and quite superior to everything around her, a feeling that had sustained her many times before on this perilous, confusing, and utterly maddening job, first with the Frenches and then with this Lebanese pirate.

The job had taken her through many strange scenes, some of them in quite respectable places like Washington, D.C., or Paris, or here on the Riviera, some in out-of-the-way and horrible locations like Athens. And would she ever forget Caracas?

High in the mountains. Hard to catch one's breath, it was. And the air polluted, simply stinking of auto fumes, Brassington remembered. Not from the parade of limousines at the governors' convention as much as from a blanketing smog that made one's eyes red and brought a cough in the mornings.

She had dressed Mrs. Leslie French in a lightweight summer outfit of pale pastels with a large lawn-party hat that she carried for protocol's sake but didn't wear because it was sure to crush her hair out of shape.

Would Brassington ever forget Caracas? That morning? Those crowds? The band playing? The long black limousines and the motorcycle escorts? And then, suddenly, the bright flash of orange and the billowing blast of smoke and shrapnel that came *before* the sound, *before* the explosion, *before* the Secret Service could rally, *before* the guards could close in and protect the young Texas governor with a wall of their own bulky flesh.

The blinding star of orange seared her retinas. She lunged forward toward the limousine as his head, spout-

172

ing blood from the severed neck, rolled out onto the pavement with the ongoing momentum of the automobile and the grenade blast.

Brassington's eyes closed as she stood over her ironing board in the cabin of the *Maria*. All about her was silence. She opened her eyes, gathered the clothing on its hangers, and left the room, moving quietly along the carpeted corridor toward her mistress's stateroom.

The door was ajar. Perhaps Madame and her sister had decided to go into town after all with the rest of the party? Brassington pushed the door halfway open. No, there they sat on the bed. Naked as schoolgirls. Facing each other.

Not a stitch of clothing on either of them. Giggling slightly. Facing each other, embracing. Brassington turned away and started to close the door behind her.

Then she realized there was a third person with them. Lying on the bed. A man, by his legs. Not much more to be seen of him. Madame Kerem straddled his midriff, riding up and down. Lady Drew sat on his face.

They were kissing each other as they moved up and down in a kind of rough rhythm, the two sisters embracing and kissing as if the man had been forgotten in their—

Brassington drew a sudden blank.

She was back in her room. The clothes still hung over her arm. She couldn't remember returning down the corridor. She couldn't remember what she had seen in Madame Kerem's stateroom. Her mind refused to link together the images her eyes had collected.

She had forgotten the whole thing. Just as she had forgotten Caracas.

173

Chapter 22

Judi had pretty well decided, not so much on the basis of the dull, dull, dull dinner, but more because of the scene her hostess and her sister had performed at the end of the meal, that she'd had about enough of American cunts.

As though each of them at the dinner table hadn't put in a hard enough day, especially Judi herself, with the flight from London and the dull afternoon in the stateroom with Jim. And on top of it all, that crashingly boring dinner.

Not that Leslie Kerem wasn't bored, too. She'd made it quite clear, thank you, that she was not only bored with the dinner but didn't intend to stun herself into further boredom by an evening at the casino.

Waiting for the gentlemen to regroup and take them all off the *Maria* to the cars, Judi found herself next to yet another flower of American womanhood, Elizabeth Blot, whom she was quite prepared to detest on the instant basis of guilt by co-citizenship.

"I get terribly tired these days. Can we sit down?" There was a note of pleading in Elizabeth's voice which prompted Judi to move with her to one of the big white sofas. "It's because I'm pregnant," she confided in a murmur.

Judi looked at her afresh and decided that under the circumstances she would be nice to her. "How absolutely super," she enthused. "When will it happen?"

"Shsh," Elizabeth whispered. "Jensen has told me to say nothing to anybody. We gather from Ali that Mr. Kerem has a thing about pregnant women. If he knew he'd probably have me flown back to America."

"I won't tell a soul. Why don't we go and buy some of those super layered dresses? They will hide you beautifully and they're all *the thing*. Let's go shopping tomorrow."

"What are you two whispering over?" Ali asked. "Men?"

"Shopping. Will you take us tomorrow, Ali?" Judi realized her play for him had to be discreet. Jim was proving himself such a pompous bore that she had to find some fun, and the godlike steward wasn't interested.

"I shall be delighted," he replied smoothly. Then, as one well versed in the ways of high society Mediterranean style, he added: "If my uncle can spare me."

Judi pouted, getting the message. Business first, Ali had signaled, pleasure when convenient and never be so stupid as to tread on the toes of one of Uncle Kee's useful business contracts like Jim Butler.

She drifted out on deck to where Jim and Kerem stood talking. They were pulling on fat cigars. The air around them was blue and acrid.

"Are we going to the casino?"

"Whenever you're ready." On his feet Kerem looked entirely ungainly, like a stork. At least Jim Butler *looked* physically together. Nobody would guess that nothing ever happened between them.

"Do you need your coat?" Jim asked them. "I've got our passports."

175

"No," said Judi, because she didn't own anything that could go over what she was wearing. She had never been to a French gambling casino and didn't know that everyone had to be signed in, with the number of their passport noted.

"Wait," she said. "I'll get the Blots."

She dashed back inside to her new friend, the pregnant Elizabeth. "Don't forget your passport, lūv," she told her.

Elizabeth frowned, obviously at her wit's end over this new complication. "But we're not leaving the country, are we?"

Judi bugged her eyes and gave a God-knows shrug. "Nothing about these people would surprise me, ducks. They're not your sort, either, are they?"

Elizabeth finally cracked a smile, her first of the evening as far as Judi could see. "No way," she agreed. Then: "Go on ahead, Judi. I'll be fine. See you at the casino."

Judi dashed out on deck again. Heavenly night. Great to be alive. And *not* preggy.

Sitting between Kerem and Jim Butler in the back of the limousine, Judi felt quite excited. After all, *anything* could happen. She hoped one of her worst enemies would be on hand to witness her arrival at the casino. Being escorted by two of the world's richest men had a certain pizazz, didn't it?

The car spun round and came to a halt outside the Summer Casino. The doorman jumped forward, recognizing Kerem. He bowed low and, as an afterthought, bowed to Judi and Jim.

At the reception desk it was Kerem whose nod was responsible for a mere courtesy glance the security man gave both their passports. It was Kerem whom the Chef du Casino fussed over, assuring him of an interesting game of baccarat within a few minutes.

"In the meanwhile, would Monsieur Kerem and his guests care to sit here and take a cognac?"

Judi, followed at a few paces by both men, was led to a corner table in the bar. Napoleon brandy came in balloon glasses as they sat waiting for the big game to be arranged.

The room was brightly lit, almost garishly so, Judi thought. And the people who drifted to and fro near the bar, or those seated at the other tables, looked somewhat dingy. Most of the men were in suits with ties, the women overdressed, all of them decidedly middle-aged. From feeling excited by the prospects of the evening, Judi now felt her express train had been shunted onto a siding.

She looked up to see a young woman standing before her at the table.

"Hello, Judi," the girl said. "You're looking well. Aren't you going to introduce me?"

It flashed through Judi's mind that perhaps this was somebody whom she'd gone on a modeling job with. Yet she couldn't place her face, much less a name. "I'm sorry."

"Don't you remember me?" the girl persisted.

Judi looked again. She didn't have that bad a memory, did she?

"I really don't think we know each other," she said at last.

The girl stood there, eyeing Kerem, who was totally occupied in studying the amber liquid in his glass. Jim made no move either. The silence grew tense.

"You must be muddling me up with someone else," Judi suggested.

With an irritable shrug the girl drifted back in the direction of the roulette tables, and Judi turned to Jim. "I'm very sorry. I've never seen her before in my life."

He roared with laughter as did Kerem. "My dear, you will have to get used to such things," Jim said. "They happen all the time. The price of fame."

"But she knew my name."

"Very difficult to find out." He laughed again. "All she had to do was ask one of the boys in reception. In fact, she was probably tipped off. They're on the game. Judi, my dear, I believe you're even more innocent than you look."

The remark annoyed Judi, as did the hand that went on her arm. She sipped little gulps of brandy, miffed at the two old men with her. It was with relief that she followed the Chef du Casino to the Salle Privée where a big-time game of baccarat had been set up. An official of the casino provided a large pile of chips for Kerem and another, equally large, for Jim Butler.

Jim turned to Judi. "Would you rather sit by me and watch the play or see what you can do for yourself?"

"I'll play a little roulette." Judi looked pathetically down at his money, one finger just tapping the corner of the big square plaque. "Can I have just one?" Her voice was childish and pleading. Nobody had ever before refused that look and voice.

Jim none too graciously gave her a chip, warning her that it was worth a lot of money and that she had better change it into smaller denominations, as it was all he was about to give her. A mean pig, too, thought Judi as she looked about for the *bureau de change*.

As it turned out, Jim had parted with what amounted to about a hundred pounds sterling. Prudently, Judi changed three quarters of the money back into French fifty-franc notes, stuffing them down inside her purse. The balance she took in small ten-franc counters to try her luck at the roulette tables.

In the less elite section of the casino things were jollier. People bustled about, slapping down counters and playing at two or three tables at once. Nobody cared much how they dressed, Judi noticed. A young man in a dark T-shirt offered to buy her a drink. She accepted but when he discovered she was staying on the Kerem yacht he made a polite excuse and bolted back into the crowd around one of the tables.

Judi discovered that around the low-chip tables there was always a crush. You had to play for big stakes to gain comfortable standing room. She moved on to a card game which she didn't understand. It appeared to attract a serious sort of person. Those seated were making little graphs on pieces of paper, while a man sat dealing the cards. His deft fingers dealt one line of seven cards, followed by a second line. As he dealt, he calculated aloud in French. Judi watched, fascinated, but never understanding why a line of cards won. She had no idea how the decision was made, but noted that all bets paid off at even-money odds.

Just as Judi was about to turn away, an old man at her elbow placed several chips on the black. On a hunch Judi did the same, feeling her heart pound with excitement as the dealer dealt a line of cards.

Up came black. The old gentleman took off his winnings plus half of his stake money. Judi did the same. Black came up again for three more turns. Each time Judi followed the old man's play. Each time they won, until finally she had a nice pile of counters.

The old man smiled at her. He pocketed his chips and drifted into the room. Judi went to the *bureau de change,* cashed in her winnings, and placed them neatly along side her other money before wandering through into the Salle Privée.

She calculated that she had almost enough money to go shopping, but she'd never tell Jim that.

A chair was placed at his side. She sat down, again not really understanding the game. There were two other pretty girls at the side of men old enough to be at least their fathers if not their grandfathers. It was all mildly depressing. Kerem was engrossed in the game. So, too, was Jim. Both men seemed to be winning, since they had large piles of counters in front of them. One of the casino servants brought Jim a brandy and asked Judi what she would like.

A nice young lad to go dancing, she felt like saying. Instead, she accepted a brandy.

It was nearly three o'clock before they finally left the casino. Both men had won. For them it had been exciting. It had been a drag of an evening as far as Judi was concerned, and she managed to convey her feelings to Jim.

"I'll make it up to you." He patted her knee fondly.

The car twisted down the hill out of Monte Carlo to the harbor. Across the *Maria*'s gangway lay a bar which had to be lifted to allow them to get aboard.

"It's necessary everywhere these days," grumbled Kerem. "Even when we're moored off one of my own islands we have security problems. All the fault of the press." The two men made a breakfast date to talk further. "Sleep well." Kerem sounded quite fresh as he made off in the direction of the radio room.

"Incredible fellow." Jim's voice was full of admiration. "You realize he's going back to work?"

Judi didn't. And she didn't like to think about it. She walked ahead of Jim toward their cabin, wondering what if anything would happen. As she stepped inside, she saw that the double bed had been turned down on both sides, all very cozy.

"I hope you weren't too bored." Jim took her in his arms. His kiss, without any buildup, seemed almost clinical.

"Get undressed," he said, standing over her without even removing his jacket. He was, Judi noticed, fiddling with his fly, but nothing else gave her much of a clue. She unfastened her skirt, stepped out of it, and sat down on the edge of the bed. Matter-of-factly she pulled her Indian blouse off over her head.

In the half-light Jim bent down slightly and fondled her bare breasts. "Lovely," he muttered.

Judi started to get up. "Don't move." He had opened his pants and now loomed over her, pushing her down on her back, her legs still over the edge of the bed.

Like a doctor's examination, it was over in a few moments, and meant about as much to her. She frowned,

180

wondering if, indeed, he had actually entered her. Jim Butler was on his feet again, tucking his penis back inside his trousers with such a self-satisfied air that Judi decided something really had happened, but she'd be the poorest witness to testify on its behalf.

Jim was humming to himself as he left for the bathroom. Judi sat up on the edge of the bed, from which she'd barely moved more than an inch or two. Had he or hadn't he? she wondered.

Well, one thing was certain: He was easily pleased.

Chapter 23

The whole party aboard the *Maria* had been invited to a luncheon given by Prince and Princess de Reconski, the custom of Mediterranean jet-set society being to accept entire households on a package-tour basis. This was on the strict understanding that such invitations would be reciprocated in kind.

The wise hostess with an eye to the main chance and making gainful contacts for the coming winter selected her August house party with care. Rich and influential people were preferred house guests, but if a hostess could toss into the mix a couple of handsome extra men—never mind if they were gay or not—and one very decorative girl who did not mind the company of older men, she was set. Their group would be invited everywhere.

The formula was much the same as the one for preparing packages of mixed nuts: so many pecans, so many Brazils and cashews, so many almonds plus peanuts galore to make the weight.

That the *Maria*'s party did not wholly comply with the standard social requirements could be overlooked. There were far too many peanuts, but everybody was anxious to meet the expensive sun-roasted almonds, Kerem, and his beautiful wife. What came with them was the luck of the draw.

In this instance, however, the De Reconskis' invitation was somewhat different. The prince was a friend of long standing of Philip Drew. He had backed Philip's plays. Both were proud of the other's friendship. Both were capable of fierce loyalty.

Dressing for the luncheon, Doe realized that she would need to tread very carefully. The De Reconskis were not powerful. The prince's personal dislike of her could have no strong bearing on her real future, since they lived most of the year in their splendid house at Rocquebrun, perched high over the Riviera. But if he'd heard of her rift with Philip, De Reconski might possibly influence Kee against her. It could make things momentarily difficult.

Doe padded barefoot out of her cabin, across to Leslie's room. She found her twin seated in front of her dressing table. With shaking hands, Leslie was trying to put the final touches to her eye makeup, and not really succeeding.

"I feel drained. Exactly as though I'd had a blazing row with somebody. Whereas Walter was absolutely sweet. He stayed after you left last night." Leslie giggled. "He told me he loved me. As a matter of fact, he said after you'd gone that it was because he loved me that he didn't want to—you know—make it with us together anymore."

Doe shrugged. "It's not the kind of reputation that either of us can afford. Is he reliable?"

"Walter is really in love. That's what I'm trying to tell you." Leslie rose from her dressing table and kissed her sister. "Now for important decisions. What are you wearing?"

183

Doe went into the walk-in dressing room with Leslie, where a long line of clothes hung waiting. "Nothing seems to turn me on. I'm distracted."

The De Reconski party might well have sinister repercussions, Doe thought. She dragged on her cigarette and ran her hand along the neatly hung line of sportswear, looking for something new. Her eye lighted on a crisp pale blue linen outfit.

"What's this like?"

"Can't remember. Would you like to ring for Brassington?" Leslie scarcely looked up, her attention once more riveted on her eye makeup. "Do you think last night shows?" she asked anxiously. "Ravages of sin?"

"Don't be stupid. Anyway, you can always wear your dark glasses."

Doe came back into the room with the blue outfit. "I think I'll borrow this if it's any good. What are you going to put on?"

"I'll get Brassington. She'll think of something."

"Not with me around she won't. Can't you do anything for yourself?" Doe was finding her sister particularly exasperating today. Finally she said, "By all means have the maid dress you, but do remember we're liable to meet intelligent people at lunch today."

She flounced out of the cabin, irritated with her sister and with life in general. If only she had been the mistress of the *Maria* what a difference that would have made!

As she dressed herself in Leslie's new blue outfit, she realized, not for the first time, that she should have married Kerem. They knew each other. They understood each other's quick desire, total ambition. Since that could no longer happen, she wanted Kerem's public support of her divorce. In return . . . well, she would be around, filling in where her sister failed, the intelligent half of the famous pair. As a shrewd business brain, an entrepreneur in her own right, she would have been a fantastic help to

Kerem. But . . . perhaps . . . . There were other men who enjoyed business as much as Kee did. Perhaps Jim Butler?

By the time she had finished dressing she felt she looked cool, serene, and elegant. Spraying herself liberally with scent, she went back to see if her sister was ready.

Leslie still sat in front of her glass working on her eye makeup.

"My God," said Doe. She glared at Brassington, who was standing behind Leslie's chair. "Get her into *anything*. We're hours late."

"I've decided to dress in white, Doe, all summer."

"Excellent," snapped Doe. "Put on the dress and come along. You know how formal the De Reconskis are."

Leslie paused and stood up in her shift. She picked up a belt. "I'd no idea we were going *there*. I can't face a formal lunch. There may be press. I can't *go* like this."

Doe picked up her sister's dark glasses and her bag. As she pushed her through the cabin door she called back to Brassington over her shoulder to telephone the princess and explain that they were a bit late but on their way.

The rest of the party sat drinking on the aft deck when the sisters arrived. Kerem, who'd been engrossed in conversation with Jim, seemed unaware that they were more than an hour late for a formal luncheon.

The cars stood at the foot of the gangplank waiting. Kerem, Leslie, and Doe climbed into the first car. Jim and Judi left on their own with their own chauffeur, while Ali drove his Lamborghini, into which the Blots fitted.

Doe suspected they were liable to receive a somewhat frosty reception. The De Reconskis prided themselves on serving some of the best food on the coast. Now that the prince's father-in-law was dead, and there was no lack of cash, he had returned to formality a regal life-style.

She hoped he wouldn't go into too much detail as to why Philip wasn't with her.

185

When their car drew up at the opulent iron gates, guarded on either side by massive stone lions, a servant was there to greet them and announce that the party was being held in the beach chalet. This involved them clambering into an elevator to descend several hundred feet of sheer rock. There was, of course, a rocky stone path with many steps. The servant spoke in slow, careful French, obviously used to dealing with foreigners.

They alighted at sea level on a wide space of rock cut out of sheer cliff. A lavishly furnished beach house looked out over the Mediterranean. Tables had been laid beneath the shade of vines, which no doubt had to be replaced annually since they would be totally exposed to salt air and winter gales. Music played as waiters circulated with drinks.

Doe counted half a dozen other guests, who by now were thoroughly tanked while waiting for the latecomers. She noted one or two more people and a young Arab sheikh who could probably buy and sell the whole lot of them, Kerem included.

Doe's smile was a trifle sharklike as she realized with some satisfaction that the De Reconskis were perfectly prepared to swallow their chagrin at the late arrival of the Kerem household. Money did make a difference.

The prince came forward to embrace them, a big warm-hearted man in his sixties, dressed in white ducks and a brightly printed cotton shirt. He held Leslie and Doe in his arms, a theatrical gesture. Then he hugged Kerem, his true friend. He paused, and then came the inevitable. "Where's Philip?"

"Delayed on business." Doe hoped it sounded convincing. With luck no nasty gossip had so far seeped into the local press. That was one of the problems about the season—there simply wasn't the time to read newspapers. It was hard to know just what tidbits other people had been reading.

Doe looking round the familiar group of regular South

186

of France freeloaders and decided that nobody beyond the prince was likely to give a damn about the absence of her husband. She took a glass of champagne and drifted toward a couple she knew quite well, but whose name, for the life of her, she couldn't remember. They spoke politely for a moment. Then she felt the prince's hand on her arm, drawing her out of the group.

"Tell me, darling. There is nothing wrong with Philip? No problem with the new *Lear*?"

"Only business." Doe looked into the tired brown eyes, surrounded by wrinkles. Normally they laughed, but they could flash with cruelty. He was of exactly the same breed as Philip. But the word "business" had diverted his suspicions.

"The dollar!" he said, "My God, it's another revolution." The prince slapped his chest and looked heavenward. Over their heads fluttered two flags, one the Stars and Stripes, the other a prerevolutionary Hungarian flag. "But you and Philip will survive, you have Kerem in the family. What a man! And your sister, what a beauty!"

Doe was trapped by her host, who pushed her in the direction of the pavilion. "Say hello to Louise, yes?"

The hostess sat on a cushion-covered cane seat that ran the length of the wall. She wore a beige sundress, dark glasses, and wide hat. On either side of her sat a man, one small with bright ginger hair, who seemed to be keeping up a running stream of conversation. On her other side sat a dark young man in silence. Prompted by the ginger-haired man, Louise raised her pale hand and smiled vacantly.

"Louise always loves to see old friends," bellowed the prince, his arm around Doe. His wife's eyes went in and out of focus blearily.

Both young men picked up their cue and asked after Doe, and her husband, her sister, and both stressed how lovely it was to have them all here for lunch. The conversa-

187

tion gave every impression of having been taped in advance. After a decent interval Doe drifted back to the mainstream of the party, realizing that other families had their problems, too. At least she and Leslie didn't have an alcoholic member of the team yet. In Texas, of course. But not on this side of the Atlantic.

Two young bikini-clad men climbed up the iron steps from the sea, dripping water, extolling the freshness of the sea, and issuing a general invitation to swim.

"I'd like to," Judi said to the surprise of everyone. She stripped off her candy-striped jersey dress and revealed a tiny black bikini. Turning to one of the men, she said, "Dive in with me?"

Both young men followed the arrowlike form of Judi, who managed to execute one of her better dives.

"The soufflé! We were just about to lunch." The prince sounded a petulant note. Youth and its ways clearly put his nose out of joint.

"Who is she?" he inquired.

"My girlfriend," said Jim Butler. "Rather impetuous, but nice."

"Why, yes." Politely, the prince forgot the soufflé. Like everyone else, he respected power and money and men like Butler, who had both. At times it did manifest itself in some strange forms, like young girls plunging into the sea just before luncheon was served. The prince smiled reassuringly at Doe, who had come to sit in the shade beside her sister.

"I should really have had my movie camera," said the prince, clearly making an effort to get the party spirit going. "Her diving form was perfect."

"Come and sit with us," Doe invited. She too felt the burden of age at the moment. At Judi's age, of course, she and her sister might have done the same thing.

"How very charming." The prince had his eye on the two young men and Judi, now with dripping black hair, as

188

they made their way back through the elegant throng. He patted Doe's knee absentmindedly. "Very charming."

She followed his gaze, controlling her anger. To think it was one of their party who was making such an exhibition of herself! She would speak to Judi later, explain that such a display just got her a bad reputation.

Doe turned away, annoyed and jealous. Youth, she thought sourly. And, really, what was the point of telling her anything at all? It would only annoy the girl, thus angering Jim Butler, thus upsetting Kee.

Wheels within wheels, Doe thought. Better just let the whole bitched-up thing alone. For now.

Chapter 24

Judi was quite determined not to return to the yacht immediately after lunch was over. For the first time since she had arrived in the South of France she was really enjoying herself.

She sat at a table in the sun with her two new swimming companions and Ali, who had pulled off his T-shirt to match their stripped-down appearance. He was being very amusing. The sun was warm on Judi's skin and she ate greedily of the glorious food that was being handed around.

One of the young men was an American, a nephew of Louise de Reconski, and spending his vacation with his aunt. Judi's eyes grew thoughtful as she anticipated dates for beach parties along the coast and car drives into the mountains. He probably had a Lamborghini too. And he was her age.

It was a lovely day and a magnificent house. Judi could

have spent the rest of the afternoon lazing in the sun, diving in and climbing out of the water. To her it was incredible that only the three of them had actually taken off their clothes and used the beach house for the purpose it was built. The older generation—what where they so shy about? Their flabby bodies?

At the end of lunch the prince was at Judi's side. "I'd like to show you around my house. It will amuse you."

Judi rose, reluctant to leave the sun, but felt that to refuse would be rude. She was no sooner on her feet than she realized the invitation included Jim. How men clung together, she thought. Immediately Judi felt trapped. The older generation had outfoxed her again. She was bored by the prospect of being dragged round an ornate showplace on a hot afternoon when she could be enjoying herself with men her age.

The prince, however, was determined. Clearly any newcomer of consequence had to be treated to the ten-dollar tour.

"When Louise and I first bought it back in sixty-two everyone thought we were crazy. I had then cut the steps in the cliff." He paused while the elevator shot up the cliff face.

"Louise and I like to live simply. We entertain alfresco, just a few friends. Everyone doing what they want."

Judi moved to avoid his hand on her buttocks. She felt Jim looking at her but she kept her head down.

"So here we are."

They alighted from the elevator at garden level. "This garden simply did not exist," the prince droned on. "Louise and I had to put every plant into the ground." He swept his arm with a magnificent gesture to take in the luscious vegetation that now grew in profusion around the house and up its walls.

"Our reception room we use in winter. I hope, now that

191

we are acquainted, you will always let me know when you are in these parts." The invitation was to Jim, who nodded politely.

They stepped into a period room, Louis XV with soft yellow silk furnishings and some Impressionist paintings on the wall. The overall effect was that of a decorator who'd been allowed to spend a lot of money but had not been equipped with much taste or imagination.

There was nothing to be done but murmur words of admiration. Mostly to amuse herself, Judi asked what the bedrooms were like.

The prince spread his hands. "Alas, they are just where we sleep ourselves. We never invite houseguests."

Judi saw a trolley being wheeled out of the other elevator—the kitchen elevator they had not used. On the cart was a large mound of pale beige fabric from which moans were coming. Two earnest young men, one with very bright ginger hair, pushed the trolley load out of sight. "What's that?" Judi asked and instantly got Jim's elbow in her ribs.

"Just the remains of the party," said the prince, reaching for a handkerchief to mop his brow. He wandered after the trolley a few paces.

"Idiot," Jim hissed into Judi's ear. "That was his wife. I thought you'd been introduced to her." Judi shook her head, making a bad job of suppressing an attack of the giggles.

Later, alone in the car, Jim turned to Judi. "I thought you knew. He's married to an incurable drunk."

Judi still shook her head. "Then why this Louise-and-I bit?"

"That's a face-saver, my dear. The prince was penniless when he married her. It's Daddy's money from Detroit that pays for the whole bloody show, Renoirs and all." Jim watched her moodily for a long moment as if wondering, perhaps, if Judi might turn alcoholic. Then abruptly he changed the subject. "We have some errands." He issued instructions to the chauffeur and reached for Judi's hand. "I hope you're not in too much of a hurry for your siesta?"

With you? You're joking, Judi thought but didn't say. What she actually said was, "In fact I need to do some shopping."

The car wound its way first along the coast in the direction of Nice, but before reaching the town turned sharply right.

"I know a good little spot where we'll all dine tomorrow night," Jim mused. "I've checked with Kerem. We're not invited to anything else."

The car came to a halt in a pretty old village perched on a rock outcropping. A group of hikers with packs on their backs gathered around the noisy open-air café opposite the bus stop.

"Afraid it means walking a bit." Jim helped her from the car and they walked up some steep cobbled steps, through a narrow arch, and past an art gallery in whose doorway sat a bearded young man. They climbed past a postcard shop selling minor gifts to an old wooden door from which swung the sign, LA CHÈVRE D'OR.

Inside, Jim was greeted by a fattish man wearing an apron over dark trousers. He led them to a very frail old man seated at the now deserted bar.

Jim introduced Judi to the owner. Then Jim clasped the old man to his chest before he began chatting in French. Cognac and coffee arrived. They toasted each other, the old buzzard running an expert eye over Judi and punching Jim in the ribs. Despite the obvious sign language, Judi decided that she had to learn to speak French. Tomorrow's good resolution.

She sat back and watched Jim make the arrangements for the party. When he spoke French she found it far easier to follow. It appeared that quite a feast was being planned. When all the details were settled, including some precise discussion of the right wines, the old boy turned to Judi and asked her in English to name her favorite color.

"He wants to decorate the room to please you," Jim explained.

"Goodness, how nice, Does he know you've invited Leslie Kerem?" Judi felt really warm toward the old man.

"As a matter of fact, no. It would be unfair in case someone from the press were to 'kneel on his chest.' He knows it's a party of beautiful people, and he's told me you're the best specimen he's seen this season."

"I'd like just yellow and white flowers, please." She smiled. "Daisies or simple things." Then, catching Jim's eye, she added, "I *really* like simple things, unlike our lunch today."

She produced one of her virgin-next-door looks, all wide eyes and slightly quivering lower lip. It had driven more than one photographer to moans of ecstasy because a girl who looked like this could sell absolutely anything to absolutely anyone.

Driving back in the car, Judi felt that she had Jim in a sufficiently mellow mood to broach the question of serious shopping.

"It's not that I'm pushing you, darling," she went on, "but I just can't go out in the same dress. Not with *them*."

Jim said he quite understood. He asked the chauffeur to drive them to the line of Monte Carlo shops that ran down the hill from the Hôtel de Paris.

Jim helped her from the car. "Let me park you here while I leave a message for some people. I'll be back in about half an hour to bail you out. Don't strip the shop bare." He patted her affectionately on the behind as he spoke to the *vendeuse* in French, a slim brunette nearing fifty.

As soon as the shop door was shut behind him, the woman beamed at Judi. "*Chérie*, you and I, we make beautiful music together, no?"

194

Judi looked at the expensive sports clothes, the too-elaborate evening wear. Nothing was her style.

"Is this *all* there is?" She was unable to disguise the disappointment she felt.

"No, *chérie*. My sister has a small boutique in the old part of town. But I think Monsieur wishes you to have elegant things." Her cigarette bobbed up and down in her lips as she spoke.

There was a pause while Judi and the *vendeuse* took stock of one another. The older woman smiled encouragingly.

"*Chérie*, this I shall do for you. I shall telephone my sister to rush over with *les plus belles choses très* avant-garde. We will also find something from here that Monsieur will like. An elegant dress *pour la grande soirée, une très chic robe pour la plage*. We shall mix things so that both you and Monsieur are happy."

She picked up the telephone and rattled French into it, at the same time indicating to Judi that she should rack through the dresses that hung in the closet. As soon as she was off the telephone, the *vendeuse* bustled over, pulled three dresses off their hangers, and rushed Judi into the changing room.

"Off." She pulled at Judi's dress. "Off." She indicated her bikini. "We cannot judge properly with that horrible black thing on your body." She patted Judi's breasts. "You're damp, child."

In a state of mesmerized semifear, Judi did as she was told.

"*Ah, quelle jolie!*" the saleslady exclaimed as Judi removed her bikini top. "We are going to make them even more delectable."

She bundled Judi into a pale lime-green pajama outfit that was almost see-through. Against her normal clothes instinct Judi had to admit that she looked good. When the woman belted a heavy gilt plaited belt with a big medallion in the center around her waist, it gave the outfit a lift Judi would not have guessed from seeing the thing on its hanger.

"Have you been with Monsieur long?" The woman was watching Judi, studying her reflection in the mirror.

"It's our first holiday together."

"He's rich, though. I've seen him before."

Judi felt an unexpected wave of irritation. Quite irrationally she was annoyed to think that Jim had brought another bird or perhaps his wife to this shop. The woman took over again, talking as she zipped Judi into another outfit.

"We shall take this one, for the smart luncheon, or for the *pêtit* bistro dinner. Now this"—she pulled Judi into a rainbow-pleated dress—"is for the party."

"Quite nice," Judi admitted.

"Where are you staying?" The woman was studying Judi closely, the cigarette still bobbing up and down on her lips. "This I like for your coloring. It needs just a little nip at the waist. Don't be nervous, *chérie*, it shall be done immediately."

She darted from the fitting room. Screeching in French, she returned to repeat her question. "At which hotel, *chérie?*"

"On board the *Maria*." Judi enjoyed her moment of triumph.

The woman rewarded her with *whoooing* noises. "No wonder Monsieur wants to dress you with class." Her face grew very grave. "There are many, many favors I will be doing for you. You shall do me one. I shall give you a very elegant scarf with my name on the box. You will give it as your gift to Madame Kerem. And, *chérie*, please tell the lovely Madame Kerem where you buy all your lovely clothes."

She paused to instruct the bent old woman who appeared, wrapped in black, where the alterations were to be

196

made. Both of them smoked as they pinned up tucks in the dress.

"So, now we wait for your avant-garde clothing, the King's Road style. You enjoy the King's Road? I never have been to London. My sister buys these things at the *prêt-a-porter*. Very mod-mod."

Judi pulled her candy-striped dress around her like a towel to hide her naked body. She tried not to giggle.

"How long have you been with Monsieur?" the *vendeuse* demanded again.

"I told you. Not long."

"So. Let me do the first of my favors, some good advice. I like you, *chérie*. I feel for you, as if you were my own daughter. You are beautiful and you have the big opportunity. Do not be stupid. Do not run after young men. Avoid them. If you get bored, come and see me. Tell Monsieur that you must visit Amie. That's me, Amie. Tell him you need more dresses. I'll find you more dresses while you make love with your young man in the back office. Nowhere else."

She paused and lighted a fresh cigarette from the old one. "You are **grand luxe** now, *chérie*. You must be very *sage*, very intelligent with Monsieur, as the fisherman is with the fish, no? Look at the lovely Madame Kerem. Look at her jewels, her yacht. Never does she wear the same dress twice. I tell you, *chérie*, she is a very clever one, that one."

"But Leslie Kerem isn't like me," Judi protested. "She's—"

"Exactly like you, *chérie*, only twice your age." The saleswoman stared somberly at Judi's breasts and belly. She seemed to grow moody as she inhaled smoke fiercely. Then she jumped to her feet and ran to the telephone to volley off more French.

"Good. My sister brings. We wait."

Judi considered her naked reflection in the mirror. Quite like a doctor's waiting room, eh? She pulled her dress around her bottom half.

"You smoke, darling?" The woman reached for her bag, extracted a packet of tipped Gauloises, and offered them to Judi.

Judi shook her head in silence. What was the old girl? A dyke? A procuress? The dialogue had been too improbable so far to be true.

"Relax, *chérie*, the other things will be here in a minute."

Judi fell into the fitting room chair as the *vendeuse* eased herself into the other tiny leather armchair, puffing thoughtfully on her cigarette. There was a long pause before she continued.

"So you haven't been with him long enough to get *anything* arranged?"

"What a question to ask." Judi stood on her dignity.

"Darling, I ask for your own good. He has not talked seriously? Not given you any money or jewelry? Never mind. We reel him in slowly because he is a *big* fish."

Judi tried to speak, but the woman held up her hand to silence her.

"I shall put some money into an envelope, telling you that it is extra buttons. I cannot add too much on top of the bill this time, but it will grow larger in the days to come. When you look beautiful in your new clothes, speak with him. I know a jeweler. He will make the same arrangement with you, in cash."

The woman's sister appeared with hangers of clothes. Together they selected three more items they considered suitable for Judi. She felt herself powerless among such high-pressure professionals and made feeble mental efforts to justify her behavior. But why not let him pay her? Hell, he was rich, and, by the sound of things, she wasn't the first bird he'd brought to the South of France.

Judi redressed and combed her hair. The woman had

198

mercifully left her alone for a moment, during which the shop door opened and Jim spoke in French. Judi wished she could understand. She'd have given anything to know his reaction to the bill, which would be big enough, even without her cash bribe added on. But when she emerged from the fitting room all he said, in a very British voice was, "Our timing seems good."

Two large dress boxes were handed to the chauffeur, while Amie, preening, said: "Your little gift for Madame Kerem and your extra buttons, Ma'moiselle." She winked at Judi, turned, and smiled at Jim. "It was a pleasure to see you again, Monsieur."

Judi fought back the flash of annoyance. Why the hell should she mind that he had taken her to a shop where he was known? Still, the woman's schemes were a bit shoddy, weren't they? This place wasn't quite the dozing old folks' retirement town it seemed on the surface.

They drove down a steep hill to the yacht. The sea sparkled in the late afternoon sun, little whitecaps gleaming yellowly. "What's that wall over there?" Judi pointed to a high rampart above the day.

"The home of Princess Grace and Prince Rainier." Clearly no sightseer, Jim sounded a bit bored.

"Do you suppose the Kerems will invite them on board?" Judi knew she sounded naïve, but it wasn't every day that you lunched in a palace or had someone spend a fortune on you for new clothes. Nor get bribed by a saleslady. It was all happening, wasn't it?

"That was sweet of you to think of buying Leslie a present. You're a nice girl, Judi."

Judi smiled back blandly. There was no point in not taking credit for the gesture. In the envelope she could feel three buttons and something crinkly, money. She was dying to lock herself in the bathroom and find out how much the woman had slipped her.

Chapter 25

Up on deck, Leslie knew, her husband was busily turning the deck of one of the largest and most luxurious private yachts in the world into a sleazy Beirut café. He had issued instructions that the supper would be a Lebanese buffet and dress would be informal. Leslie knew from long experience that this meant Kee would neither shave nor dress. He had, in fact, invited several old Beirut cronies to play *trictrac,* among them Zaki.

Lying on her bed in the darkened stateroom, clad only in a thin cotton nightdress, ready for a siesta, yet not tired enough to fall into slumber this early in the evening, Leslie listened to the faint scraps of sound that occasionally filtered through the jasmine-scented air-conditioning ducts, a vague whisper of shouted conversation, a hoot of laughter, the *ding-ding* of a ship's bell, muted, faraway, as if produced by tiny people no bigger than dolls.

She did not like Kee when he was being at his most Lebanese. She especially didn't like him when he sank up to his eyeballs in Levantine folksiness with a few of his long-time friends. And she particularly hated Zaki.

What was he, a hanger-on, a drifter, making his living at cards, no more than a beggar really? Yet he had a powerful mystical hold on one of the richest men in the world.

Perhaps it was simply that he'd known Kee forever and they spoke the same village dialect as Elly and Ali. Perhaps it was that Zaki's gypsy life appealed to some raffish strain in Kee's character. "There but for the grace of my own Godlike brain, go I."

She sighed unhappily. Walter would be busy now for hours, serving and clearing and doing all the menial things that kept him tied to the *Maria* . . . and to her.

Why did the image of Zaki haunt her? Perhaps there was something mystical about him after all, some hold he had on her as well as her husband. Perhaps he was psychic. The Levantines might think so, of course. There was a tradition of that in Mediterranean lands, the wandering gypsy witch or warlock.

But those chilly gray eyes of his that looked right through her were not Lebanese eyes.

Leslie shivered and rolled sideways to get under the bed covering. She pulled the thick blanket up under her chin and stared with her eyes unfocused at the ceiling of her stateroom. She'd asked Doe several times if she, too, felt this strange power about Zaki, but her sister had merely shrugged it off in her usual businesslike way. Her usual imitation, Leslie corrected herself, of a businesslike manner.

"He may spook you," Doe had said, "but he's got nothing on me."

Got something? Leslie frowned in the dark. Doe had a better memory than she did. She was referring to something about Zaki that Leslie had forgotten. It had to do with Maurice, that much she remembered. With Maurice's death. Something Zaki had said about it to her, or perhaps simply the way he had looked when he said it. Perhaps the old Levantine gambler thought widows brought bad luck. He and Kee were a superstitious pair. Or was he of Syrian origin, in which case it was her blond hair that would be considered so unlucky.

She wished she could pick up the telephone and summon a cup of tea, complete with Walter, but she knew at this hour it would be another who brought it. In fact, she didn't dare ask for Walter by name at any time. But if he were only here now. If Doe were only here.

Leslie didn't mind being alone, that wasn't it. She rather treasured her privacy, if it came to that. But when she wanted an intimate companion, she wanted him—or her—at once. She didn't like to wait.

He was really so darling, Walter. Of course he'd been quite shocked at first. For all his European background, he wasn't as sophisticated or as corrupt as he thought. And he still preferred to be alone with her. But she owed it to Doe to share him. He was simply too delicious to keep locked to herself alone.

August was, on the whole, turning out quite well for her. And, as for the boy, it would be a summer Walter would never forget.

Smiling now in the darkness, she let her large violet eyes close, as if of their own weight. She tried it a second time, enjoying the feeling of her lids lowering slowly and a deeper shade of black sweeping over her. She did it a third time, even more slowly, and then a fourth.

After a while, far away and as small as an elf's thimble, the ship's bell sounded, but Leslie failed to hear its faint echo in the air ducts. She had fallen asleep. The very slight up and down motion of the *Maria* at anchor was soothing in such a subtle way that most of its passengers didn't even realize they were being gently rocked with a long, slow, full, almost stately motion.

In the extremely faint light that came under the door of

202

her stateroom, Leslie Kerem lay motionless, only her face showing. Behind her closed lids there were vague stirrings as her eyes raced left and right.

She had managed to spread the large lawn-party hat on the back seat of the open black limousine. There was quite a lot of room between her car and Maurice's car as the cavalcade of governors sped along.

She knew from past experience that it was expected of her to put some distance between them when they rode this way along public thoroughfares in open cars. One of the public relations men had patiently explained it to her. "The crowds don't know whom to look at if you sit in the same car," was the tactful way he had put it. What he meant, Leslie realized after several of these ceremonial parades, was that the public didn't get a clear view of Maurice French unless he had a lot of space around him.

There had been a sharp wind at the airport as the governors reviewed the Venezuelan troops lined up beside their plane. Fortunately for Leslie's long, loose blond hair, the wind had died down as the party got into their long line of limousines. The marching bands had led off the procession, playing something very sprightly. For most of the trip from the airport, however, they marched silently.

Now the cavalcade of governors was entering Caracas itself. The band struck up another lively tune. The lines of people at roadside were two abreast, then four, then eight. Now there were real crowds and they were shouting.

Vi-va! Vi-va! Vi-va!

Behind her lids in the darkened room, Leslie's eyes darted this way and that with sudden urgency. It was about to happen again. There was no way she could stop it from happening. She knew what it would be, but she was powerless, even more powerless now than the first time it had happened.

They had turned the corner onto the main avenue. A standing band across the plaza had begun to play, the music amplified by loudspeakers. The motorcycles snarled in lower and lower tones. The speed of the parade had begun to slow.

Vi-va! Vi-va! Vi-va!

Dreading it, knowing what it would be, Leslie watched herself reach over to the hat. It had begun to slide off the seat and in another moment it would be on the floor of the limousine, getting dirty.

In the car ahead, Maurice's arm was up and his hand waving. His grin filled the sunny air. He nodded and waved as the crowd warmed still further to him.

Vi-va! Vi-va! Vi-va!

Out of the corner of her eye as she lay sleeping in her stateroom aboard the *Maria,* Leslie Miles French could see the man's right arm go back, far back, as if he were yawning and stretching.

She could see him between two khaki-shirted soldiers with Thompson submachine guns, two of the thousands who lined the parade route. She could see the man's right hand go far, far back and she could see that he was holding something in his hand.

The beautiful pale pastel lawn-party hat was falling, falling. Leslie leaned forward to stop it. Such a lovely, lovely hat.

She was awake and halfway off the stateroom bed, her face and neck dripping with sweat, eyes staring wide into the darkness.

Sitting on the edge of her bed, Leslie began to shake with cold.

204

Chapter 26

A buffet supper had been set out on the aft deck of the *Maria*. The menu was Lebanese, since Kerem expected two of his cronies. He knew that Elly, with her proverbial tact, would add some rabbit food, as he was given to calling the American salads his wife enjoyed.

He felt in no mood for adjusting to any guests but his Lebanese friends. Not bothering to speak any other language.

On an impulse now, he had asked his radio operator to put a call through to Leda in Athens. He might just fly in and spend twenty-four hours with her, if the airport was open again.

He deliberated as to whether to invite Zaki to Athens. Do him good to get away from the card table for a night. Then Kerem thought better of it. He would have enjoyed Zaki's company on the flight, but what would the old gambler do in Athens? He didn't speak Greek.

Kerem wanted to take Ali. But that meant he would be leaving the *Maria* at the mercy of every freeloader in Monte Carlo. While he was aboard, people were afraid to take liberties, and Ali kept things in order.

Elly appeared for a moment to show him a guest list for a party he was giving—Leslie was giving—soon. "The archduke has accepted," she told him.

Their glances locked and their almost identical smiles were ironic. "Re-ah-ly?" Kerem drawled in British English.

"Quite," Elly returned.

"How lucky," he went on mockingly.

"For us." Her smile broadened. "He could hardly refuse your illustrious company. And the free booze."

"And the illustrious company of my legendary wife." He laughed. "My dear Elly, when you marry into the Texas financial aristocracy, provided you have the cash to pick up the tab, society is all yours. I wish to God we weren't giving the party."

"Want to cancel?"

"Too much explaining."

Kerem stretched himself in his canvas chair. It was peaceful with everyone at their siesta. His mind drifted back to the summer he'd cruised the Mediterranean with Leda. Together they had discovered bits of islands, nothing more than rocks sticking out of the sea, other islands on which sheep grazed and a handful of peasants eked out a living. They had lain in the sun, indulged in all the pleasures, including good peasant food and good peasant sex. His romantic thoughts were brought to an abrupt halt as Lady Drew swayed barefoot across the deck and planted a kiss on his bald pate.

"Kee, darling, I had a hunch I might find you alone."

It went through Kerem's mind to pretend to be asleep. In no way did he feel up to Doe in one of her organizing moods. He did not want to discuss their on-and-off affair, not even to analyze why from time to time he was overcome with carnal desire to possess her. He knew perfectly well that she was a scheming bitch who manipulated every-

206

one to suit her own ends. He'd been a fool even to let her on board. Her influence on her twin was disastrous. Except that his wife was usually so far underwater that influences rolled right off her, leaving her untouched.

He yawned in her face, stretched again. "Well?"

"I think we should have a little chat." The wheedling note in Doe's voice was particularly irritating.

"What about?" He still had his eyes closed against the setting sun. He hoped his voice sounded gruff and unencouraging.

"There's us. But I'm really worried about Leslie."

"Be worried instead about you . . . and Philip."

"Oh, Kee."

Kerem struggled from his reclining position, pulling himself up by the sides of the deck chair. He thought to himself that it was family ties and commitments that gave a man a stroke. He sat straighter in the chair now.

"What happens within the family is family business. We're giving a big party, I want your husband here." Kerem noted with satisfaction that he had struck an unhappy chord. He watched Doe light a cigarette.

"I should have thought you, of all people, wouldn't want Philip here," she suggested, letting her voice lower to a sultry note.

"So we can fuck?" He grinned at her. "Are you that good, my dear?"

"Bastard." Her mouth twisted through several contortions until she produced a grin that matched his, reckless and quite evil. "If you'd like Philip here, write him yourself, darling. He hasn't started rehearsals yet."

"I'll do just that." His grin faded. "And you'll be lovey-dovey to him when he arrives for the party. Understand?"

"Bastard."

"And, another thing." He tweaked the live cigarette out of her fingers. "You smoke too much." He watched her stalk over to the rail.

Kee Kerem sank back to snooze, leaving Doe to drape herself along the rail and gaze across at Monte Carlo. Kerem watched her from under his eyelids. He liked Philip Drew, a man who had once fallen on bad times but had remade his life, and was now successful.

What Kerem admired most about Philip was the way he was prepared to do a job, and a good one. He didn't expect leavings from the rich man's table without pitching in with his own contribution. Doe was a fool to lose such a man. A gentleman.

Zaki shambled onto the deck, carrying his own backgammon board. Kerem rose, this time without effort, and clapped both arms around his Levantine buddy. As they embraced each other and kissed each other's grizzled cheeks, Kerem saw distaste in his sister-in-law's face. He hugged Zaki even tighter.

The young German barman was setting out the drinks. Kerem called to him in German to bring them a couple of scotches, deliberately not inviting Doe to join them. When Walter came with their glasses on a tray, Kerem patted his arm. "You're doing a good job, Walter. In a menagerie like ours, it's not easy. Now, offer that sister-in-law of mine a drink."

Walter clicked his heels and went.

Zaki had the backgammon counters set out. Kee began to toss the dice, his problems forgotten. Halfway through their first game, he got his telephone connection to Athens. Speaking haltingly in Greek, and winking at Zaki, he carried on a conversation with Leda, keeping his eyes on Doe.

It pleased him to be making telephonic assignations with his mistress under the nose of his wife's sister and his own sometime bed companion. The irony of the situation was even sweeter since only Zaki understood what had been going on and Zaki didn't really give a damn. He was the perfect chorus for this tragicomedy, disinterested, remote.

"Dumb," Kerem murmured in Lebanese to his gambling companion. "She thinks that marrying a gentlemen gives her style."

Zaki frowned and murmured something in return about skinny bitches being bad in bed. Kerem got to his feet with a roar of "Where is everybody?" He winked again at Zaki. "Did you see our plump little American chicken, the wife of my broker?"

In ones and twos, people drifted back toward the buffet and the noises Kee Kerem was now making, noises that were meant to sound hospitable but which someone who really knew him, like Ali or Elly, would know to be camouflaged hostility.

He reached out for Elizabeth Blot and pulled her over to Zaki now with the air of an Arab slave trader selling off a particularly soft-assed teen-age boy to an oil sheikh. "Here's a lot of meat," he told his crony. "U.S. Grade A Choice," he added in English for Elizabeth's benefit, and was happy to watch a dull red glow suffuse her cheeks.

"Keep her under you, my boy," he told Zaki in Lebanese, "and you'll never need a mattress." His hand cupped around Elizabeth's buttocks and jiggled them softly, almost impersonally.

Zaki's filmy eyes sharpened as he glanced over Elizabeth, quite as if measuring her milk output or the number of steaks he might carve from her haunches. Slowly, the old gambler's face went blank. Then he frowned very slightly, a poker player's expression, and turned to say something to Kerem, who had wandered away to talk to the English financier.

The frown on Zaki's forehead deepened. He sought out Ali, who was busily chatting up Judi. "Young prince," be began in Lebanese, "does this girl understand our tongue?"

"Only," Ali responded in Lebanese, grinning slyly, "when it is inserted in her rosebud orifice."

"Why has no one told Kee the blond Yankee cow is pregnant?"

The grin disappeared from Ali's face. "There was no chance, old man," he explained guiltily. "We were on the high seas, and what were we to do, throw her overboard? And now it's too late. Anyway, it's a silly superstition."

Zaki nodded. "But you did wrong not to warn your uncle. And because I love you as I love him, I am also not going to tell him for fear of getting you in trouble."

"A thousand thanks, old friend."

The gambler's milky eyes seemed to unfocus, as if he were staring into a wilderness of future events. "Someday. . . ." His words stopped, but his meaning was obvious. Someday Ali would stand in his uncle's shoes. And Zaki wanted the Kerem patronage to continue. To remain a friend of the nephew, he would neglect to tell the uncle about the pregnant one.

Jim Butler picked up a glass of pale yellow wine. "A good peasant wine, to accompany what makes for a very pleasant change, this good Lebanese food."

Kerem saw with pleasure that his little charade, which had so often intimidated other guests, was having the reverse effect on Jim, who actually seemed to enjoy the peasant provender.

"I am by no means a connoisseur of wine," Butler was saying, "but I do enjoy the local vineyards on holiday."

"I suspect you enjoy a lot more than wine."

"Should we then agree? The French have built up such a mystery about wine, and the ordering of the correct bottle at every meal, that to break rank and openly enjoy foreign grapes is to break with the social graces themselves."

"You sound like an educated English gentlemen." Kerem roared with laughter.

Leslie Kerem appeared then, drifting across the deck in a cloud of white, the sleeves of her dress reaching almost to the hemline of her nightgownlike garment, her pale blond hair floating to her shoulders. She took up a pose at Jim's elbow, looking intently at Kerem.

"Aren't we doing *anything* tonight?"

Kerem chose to ignore the discontent in her voice. He made one of those all-women-are-the-same gestures as he turned to Jim, saying, "Ali plays excellent *trictrac*. Why don't we have a partnership game?"

"Some of us might like to play, too." Doe directed her comment at Kerem, making no effort to disguise her annoyance.

"Why don't you, then? Set up your own competition."

Ali appeared with a second backgammon board and whispered in his uncle's ear. "The plane will be at the airport in the morning."

"Capital." Kerem clapped him on the shoulder, waving him to a chair opposite Jim Butler. He summoned Zaki and the four men sat down to their backgammon boards. It was almost, but not quite, as good as if they were back in Beirut, thought Kerem happily. It was amazing how with a bit of booze and some cigar smoke one could turn the deck of this luxury tub into a sleazy Mediterranean café.

He yelled for more drinks, deliberately shouting loudly to annoy Leslie. He hoped she'd notice him sweating. She disliked the body's natural juices, as did Doe. Overwashed American bitches, the pair of them.

He settled down in earnest to roll the dice, in an effort to beat his lifelong opponent Zaki. He saw that the old gambler's glance shifted from the backgammon board to the plump Elizabeth Blot. She seemed to bother Zaki.

Kerem smiled privately. He'd never known Zaki to let a woman interfere with his gambling. Maybe there was more to Mrs. Blot than met the eye.

Chapter 27

It was six A.M. Kerem, the sole occupant of one of his own bank's DC-9's, rose like a great bird above the runway of the Côte d'Azur airport. Below lay the jagged coastline and the old town of Nice—a series of multicolored rooftops in the early morning sun. Farther along the coast, just before the rugged cliff face almost met the sea, lay Cap Ferrat, an elongated green strip covered with white villas, like some architect's model for housing development.

High-class overcrowding, Kerem thought, turning back from the porthole. He strode into the cockpit as the craft headed out to sea.

"Want to dip a wing over the *Maria*?" The pilot, who had flown Kerem on many occasions, thus reminded him that he used to do this in the days of Leda's reign aboard the yacht.

"Those days are . . . in cold storage." Kerem laughed, patting the man on the shoulder. How good it was to be speaking in Arabic again.

He went to his seat and accepted the strong black coffee the hostess put before him. Solitude. He ran his hand over his stubble cheeks. A few minutes before he was due to land in Athens he would ask the girl for an electric shaver.

He snapped open his briefcase and began making notes. Sending for the steward, he had him cable his London public relations man to be in Monte Carlo for the party. He wished he could pinpoint why he felt bothered about holding the party. Yet he did. He sensed that when the night arrived it would be an unhappy occasion.

He shrugged. He was capable of not attending the thing. So what *was* he worrying about? As to the café-society that his wife chose to call their circle of friends, he didn't care if he never set eyes on any one of them again.

At least, relaxed and ten thousand feet above land, that was what he assured himself. There had been a time when princes and titled people had been of considerable importance in his scheme of things. In the days when he had first entered the resort development business, social names had mattered. He had, for example, tried to maneuver a duke into a business partnership.

What a golden venture that might have been, he mused, but the duke had regarded his social position as something verging on holy. His name was to be preserved at all costs, however fading his grandeur. He shunned such upstarts as Kerem.

We both missed out on a very good deal, Kerem mused now. It was his guess that the duchess was not about to let her husband's property be turned into another Las Vegas. Yet her scruples were for nothing. They would have done far better to have turned professional than to turn an amateur's blind eye to all the call girls and cheapskate gamblers who swarmed through the overpriced skyscraper tax sanctuary.

Odd, how nobody faced up to fundamentals. Kerem made a note in his pad to check current prostitution figures. It amused him to trot out such statistics in the middle of some pompous occasion. His own party would be the place for a quip like that. It made the wearing of his dinner jacket, and the undeniable expense, worth it.

And it would enrage his wife.

There was supposed to be one hotel in Monte Carlo that operated twenty-four-hour call girl service. For no reason he found himself reliving the casino evening. He recalled Judi's face. He wondered if Jim Butler had long-range plans for the girl. Stupid, if he did. He made a note on his pad to ask Ali if he had scored with the girl.

Kerem began to write out a list of items he wished his jeweler in Athens to supply. He was going to get behind his promotion of gold in a massive and obvious way. All the women on board his yacht would get a present. Get the word "gold" into print.

There was Jim's girl. He would give her something nice. He wondered who had given her the bright idea of bringing Leslie a present. Young people weren't like that. Someone else's brain at work.

Elly. What could he give her? She was worth all the gold in South Africa. But he'd already settled quite a trust fund on her, not that she knew it, of course. Something expensively golden but very delicate and simple for his darling Elly.

Then he wanted one heavy, utterly vulgar piece of ornamentation, if possible a necklace that would be actually painful to wear. That for Leslie. Let my wife suffer, he thought, to remind her with every twist and turn that I have given her yet another present.

Doe? She must have something tinny. Something that was large to look at but had absolutely no resale value.

Elizabeth Blot? Something nice. He might even have a go at her when he returned, see if that plump U.S. carcass was worth a bite or two. Something plain and very expensive for her before he pronged her a few good thrusts.

Having made his list, he then had the steward cable Michaelous in Athens to meet him at the King George Hotel with all this jewelry. But most important of all, he was to bring his currently most lovely piece in gold and lapis lazuli.

That was for Leda, her favorite stone.

The steward brought him an electric razor. They were about to make their descent into Athens.

Kerem found his bank's car and chauffeur waiting in the morning heat. The airport was all but deserted, and no wonder. What foreigner in his right mind would willingly risk being caught up in the frenzy of a political demonstration?

Crazy people, the Greeks, thought Kerem. He wondered in what frame of mind he would find Leda. What political party would she have tied herself to now that she was back? Surely not to Karamanlis. His charm for Leda had always been his exiled status. Now that Karamanlis was back in Athens Leda would ignore him. Or would she? Leda was unpredictable, and jealous to boot.

My God, thought Kerem, she could be jealous over the most irrational details, insignificent things. Certainly, by now she would be feverishly behind her onetime friend, Karamanlis, or already denouncing him as undemocratic with nasty French habits.

It was Greeks like Leda, emotional and changeable, that made Greek politics so unpredictable. Whereas in Lebanon the ages-old implacable hatred between Christian and Moslem was as unchanging and as deadly predictable, as the heat of the desert or the slow tides of the sea.

He had booked a suite at the King George Hotel, preferring it to the Grande-Bretagne next door. It had the added advantage that Leda had already installed herself there. But he had always favored the King George for liaisons for a simple and very practical reason. On its rooftop was one of the best restaurants in Athens. Therefore, to be seen getting in and out of an elevator at the King George did not bring about the normal raise of eyebrows.

It just crossed his suspicious mind as his limousine arrived at the hotel that this too could be the reason the dynamic Leda had also chosen to say at this hotel.

The lobby was old-fashioned, furnished in reproductions of a French style of eighty years ago. A massive arrangement of pink gladiolus graced the hall table, but only one other guest could be seen in the empty lobby.

Kerem called Leda on the house phone. Her voice was throaty with pleasure as she invited him to her first-floor room. She opened the door. She was dressed in a flowing peignoir. "Darling, how marvelous." She pulled him inside. "It's so early, I'm not even dressed."

Kerem was surprised to see that she had installed herself in a small single room. It was nicely furnished, had a bathroom *en suite*, but was far from her normal scale of living. It crossed his mind that she was short of money. Yet he knew, or thought he knew, this was impossible.

He sat on the unmade bed, there being several books on the stool at the desk. The only other chair was piled high with Leda's clothing.

She locked her arms round him. "This is the most fantastic good luck. How long will you stay?"

From the square below came singing and shouting, the noise gradually growing louder. Disregarding the air conditioning, Leda threw open the door and stepped out onto the balcony.

"Come, look, see how they adore their freedom." Beneath in the square about two hundred students, mostly boys, were carrying anti-American banners. They went singing past the hotel, across the road, to plant their banners on the steps of the Assembly Hall.

At this, uniformed police remonstrated with them, pulling down their placards and dispersing them in an almost friendly fashion.

"The brutes." Leda closed the window and turned back into the room.

216

Kerem mopped his face. The heat from the square had been insufferable. He was glad to have the room cool again.

"Politics can wait," Leda said, holding out her arms.

As far as Kerem was concerned, Greek politics could take a back seat forever. He locked the bedroom door and removed his blue flannel suit.

Leda lay invitingly on the single bed. Again it went through his mind to ask why she was living so modestly. Later, he thought, I'll raise the question over lunch. Perhaps it's sheer peasant practicality.

He forgot about the smallness of the room, his gamble in dollars. His mind went back in time to their honeymoon summer, alone in the *Maria,* as he lay down beside her. The telephone rang. Leda looked at the ringing instrument, then at Kee.

"Answer it," he said. "Perhaps the students have sparked off another revolution."

She flashed him a warning look. She had no sense of humor where her precious Greek politics were concerned, he observed. There was a half-eaten box of French chocolates by the bed. He bit into one.

"Ambrose," said Leda guardedly into the receiver. There was a pause, then her throaty laugh. "It's Michaelous. He has a packet for you. Buying more gold?" She laughed.

"Tell him to wait for me up in the restaurant." Kerem stuffed another chocolate into his mouth.

Leda passed along his order to the jeweler and hung up the telephone. Then she clicked the instrument up and down several times until the hotel operator answered. "No calls until further notice," she said, smiling broadly at Kerem.

He lay back naked and cadaverous-looking on the bed and picked yet another chocolate out of the box as she stood up and slowly, as if onstage before an audience of thousands, let the filmy peignoir slip from her shoulders. It fell in a heap at her feet and she stepped free of it, her breasts jutting out at him as she fell forward across his body.

"Those chocolates are loaded with aphrodisiac," she teased.

"Mount me and ride," he ordered.

She started to fit him into her, then stopped. "Don't be such an old man, darling. It's being the jockey that keeps a man young."

She rolled off him and lay face down on the bed, her buttocks raised slightly, invitingly. "Mount me and ride," she mimicked in a gross imitation of his command.

"The doctors in New York—"

"Have never made the beast with two backs," she finished. "Mount me," she commanded.

"The erection—"

"Besides," she taunted him, "it's the way to make a boy, didn't you know that?"

"You pregnant? With my son and heir?"

"Why not? Get going. Now."

The order excited him suddenly. He rolled over and entered her from behind, holding onto the smooth globes of her buttocks and squeezing them powerfully as if they were the giant breasts of some great primordial earth goddess, rank with the reek of lust.

She moaned as he thrust home. He could feel his heart thud with excitement at the harsh angle of entry. Closing his eyes, he thrust home again and again. He could feel his body come alive, tingling with strange movements inside his veins, as if he were being caressed from within by his own blood. Leda pregnant. With his son. His *son!*

Again. Again. Deeper, higher, further. He was gasping with joy, thrilling with each thrust. He would go on like this for hours. He would live forever.

He would keep her pregnant for years . . . all boys!

On the next thrust—

218

Chapter 28

Although the stern deck of the *Maria* had been screened off by canvas panels so that sunbathers could not be seen from shore or from other ships in the harbor, Leslie Kerem knew from bitter experience that nude sunbathing was impossible for her. The ingenious *paparazzi* had been known to rent helicopters and, with powerful telephoto lenses, snap pictures that could never be mistaken for anything but the real thing.

Five berths along the dock the Onassis yacht was moored and the photographers stalked it like panthers, waiting for a glimpse of Jackie or Ari or anyone else whose photo would bring money from gossip editors.

Dressed in the barest of bikinis, Leslie lay on her stomach and felt the sun beat down on her body. It would bleach her hair even paler. They said the sun was the great god of fertility, she mused sleepily. She turned slightly to look at Doe, lying beside her.

"Doe," she murmured, "didn't the ancient people believe—"

But her sister was asleep. No sense asking her anything. But Leslie could vaguely remember something about the sun fertilizing a woman's womb and producing a boy. The fertility rites of the ancient religions. The Virgin birth itself. She frowned at the exertion of so much thinking.

Leslie sighed. She really was not cut out for thought. She stared now past her sister's sleeping body. Doe was the thinker, the planner, the schemer who could create the most improbable things out of her brain and make them come true. Past Doe's breasts in their bikini top, rising and falling faintly as she slept on her back, Leslie could see the bar set up under the awning.

Poor Walter stood stiffly behind the bar polishing glasses, not daring to look in her direction. Lolling easily on barstools, Ali and Jensen Blot muttered together quietly, almost good-naturedly now that Kee Kerem wasn't there to ride herd on them.

Blot kept ticking off points on a pad of paper attached to a clipboard. Ali, still juggling bits of paper torn from the telex printer, conferred with him, squinting at the writing on the pad. Vague snatches of their conversation drifted to her through the hot sunshine.

". . . Basel signals are all go."

"Then we go. But Uncle Kee isn't . . ."

". . . have his power of attorney on this."

She caught Walter's eye. He stared at her past the two men with such a burning glance that Leslie felt as if she were turning on a spit. She blew him a kiss with her soft, full lips.

At that moment Judi arrived, sleek and dark-haired, in a terrycloth kaftan. She glanced once in Ali's direction, then unzipped the kaftan and revealed herself naked to the sun. The brilliant Mediterranean light glinted in the dark muff of her pubis before she lay down on her stomach and matter-of-factly closed her eyes.

"My dear," Leslie murmured softly, "you don't seem to understand."

She could see that Ali was examining Judi's nude body with more than routine interest but she had the feeling it was only Kerem's nephew for whom the display was intended.

"Judi," she whispered, "this place is swarming with photographers. You'll have to— "

"Crikey!" The British girl jumped to her feet, turning so that her small breasts ponted toward Ali. "I had no idea. And I didn't bring anything but the kaftan." Giggling, she bounded off naked into the salon.

Ali slid off the stool and walked slowly toward his uncle's wife. He grinned down at her. "Did I just see what I just saw?"

"She doesn't understand about the *paparazzi.*"

"Never mind the *paparazzi,*" he countered, "what about me?"

She smiled up at him, only slightly less naked than Judi had been, but feeling somehow less vulnerable with her tanned color. "I had no idea you fancied the model type, Ali."

He shrugged. "To each his own dirty taste, as the French say. I notice that it didn't faze Jensen Blot for a second."

She closed her eyes, hoping to dismiss him. "Of course," Ali added then, "our American friend doesn't really notice much of anything when you're available for ogling."

"Really?" She made it sound as languidly disinterested as she could. "I wonder how Jim Butler would feel watching you ogle his poopsie."

Ali snorted with laughter. "*His* poopsie?" He leered at her with such force that she almost felt the look and opened her eyes. His teeth in his dark face were dazzling. "I doubt if Butler's even been in."

"Ali," she began in a warning voice.

"Right. No sex talk. But if ever I saw a proper English faggot who wouldn't know what to do with it if it jumped up and pissed in his ear, that's Jolly Jim Butler."

221

Doe grunted uneasily as she awakened. She stared at Ali. Then, in a small, sweet voice, like a proper little daughter of Texas high society she said, "Ali, you dirty little Levantine shit, fuck off."

"Ladies, ladies," Ali said soothingly. "The minute Uncle Kee is gone you just can't help reverting to type, eh, Doe?"

Before either Leslie or Doe could respond, Judi returned in a bikini and lay down beside them. "Sorry about that," she said to no one in particular.

"Don't apologize," Ali assured her. "I loved every inch of it."

"Words," Judi countered. "Mere words."

Doe now turned over on her stomach with such finality that, after a wink at Judi, Ali turned back to the bar. In the silence that followed, Leslie could hear him pick up the threads once again of his conference with Jensen Blot, as if nothing at all had intervened.

". . . unload in London and Amsterdam first?"

"The New York sales will be much . . ."

Leslie found herself wondering why men were so much different from women when it came to sex. Even Maurice could never quite stop thinking politics in bed with her. And she was sure that as she serviced Kerem's ugly lust his mind was probably on his financial schemes. It was all just a sudden muscle spasm for men, wasn't it? Just a rub and a spurt and back to business again.

She tried to consider if Jim Butler was the same sort and decided he was.

But if Ali was right, Jim had even less interest in sex than most men. Which was all to the good, after all. One really didn't marry for sex. She, for example, would never dream of marrying poor Walter. It would have only one effect, that of utterly spoiling sex between them. How could she share a husband with Doe, for example? Of course, she knew Kee and Doe occasionally. . . . But that didn't count, since Doe had been there before her.

222

The sun beat down on her with an almost sexual force, hammering at her flesh insistently, like a lover. She could feel herself sliding under. The great thrusting prick of the sun impaled her. She shifted luxuriously in her sleep.

It hurt this high up. Caracas was much closer to the sun. The air, even as polluted as it was, was thinner here in the mountains as the cavalcade of limousines moved through the streets.

Viva! Viva!

The open cars let the sun beat on their heads, glinting on Maurice's smile, on the clenched face of the man with the arm pulled back as if to throw something.

Viva! Viva!

See his smile explode!

"Jesus Christ!" She heard her own scream in her ears as she awakened, half sitting, on the sunbathing mat. Ali and Jensen Blot turned to stare at her. *"He's dead!"* she screamed.

Viva!

Chapter 29

La Chèvre d'Or perched high on a rock overlook-
ing—overhanging, in fact—the seacoast. Although it was
situated in the tiny French village of Eze, it looked down
on Monte Carlo and the Principality of Monaco below it.

Eze was a perched village, placed there in the early days
to avoid the attacks of Saracen raiders along this sunny
coast. Now that the sun was starting to sink in the west behind the low massif of hills that lay at the end of the Riviera, diners began to thread their way through the curving
streets and alleyways of Eze toward La Chèvre d'Or.

Not all of them were bound for Jim Butler's party. Some
actually lived in the tiny eight-bedroom inn that was part
of the popular restaurant. Some were simply cocktail-hour
visitors here to enjoy a glorious view of the Côte d'Azur
with their predinner drink.

The first to arrive for the Butler party, by an odd coinci-
dence, were the host himself and a woman who was not

Judi. She had disappeared after siesta to go waterskiing with Ali and neither one had yet returned to the *Maria*.

Butler had gone up ahead of his party to make sure all was in readiness. Seeing him leave, Doe Drew had followed in her flowing, floor-length evening dress of a pale chartreuse bordering on the yellow of early willow leaves. After helping him check out the details of the dinner, she had invited him up to the next higher level of La Chèvre d'Or, where a tiny swimming pool occupied part of a courtyard. There they sipped martinis and chatted idly.

"About Judi," Doe said then.

"She's all right," Jim Butler assured her. "It's not as if I'm engaged to marry the little bint."

"Then you realize what she is." Doe felt quite pleased at having gotten the conversation off on such an intimate level so quickly. It wasn't that easy with anyone, but especially not with a moneyed Englishman.

"I do." He frowned at her. "Do you?"

Doe shrugged airily. "Bit of a party girl."

"Yes," he agreed judiciously. "Hardworking model, too. Our generation doesn't understand her attitudes toward sex, of course."

Doe decided she didn't at all like being included in Jim Butler's generation. What was he, crowding sixty? "If you mean total promiscuity," she began.

"Oh, rot." Butler sipped his martini and ordered another from a passing waiter. "All I want is a pretty bit of fluff on the arm, so to speak. Something to match the fearsome Kerem at his own game. I'm not asking her to love, honor, and obey. Or even behave."

"I see. Then it won't disappoint you if you learn—"

"That she's been screwing the whole French navy this afternoon?" Butler finished. "My dear Doe, I did make it clear, did I not, that she's no candidate for wife?"

Doe smiled, making the movement of her lips soft and a

bit pouty. "I understood some lucky woman already had that title."

He shook his head slowly and, taking a fresh drink from the waiter's tray, handed it to her. "The divorce became final last spring."

Doe sipped her second martini. She decided a total change of subject was in order, and quickly. "Do you know," she said then, "I believe dear little Mrs. Blot is a bit preggers."

"Elizabeth Blot? Now that you mention it—"

"If Kee finds out there will be utter unholy hell to pay. He has a *thing* about pregnant women. It's very ancient and archaic and Levantine, if you know what I mean. Super-superstitious."

"Even if it were his own wife, your twin sister?"

Doe made a face. "Leslie would cut her throat rather than bear a child of Kee's."

"And you, my dear? Any little Drews about?"

Doe turned her hands out in girlish helplessness, as if she would be happy to oblige if she but knew how the trick were done. "Alas, no. Philip is . . . not . . ." She let the thought die.

"Surely those virile actor types are—"

"Not all of them," Doe cut in quickly.

"But, forgive me, my dear, it's not from lack of—of—"

"Of trying?" Doe watched him finish his second drink. She timed the effect for maximum impact, slowly draining her own martini as well in a growing moment of sheer drama. Then, with a sob, she buried her head against Jim Butler's chest. She was careful not to produce tears, but only the sound of sobbing, tiny and helpless for a moment.

"My dear girl," Butler began.

"If you only knew." She let the rest of what she was saying come through shakily, not in sentences but in phrases softly racked by sobs, confident in the knowledge that he couldn't see her face. "Brink of divorce . . . a thousand times I've begged . . . body burning with desire . . . tor-

ment no woman could ever bear . . . suicide is the only . . . not worth living if . . . thought that somewhere a
man would take pity . . . too much to expect of . . . cruel
sort of life but. . . ."

At the very end she broke free of him, aware that he had
put his arms around her. She stared up at his face, her dry
eyes searching his. Then she pressed herself against him
and they kissed.

She let her lips open slightly. After a long moment his
tongue entered between them, experimentally. She took it
all, pulling it into her mouth, moaning with ecstasy. He
tasted of extremely good gin, and more faintly, of extremely fine vermouth.

They moved through the arched doorway and found
themselves in a bedroom. The martinis had been strong
enough, Doe saw. She reached for his fly and began to un-
zip it, at the same time turning her left wrist so that she
could read the time on the tiny dial of her diamond en-
crusted watch. They had at least fifteen minutes before the
guests arrived.

She reached inside his fly and caught his penis in her
hand, watching his face as she did so. His eyes seemed for
a moment to turn up in his head, as if she had plunged a
dagger into his abdomen. He pulled her down on the bed
with him, but they missed the edge of it and went to the
floor.

Fair enough, Doe thought. Nobody can see us at this level. No sense giving away my hand to any spies Philip has
planted nearby.

With her free hand she slowly pulled her long skirt up
over her legs. She was wearing no panties. She decided to
give her next husband as much of a look of it as he wanted.
But, at this point, all she would let him do was look. Jim
Butler was a lamb led to slaughter. If there was one thing
she'd learned in business it was not to give away a salable
item. He'd probably never before in his life gotten the full
official Texas cocktease. He would now.

227

Chapter 30

Carefully laying a slightly moistened towel over the delicate fabric of the long gown, Brassington lightly touched it here and there with the hot sole of the traveling iron.

It was either too hot, she noted, or never hot enough aboard this accursed ship. Something about the generators on the *Maria*—they were never quite stable enough to produce electricity one could rely upon. But, then, what could one expect of a non-British ship, and a Lebanese vessel at that?

Brassington glanced at her watch and saw that her mistress, Madame Kerem, should at this very moment be at La Chèvre d'Or where that extremely nice, very friendly, and utterly suitable Mr. Butler was holding his party.

She really could find nothing at all to complain about Mr. Butler except perhaps that his name appeared in the newspapers a bit too often. Judi she did not really hold against him. Brassington understood Judi. She also understood men.

With the possible exception of Walter, the German steward.

It was, in fact, Walter who was now responsible for delaying her mistress. Brassington understood quite well that if Leslie Kerem didn't wish to be delayed, or had perhaps for the first time in her adult life some vague desire to be on time at a party, then no servant and certainly not a pretty weakling like Walter could have delayed her.

But that was what was happening at this very moment. Brassington knew quite well why her mistress' stateroom door was closed and locked.

She knew, perhaps not with anatomical accuracy, but with a fairly good sense of geography, where her mistress and Walter were at that moment in the stateroom. She also had a fair idea of what they were doing because she had accidentally walked in on them often enough in the past week and, silently, bowed back out again without either of them suspecting her presence.

Oh, it was all quite standardized now, Brassington thought as she continued to smooth away microscopic wrinkles that were virtually invisible to anyone but her.

The only departure from the norm was the absence of Lady Slut. Brassington reckoned there had been a reason for the sister to depart the *Maria* with Mr. Butler. She reckoned the reason had to do with the rift between Doe and her husband. It wasn't too hard to understand that Sister Doe was already shopping for a new mate.

Brassington frowned. If Mr. Butler deserved anyone as a wife—and Brassington didn't for a moment believe a man as rich as Mr. Butler actually needed to be married—Judi would have been a better choice.

Judi was far prettier than Lady Doe and far younger. She did have a fatal attraction for young men but that was only natural in a high-spirited girl off on a jaunt, away from her usual London homosexual photographer friends. Brassington knew a bit about the Great World and understood that for a busy model like Judi, life in London

229

could be almost nunlike, surrounded by the high priests of her profession, artists, photographers, and advertising men who simply didn't like women.

She stopped frowning as she lifted the dress from her ironing board. Stunning. Her mistress would look exceptionally beautiful in this soft, faintly rosy-peach color that would set off her Mediterranean tan. Blondes like Leslie Kerem, she reflected, did well to wear these blushing colors.

And, after all, appearances were everything, were they not?

It was terrible to realize this about one's employer, especially when one has worked for nobility, real British nobility, not knighted actors, no matter how good they were. But the lineage, the provenance of the Miles sisters, Leslie and Doe, had been quite good as bloodlines went. It had been this ancestry, as much as the fantastic political future of Governor Maurice French, that had convinced Brassington and her father that the job in America was a good one.

Terrible to realize, Brassington thought, the iron poised in midair as she wound up the cord, that in this so-called jet-set world, the men were all great thieves like Kerem and the women were all for sale.

That was really the truth of it, sad to say. And not just the women, but the pretty young boys like Walter as well. On this whole ship, only the two Levantines, Elly and the nephew, could claim to be persons in their own right. And why? Because they had already been bought by Kerem. Blood royalty was perhaps as strong in them as the money tie. This accounted for their independent air. But money underlay their loyalty nevertheless.

Terrible, Brassington repeated to herself. Fine girls of impeccable lineage, selling themselves as openly and with as much advertisement of makeup, hairdo, and clothing as Judi sold her body to the adverts and, yes, to that nice Mr. Butler.

230

Was that what the Great World was all about? she mused. Had it come finally to that in this new age where titles were empty and bloodlines meaningless?

In this Great World, Brassington asked herself, were all the women Great Whores? Had it come to that?

She heard footsteps down the long hall toward the foreward quarters of the yacht where the crew lived. Peeking out the door of her room, she saw Walter moving slowly, wearily along the corridor. In a moment her mistress would ring and the process of makeup and dressing would begin. Within an hour, possibly, with luck and Brassington's chivvying, she might even be ready to leave for La Chèvre d'Or.

As Brassington started back into her room she saw Walter seem to stumble, then stop and lean against the corridor wall for a moment. He had raised his arm to press it against the wall, his head tucked beneath it, cheek to the paneling, as if warding off a blow.

His shoulders started to shake. Brassington realized he was crying.

As ye sow, so shall ye reap. Brassington's lips pursed tightly as she tried to smother the sudden rush within her of sympathy for the poor confused boy. He was way over his head. He was drowning in the kind of international sophistication that someone like her mistress could handle quite easily.

She watched Walter get himself under control and move off into the darkness at the far end of the hall. As ye sow, Brassington repeated soundlessly, so shall ye reap. A cruel saying.

But when was the truth anything except cruel?

Chapter 31

Jensen Blot sat on the edge of his stateroom bed and watched Elizabeth wipe off her lipstick and start over on her mouth for the third time. "Libby," he moaned, "we should be there right this minute."

"I can't get it right."

She threw down the lipstick and the mirror and stared at herself in the dressing table mirror. "My face has gone all wrong, Jess. I don't look the way I used to. It's this damned baby. There's even a name for it, the mask of pregnancy or something. A woman gets all peculiar-looking. Her features go all wrong. She becomes another person entirely."

"You can say that again," he agreed morosely.

She whirled on him. "Don't start that again, Jess. One more crack and you go to your precious party with your precious clients all by yourself."

"Is that supposed to be a threat?"

They stared at each other, each wondering if this were the inevitable moment, the ultimate argument. American couples lived in fear of such moments. With a divorce rate that effectively closed out one in every three marriages as regularly as clockwork, and with equal efficiency, American husbands and wives spent their evenings at home wondering which of the necessary domestic discussions would end up in the hands of their lawyers.

"I take it back, Lib," Jensen muttered at last. "Please get going."

She turned to the mirror and started on her mouth again. "Not that it's anything new for this voyage," she said, her words muffled slightly by her need to keep her lips motionless, "but aren't you even touchier than usual tonight? With Mr. Big off the premises, you can afford to relax. And you did most of the day."

"He's due back tonight in time for the party."

"From where?"

Jenson Blot shrugged. "Does he tell me?"

"Ali knows."

"And Ali keeps it to himself." Jensen got up and began pacing the carpeted floor. "Libby, we hit the go signal on this big dollar deal. Ali and I pulled the plug. Without consulting Kerem."

Elizabeth's hand stopped. She stared at her husband in the mirror. "Was that smart?"

"Kerem gave us power of attorney to do it whenever we got the right signal from the Basel bourse. Well, the signal came through loud and clear this morning just before lunch. So . . . we dumped."

"All those dollars?"

"Even I've lost count of how many. But it's over half a billion. Everything he could convert to cash I've converted over the last year. The only things he couldn't flog were the hotels and the bank. They're owned in Lebanon and anything you do in Lebanon gets known in hours because government officials can be bought. And are. So we had to leave his Levantine property untouched. All the rest.

though, went around noon today. The rest of it went to-night, when the markets opened in New York and Chicago. It's gone now. Every dollar's sold."

"For what?"

"Swiss francs, Deutschemarks, guilders, yen, French francs. Hell, we were even taking pounds sterling and Austrian schillings by the time we closed out the whole deal. Naturally we didn't use the Kerem name."

"And the dollar?"

Jensen shrugged again, a faintly guilty gesture for him. "We sold at the very top of the dollar's current value."

"But what about the value now?"

"Now it's night here. In Hong Kong and Tokyo they're just beginning to realize what's happened. By tomorrow morning the dealers in Basel and Amsterdam will know. It won't hit New York for almost twenty-four hours."

"And then?"

Again the furtive gesture with his shoulders and arms. "And then everybody'll know. I figure the dollar will drop at least ten percent. There hasn't been a sale like this in years. All secret, in fake names and fake corporations. Even the Russians never tried anything this big in the old days when they were trying to fuck up the dollar."

"But what the Russians didn't dare, you and Kerem had no compunction about—"

"Easy, Lib." Jensen's face had gone red. "This is business, baby. Just business. I have a job to do. I'm paid god-damned well to do it. I'm supposed to make money for my client. That's what I'm paid for. Don't forget it."

"It's hard to forget when you start reeling off numbers."

He nodded savagely. "Damned right, Libby. I figure I've made that Lebanese bastard something in the neighbor-hood of fifty million dollars today."

"Jess!"

"Well, why not? We're using half a billion plus to play with, right? And what's ten percent of that?"

234

His voice had gotten a curious defensive tone, as if the sheer numerical weight were going to be enough to justify not only this but any other deed he had in mind.

"And let's not forget one important thing," he pressed on quickly, taking advantage of his strongest suit in this game. "In addition to my drawing-account salary at the office, I get a one percent override on all profits in the Kerem portfolio. Do I have to spell that out?"

"One percent of fifty million dollars?"

He smiled at her face in the mirror, her eyes wide, half her mouth smeared red, the other half as pale as death.

"Of course we're talking in round numbers," he said, savoring the delicious delay in giving her the news. "I mean, we had to give up points here and there when we sold. And the devaluation may not reach ten percent. But on the other hand, it could drop even lower, right? And I'm not figuring what taxes I have to pay on my one percent, right?"

"Jess, in God's name!"

For the third time he gave that sneaky, half-guilty shrug, now half proud as well, and diffident as only a White Anglo-Saxon Protestant money manager can be about money.

"Oh, my take is, say, no less than . . . half a million dollars."

In the sudden quiet of the stateroom it wasn't the dollar amount that echoed in Elizabeth's ears, it was a single syllable, the word "my."

Chapter 32

"What do you think?" Jim Butler murmured uneasily in Ali's ear. The two men had left the rest of the party and moved down to the far end of the charming, old-fashioned bar that La Chèvre d'Or kept separate from its restaurant.

Ali stared at his drink. "He's been late before," he said at last. "I called the airport at Nice and they say they've received no flight plan from Athens, but that doesn't have to mean anything."

"Why not?"

Butler glanced at his watch. The sun had gone down already, flaming the Mediterranean beneath them with a hot orange that changed to crimson before it disappeared. Now the party was more than ready to move on across the court and upstairs to dinner. Everyone had had at least two drinks, some of them four or five. It was nearly ten o'clock of an August night and Kerem had yet to arrive.

"Why not?" Ali repeated, as if stalling for time. His liquid eyes, like ripe olives, shifted sideways. "With Uncle Kee one never knows. He could have flown to Milan and taken a small single-engine plane from there. Or be driving here on the autoroute. It only takes a few minutes."

"Yes, possibly." Butler agreed.

"Or he could still be in Athens," Ali concluded morosely. "There is no way of outguessing him."

"Damnably rude," Butler snapped. "And your uncle is anything but an ungracious man, Ali. I've found him the soul of friendliness and good breeding."

The nephew nodded miserably. It was obvious that he knew no more of his uncle's whereabouts than did Jim Butler. The Englishman turned to survey his guests in the half-light of flickering candles. It would be unforgivable to delay dinner much longer.

He watched the sleek, blond form of Doe Drew moving quickly from group to group. Quite an operator, that one, Butler mused. He'd never before gotten the full blast-furnace treatment from a woman determined to drive a man mad with desire and even more determined not to let him get in. She would be hell in a business deal.

Kissing, yes. God, how she had devoured him with kisses on the floor of that upstairs bedroom. And a nonstop caressing of his prick until he had to ask her to desist. And tantalizing glimpses of the promised land by the score, enough advertising to make him want to buy out the whole lot.

Which was, of course, the idea. She'd been only distantly friendly until he'd admitted he was currently single again. But, what the hell, wasn't she married to that actor? Would he *ever* understand women?

"I think we'll move up to dinner now," Jim Butler said in a carrying voice. "Our good friend Kee is delayed a bit and doesn't want us put out on his account."

He watched Doe start for him, hoping to link her arm in his for the procession to the groaning board. Instead, assuming the prerogative of the host, Butler took her sister's arm and smiled down into those great limpid violet eyes.

Her lips were soft, lovely, and the rose-peach gown seemed to ignite the pale skin over her high cheekbones with a kind of exotic reddish glow.

"You're especially lovely tonight, dear Madame French," Jim heard himself saying.

The look that slowly crossed Leslie's face was so submerged that it told him nothing. But the glances exchanged by Ali and the American moneyman, Blot, told him he'd dropped a clinker.

"Terribly sorry, my dear," Butler corrected himself. "Madame Kerem is the name you will bear down through the annals of history. It suits you."

Judi, who had attached herself to his other arm, nodded enthusiastically as a way of attracting a bit of attention to herself. "You're originally French, aren't you?" she asked Leslie.

"That was Maurice's family name. But my family was English."

Leslie glanced around the room with a lost expression, as if not sure on which of the planets she had landed. In reality, Butler saw, she was searching for that tease of a twin of hers. He wondered just how inseparable they really were.

"But, actually," she went on then after a very long pause, as if her memory had lapsed badly, "we're just pure Texas. My father's name was Miles. Captain Miles, U.S. Cavalry and the Texas Rangers."

Butler escorted both the attractive brunette and the lovely blonde out of the bar and up the stairs to dinner. "Quite a few of the old English families are French or Norman, actually," he went on, making light conversation.

"Came over at Hastings," Judi submitted as a sample of her erudition.

238

"Not my forefathers," Butler said. "All a bloody pack of Saxon savages, I should think. Probably painted blue."

"Woad?" Leslie asked.

"Ah . . . I beg your—" Butler frowned and turned to Judi for help.

"Did your Saxon fellas have horses, do you think?" she suggested.

"Doubt it," Butler responded.

"Not 'rode.'" Leslie's voice had gone throaty and muted, as if produced under the extreme pressure of shyness. "'Woad.' It's a blue dye. Body paint, you see. I'm sure our ancestors wore it." She stopped halfway up the stairs. "Isn't it?"

Butler's eyes screwed up in a movement that tried to suggest deep thought but was really his way of keeping from laughing out loud. He'd perfected it at board meetings. "Onward," he said then, urging his women ahead, "and upward."

In the *Guide Michelin* there are no stars before the full name of Le Château de la Chèvre d'Or, but there are three crossed forks, which translates in the sniffy code of the Michelin inspectors as "a very comfortable restaurant."

They have managed to squeeze out one additional, grudging statement of praise: "A picturesque site that dominates the sea." None of this prepares the casual tourist for the very excellent food served there. It is not the oversauced dishes that appeal to Michelin inspectors.

It is the *haute cuisine* of the comfortable bourgeoisie, the middle-income French families who have servants to shop daily for produce and meat brought freshly to market. It is a cuisine whose excellence is based almost entirely on undertreating ingredients, on letting the freshness and flavor be the star of the show, rather than overconcocted sauces a chef and three undercooks took days to assemble.

Yet, despite the true excellence of the food, Butler's party never really got off the ground. He had no way of knowing exactly why, except that it very much had to do with the absence of Kee Kerem.

Otherwise the mix of guests was good enough, youngsters like Ali and Judi—and the American couple—and oldsters like Kee's gambling companion, Zaki, now a bosom buddy of Jim Butler's as well. Even Elly had been invited, since she was so obviously part of the Kerem family, but she had declined at the last moment, indicating that she—or actually she and Ali—had decided one of them should be aboard the *Maria* in case any messages came through from the master.

Butler surveyed the table. He had allowed Judi to remain on his left hand and had made sure of Leslie Kerem on his right. Her sister, face set in deadpan immobility, sat across the table and pointedly addressed remarks to Butler, sending them across the flowers and napery like so many darts at a board.

Cupid's shafts they were meant to be, Butler supposed, but they had begun to have barbs on them as she realized he was determined to pay no more attention to her than to any other guest.

He wondered what Doe took him for, some sort of penis-oriented Mediterranean type, an Italian or Spaniard or Greek, who would under that kind of teasing treatment lie on his back and allow himself to be cleaned out like a corpse at a funeral parlor?

Butler frowned. He hated figures of speech like that. He hadn't yet reached his fifty-fourth birthday, but funeral parlors were no laughing matter.

For him, he realized as he sat back and surveyed his guests, a quiet woman like Leslie Kerem was entirely more suitable. She said so little, and when she did it made so little sense, that she was a positive pleasure to have on his right hand. Woad, anyone?

And now, dessert. It came as a sort of mousse made with

orange liqueur. The waiters were grave as they distributed portions of it to everyone. Judi squealed with delight as she sneaked a taste. Butler found himself enjoying Judi as he would a skittish, tomboy daughter. She was obviously no one to be serious about.

All during the party she and Ali had pointedly paid so little attention to each other that it was thoroughly obvious to everyone, or at least to Jim Butler, that the two of them had spent the late afternoon steamily pleasuring each other in some accommodation hotel in Monte Carlo where a fiver to the concierge bought peace, quiet, and discretion.

Butler found himself picturing their couplings, like illustrations from some extremely expensive book of pornography. None of it really stirred him, no more than the look and scent of Doe Drew's vulva earlier this evening.

It wasn't that Butler didn't have sex now and then, it was simply that he had assigned a lower priority to it than most other people. It was his ability to do this, he felt sure, that had made him what he was today, one of the more powerful financiers in England, a bit short of ready cash now, to be sure, but what moneyman wasn't these days?

He turned to watch Leslie Kerem on his left. Now there, Butler thought, was a great beauty who had assigned the same priority to sex as he, and profited as much thereby. She was a vision of sexual delight, but Butler had been around long enough to know that beneath the playacting exterior—a lot of it produced, coached, and directed by her sister—lay a girl who had never really been all that interested in having it off again and again and again.

Butler found himself wondering how often Kerem fucked his wife and whether he enjoyed it. To Jim Butler sex was something one did for one's health's sake. It was a quick act, like having a boil lanced. It had to be done because one's health demanded it, but one didn't have to linger unduly over it, or make a fetish of it, or assign any higher value to it than taking a good crap.

241

He smiled slightly. He had the feeling people found his smile cold. He'd been told as much by some of his wives. Yet he now found Leslie Kerem returning the smile with that full, sensuous mouth of hers, as moistly appealing as her sister's vulva had been repellent. He glanced across the table at Doe to make sure she had registered the byplay between him and her twin. Serve the bitch right.

The dessert had been cleared and coffee was being served. Since he had expected Kee Kerem, Butler had arranged to have thick Arabian coffee served, and so it was that the small espresso cups arrived, filled with grounds, ink-black liquid and the cloying sweetness of honey.

The corner of the dining room in which their party sat was a bit cut off from the rest of the place. Butler found this suitable, as he did the scene around him now, guests slowly sipping their coffee, the night outside pressing in through the glass, the corniches below like strands of diamonds in the night.

And then he heard the sound.

The flesh on his shoulders crawled at the tone of it, a moan—no, a howl of anguish. It grated in his ears like the baying of some doomed animal, powerful, laden with the woe and grief of death-in-life.

"Good God." Butler stood up. "What was that?"

Ali was on his feet, eyes wide with horror. He turned to stare at the entrance to the restaurant. There in the doorway stood Elly. From her lips the ululating sound poured like a tidal flow of utter grief.

"Elly!"

Her skirt was black, her feet bare. Her blouse had been ripped with fingers whose nails had scratched red tracks across her breasts. Her night-black hair had fallen over her eyes. Tears flowed down her face unceasingly and from her tear-wet mouth came the horrifying sound of archaic mourning.

242

Ali had dashed across the room to her. He barked dialect into her face but she remained impassive, stony, only the tears alive on her face. Then she murmured something, her eyes straight ahead, staring down the long room . . . at Leslie Kerem.

Ali's eyes bulged. His head snapped back on his neck and from his throat issued a long howl of anguish. He slammed the flat of his hand across his face. Blood spurted from his nose. He grabbed at his knit sports shirt and ripped it open across his hairy chest. In the dim light a small golden object glinted faintly there on a chain among the mossy curls of hair.

Butler was running to him now. "What's happened, old man?"

"He is dead!" Ali howled at heaven.

Butler stopped short, halfway across the room, aware as only an Englishman can be that everyone was watching the scene, perfect strangers, French, even Americans. He drew himself up.

"You mean," he began, "you don't mean—"

"The Great Whore has murdered him!" Ali howled. "She has had the last laugh. Leda has killed Zeus!"

The entire party had begun to cluster around Ali and Elly now. Elizabeth Blot stepped forward to take Elly's hand. "I'm so sorry to—"

"Unclean!" Elly screamed. Her voice seemed to peel back Butler's skin. "It was your curse that killed him! A pregnant woman! And none of us"—her voice broke pitifully—"none of us were loyal enough to warn him."

"But that's nonsense," Jensen Blot began in a businesslike voice.

"She's upset," Doe Drew suggested.

"She is right!" Ali thundered. His face was a mass of blood from his nose. The thick red stuff dripped slowly from his chin as he pushed his face forward into that of

Elizabeth Blot. "The moment we knew about you, that very instant, I should have thrown you to the sharks! Evil! Unclean! Unclean!"

His eyes turned up suddenly in his head and he collapsed on the floor in a small pool of his own blood. Elly knelt beside him, moaning and rocking his head against her breasts. Both of them were an untidy mass of blood and rent garments. The rest of the party pleaded with them, implored, begged for common sense to prevail.

Only Jim Butler stood back a yard or two from the epicenter of this wild peasant cyclone of grief. He watched for a moment, thinking quickly, but with his usual tidiness.

Then he realized one person was missing from the scene. He turned back to look at the dining table where only a moment before they had been sipping their coffee.

She sat there very erect and beautiful in her rose-peach gown, her cheeks flushed with color, her eyes wide as the sky and utterly dry. As their glances met, Leslie Miles French Kerem lifted her cup of Arab coffee and sipped it slowly, daintily, almost thoughtfully.

Chapter 33

Brassington had seen better funerals in her time.

The one for Governor French, for example, had been quite fine, if your taste ran to that sort of thing, Church of England rites in a Dallas cathedral.

But the funeral of Kemel Kerem was really quite small potatoes, when it came to that. First of all there was the quite unnecessarily large amount of trouble in getting to the tiny, sunbaked town high in the cedar-covered mountains to the east of Beirut where he had been born and had made sure his body would be laid to rest.

No trains, no airplanes, nothing but small cars could carry the funeral party in and out.

It had taken most of a day just to ferry in the widow, her sister, Brassington, that nice Mr. Butler and, of course, the whole lot of weeping, teeth-gnashing, breast-beating relatives headed by Elly—whom Brassington had once thought to have had too much good sense for such obscene displays of emotion—and Ali, who had struck himself so often in the face in the last three days that he looked as if he had been through a ten-round championship fight and lost.

There were absolutely no accommodations in the village. The people spoke some sort of barbarous dialect that not even the Levantine officials of the Kerem bank could understand.

If it hadn't been for the fact that Kerem had remodeled an ancient caravanserai, its four-domed roof like the rising teats of a mother goat, and put in some decent plumbing and electricity, there would have been no place at all to receive condolences.

Then there had been that ridiculous business with the big-shot archbishops and metropolitans who had at first refused to allow a priest to perform the necessary funeral prayers over the body of the departed.

The departed had been a very great sinner, even by standards normally applied to Levantine business successes, and should be forced to pay large sums of money to the church before his soul could be prayed into heaven. Bargaining ensued.

And, if that weren't enough, the church hijacking the Kerem family for cash, then there was the absolutely ludicrous scene over whether or not Jensen Blot and his poor, miserable pregnant wife could attend the funeral. As Kerem's right-hand financial man, Blot was locked in around-the-clock conferences with Ali and the other Lebanese. But neither Ali nor Elly—who were the chief Kerem heirs, in addition to some remote cousins—would allow Elizabeth Blot anywhere near the body of their dead master.

She had finally been installed in a suite at the Phoenicia Hotel where, Brassington supposed, she sulked away the hot days while her husband was being ferried to this tiny

246

mountain village for three days of prayer, feasting, and business bickering.

Finally, to top off the whole caricature of a funeral, there were the flocks of photographers and reporters, quite like vultures hovering overhead as a corpse putrefied or, more aptly, like flies crawling over the rotting face of carrion death.

Brassington shivered as she thought about the *paparazzi* with their telephoto lenses following her poor grieving mistress everywhere. One of them had even had the temerity to call out, in French, "Hey, Leslie baby, I've got color film. Can't you wear anything but black?"

It had drawn a hard-bitten laugh from his fellow vultures, but her mistress' face, and that of Doe, had been set in graven lines of emotionless shock. Odd how the death had taken the sister even harder than the widow, Brassington mused.

She was standing at the open window of her room in the converted Arab caravanserai, watching the funeral cortege, on foot, wind its way with its burden to the family graveyard on the rise of a hill less than a quarter of a mile away. A hot wind made the dry grass flicker. The village had produced nothing more musical for Kee Kerem's last journey than a small boy with a big drum who boomed it slowly as the pallbearers and mourners moved steadily forward up the slight hill. Above, a photo helicopter hovered in the hot sky.

Brassington observed that Mr. Butler and Sir Philip Drew were the lead bearers, one on each side, while Ali and Jensen Blot carried their burden at mid-coffin and the old gambler Zaki plus a crony of his from the village, brought up the rear of the long black box.

They moved stiffly, in time to the deep, hollow boom of the drum.

Behind them, stretching back for some distance, walked

Leslie Kerem, holding onto the arm of Elly, Doe behind her, and then a mixed party of people, most of whom Brassington didn't know. The young steward, Walter, seemed to be one of them.

Brassington turned from the window and walked down a long curving flight of stone steps to the hall where once a sheikh's entourage had eaten its meals. It was now fitted out as an immense manorial living room with sofas, chairs, tables, a great fireplace, dozens of paintings and lamps, and a Dow-Jones ticker tape and five telephones.

Judi had sunk into one of the overstuffed sofas and was glumly sipping a glass of that filthy Arab liqueur, her eyes fixed on a rather attractive young Frenchman, a reporter for one of the news syndicates, who was vainly trying to place a long-distance call from a telephone in one corner of the large hall. His common language with the operator was French, a tongue he seemed to know much better than she.

"Don't drink that muck, dear," Brassington whispered to Judi. "Rots the pipes, so it does."

Judi shrugged. "Not much else to do in this dump."

"Stick to scotch, then."

The younger woman made a face. "Ali is so changed I can't believe it. He hasn't said two words to me since that horrible night in La Chèvre d'Or. And as for Jim . . . well, between us, he's overdoing the help-the-bereaved-widow bit, ain't he?"

Brassington made a face of disapproval. She would hear nothing against her mistress, of course, but she really didn't like Judi "talking fresh" about that nice Mr. Butler, either. "He's only doing what a gentleman would do," she said, sitting down beside Judi.

"Merde!" the French journalist shouted into the telephone.

"He's doing a whole bloody hell of a lot more than a gentleman would do," Judi murmured in Brassington's ear.

"And, as for me, you'd think I'd picked up a case of lepro-sy or something. Hasn't said two words to me since that horrible—"

"I thought that was Ali."

Judi nodded, sniffed, and gulped a bit more of the anise-flavored liqueur. "The both of them. I'm off limits or something."

Brassington considered the situation. "Cheer up, dear," she said then. "Your young man has just inherited a great fortune, you know, as has my lady, too. It's enough to turn anybody stone solemn. He'll be back sniffing around again."

"And Jim?"

"Forget Mr. Butler," Brassington advised her. "He was never for you."

"Too right."

They sat quietly for a while, listening to the faraway boom of the drum. "You're wrong about Ali inheriting that much," Judi said then.

"I understood—"

"The papers have it all ballsed up, as usual," Judi told her. "He's Kee Kerem's Levantine heir, he and Elly. They get whatever the old man owned in Beirut, some hotels, I gather, and the bank. It's a lot, but there's quite a bit more."

"Why do you say that, dear?"

"I keep my ears open," Judi explained. "I heard that Blot fella talking about it with his wife back at the Sands hotel the day before yesterday. And I heard Ali moaning about it to Blot again just this morning. Some long string of complaints about dollar sales or something."

Brassington shook her head. "Dollar sales? It doesn't make sense."

Judi sighed. "He was accusing Blot of something. Every-thing being in fake names or something and only Blot hav-ing the official signature to release the funds."

Boom. boom. Boom.

The two British women sat more quietly now in the deep recesses of the upholstered sofa and idly watched the attractive young Frenchman going noisily insane over the telephone. In the distance, growing fainter all the time, the funeral drum faded slowly from their consciousness, and so did the funeral.

Only the faraway *pock-pock* of the photo helicopter could be heard, like the rapping noise in a wall when a death-watch beetle is hard at work.

Chapter 34

It was, Jim Butler decided, in its own strange and exotic way, a fitting funeral for a great man. There was certain dignity in having it here, on a dust-dry hill, under a broiling Levantine sun, the long, liquid, glottal syllables of the priest's prayer rolling forward like some barbaric chant beneath the stutter of the helicopter.

Butler was impressed. He was also impressed by the way Leslie Kerem handled herself. It was true that she rarely showed much emotion. That was, in fact, her secret charm, the sense of her not really being anywhere at all.

And, he reminded himself as the liturgy droned on, it was not as if Leslie weren't well prepared by fate for the role of the widow.

She was, in fact, on somewhat intimate terms with death, even though this was only the second husband she had buried. He had to give her credit, though. This had been the most confusing three days he'd spent in a long time. He had often enough regretted his decision to stay with the funeral party instead of doing a bunk. The whole thing simply wasn't Jim Butler's style, but neither was deserting a friend's widow in her hour of bereavement.

And what confusing hours these had been. First there had been all that business between Ali and Jensen Blot. Then there had been Blot's sudden fit of contrition just last night, in which he'd knocked on Butler's door almost precisely at the stroke of midnight and wanted to come in and talk, one Anglo-Saxon Protestant moneyman to another.

But what he'd had to say had been even more surprising than the hour he'd chosen for confession, or the fact that he'd picked Jim Butler as father confessor. The whole sordid story of the Kerem raid on the dollar had come out in one long blurt. And the ending had been a shocker for which even Butler hadn't been prepared.

It was not outside his experience in the world of finance that some exceedingly big bird like Kerem would foul his own nest in order to pull off a stroke worth fifty million dollars, with risk held to an absolute minimum. Nor was it surprising, in the dicey state of the dollar, that his raid had dropped the currency not ten but, by Blot's current reckoning, damned near 15 percent, panicking Washington, D.C.

But the part that really threw Butler into quiet convulsions was the use of what the financial fraternity called "street names," fake fronts of convenience to keep the Kerem name out of the buy-sell transactions. Precisely because of that, Ali's name couldn't be used either, since it was the same as his uncle's. It was the hitherto little-known name of Jensen Blot that now controlled the various spurious corporate shells through which the profits from the dollar raid could be reclaimed.

The hellish responsibility of it had finally cracked through Blot's normal professional façade and, near panic from the constant pressure being applied by Ali, he'd come to Butler, as a notable Anglo-Saxon Protestant money manager, for advice.

"What should you do?" Butler had replied when the last of the confessional had dropped from Blot's lips. "Sit tight, for one thing. Keep your nerve, for another. And for a third, don't tell another soul, you idiot."

Chastened, Jensen Blot had done his best to lay the whole thing in the capacious, fatherly lap of the great Jim Butler, England's foremost financial wizard. Butler had seemed to refuse custody.

"We'll work it out," he'd said, being as deliberately vague as he could manage. "You'll be taken care of properly, at any rate. One percent of it isn't enough to pay you, you know. If I have anything to say about it," Butler fantasized, hooking Blot firmly on his line, "you'll get ten percent of the proceeds and not a penny less."

Elly stepped forward suddenly in the dazzling sunlight, arm in arm with Leslie. They stopped, picked up handfuls of the dusty earth, and let the dirt fall into the grave to scatter over the black face of the coffin.

Elly broke down then, ripping at the heavy veil over her face, sobbing and clutching blindly at Leslie, who led her back from the lip of the grave and turned her over to Ali.

She stood alone now, the widow. Not even her sister, Doe, arm firmly imprisoned in her husband's grasp, could come to her side. Jim Butler watched the dry, hot wind tug at the veil over the lovely face of Leslie Kerem.

Then, moving solemnly as befits a close friend of the bereaved—one who planned very shortly to become an even closer friend—the financial wizard closed in on Leslie and took her soft dry hand in his.

They stood there, shoulder to shoulder, as the gravediggers began to bury the man who had once been Kemal Kerem.

Chapter 35

In a week the world had practically forgotten the whole thing.

The lawyers had all gone under cover. The principal players had left, the Drews for London, Judi and Ali for Monte Carlo, Elizabeth Blot for New York.

Elly had remained behind in the great caravanserai high in the eastern mountains. She was planning to turn it into a museum or shrine. In Paris, Leda Lambros was cutting an album of political songs, featuring her new guitar player.

Brassington had been shipped ahead to Texas to await her mistress, who was somewhere in Switzerland. Some said Gstaad, but there was no sign of her there, even in the villa Kerem had owned.

Jim Butler, too, was in Switzerland, people said, with Leslie Kerem, but there was no proof. In point of fact, Jensen Blot was also in Switzerland, but made frequent business trips for a day to nearby Liechtenstein.

In a week or two he had transferred every cent of the dollar deal—well over half a billion plus profits—into a series of trusts that could only be unlocked by the widow or by her official financial executor, Jim Butler. Blot was now employed by the Butler organization as an executive vice-president. He planned to get back to New York shortly but, as it worked out, he didn't return until after the birth of his son six months later. Mother and child were doing fine.

In a week or less after the funeral, if one didn't count the other Kerem relatives or the Lebanese officials of his banking and hotel interests, only one of the entire party that had been so gay aboard the *Maria* was left behind in Beirut. He was the steward, Walter.

In that week, or perhaps a bit more, Doe Drew had slipped out of London and joined her sister in Switzerland. They went everywhere together, totally incognito for at least three days until the *paparazzi* found them again. Jim Butler managed to stay out of camera range. He was really much better at it than either of the two sisters. His wedding to Leslie wouldn't take place until the following June, but for all intents and purposes, since she had a total lock on the Kerem fortune, so did he.

Only Walter remained, but not for long.

The day Leslie left for Switzerland, he had wandered around her deserted suite atop the Phoenicia Hotel. He had found a wadded-up pair of panty hose, black, left over from the funeral. She had put a run in them kneeling to pick up a clod of dirt to drop on her husband's coffin.

Pressing the panty hose to his lips, Walter had gone out on the balcony that overlooked the city of Beirut.

When he hit the pavement twelve floors below, the hose were still pressed to his lips. His body remained in Beirut until a member of his family arrived to take it on back the long journey to Germany for burial.

Lambton, Anne
The sisters.

pain received. What was it? His heart was beating faster suddenly. The look of pain . . . of pain inflicted and . . . and enjoyed?

"That will be all, Walter. Thank you."

He walked slowly back down the long carpeted corridor in the direction of the galley. He realized that beneath the Kerem uniform—white cotton trousers, white shirt, and black belt—his muscles were tensed, as if to receive a blow. He longed to light a cigarette. But no crew members might smoke except within the confines of the mess and Walter was on call until after lunch had been served.

There must be some way around the rule, he was thinking. If he were regularly to see Leslie Kerem stretched out in bed each morning, asking him to perform minor chores that gave him a direct look at her softly rounded, tanned body, he would somehow have to find a way to sneak a calming smoke.

By the time he arrived in the galley, the chef was at work preparing a buffet lunch.

"How's Brünnhilde?" The stocky little chef, his left hand covered in shredded ham, winked at him.

"Telephoning her sister." Walter helped himself to a slice of ham. "Christ, I'd give anything for a cigarette."

Privately he cringed at how crude his countrymen could be. He hated the way they referred to Leslie Kerem with a bear-garden vulgarity to express how all of them felt about an attractive women. Naturally, with his actor's good looks, Walter was taken as one of them.

"What's all this about a gale force nine?"

"You get sick?" the chef asked.

"Hell, no." Walter lapsed into his newly acquired American. "But the man in the radio room said we were heading for a real storm."

"Can't happen soon enough. By this time tomorrow we'll be serving only cups of Bovril. Imagine"—the chef brandished his knife dangerously near Walter's left ear—

"during the bloody season I'm preparing Lebanese specialties for him, low-calorie dishes for Brünnhilde, German grub for the fucking captain, and Christ knows what when a fancy guest comes aboard. And to cap it all Mabel, the Brassing-Ass, only eats grilled sole and honey sandwiches. Honey sandwiches, imagine? I tell you, sweetie, you've got it made, handing the trays and the cocktails."

Walter made a disgusted face. It was only a matter of time before one of the German crew made the first pass at him. It would come from someone higher in rank than the chef, of course, but it had to happen.

A picture flickered through his mind of Leslie Kerem, naked on that immense yellow bed. Dear God, this voyage was not going to be any picnic, was it?

Chapter Four

The telephone pealed through the Drew penthouse. Brassington, who had been enjoying the *Tonight* program on television, switched off the set before crossing the room to answer it. But apparently she was moving too slowly.

From the open bathroom door came the irate voice of Lady Drew. "For God's sake, Brassington, answer the phone."

About to lift the receiver, Brassington allowed the telephone to ring once more. Somehow Mrs. Kerem's sister had to learn that she couldn't be treated like some ordinary cleaning woman. Brassington pursed her lips, took a long composing breath, and waited yet another moment before saying into the reciever in her grandest voice: "The Drew residence."

"We have a call from the ship *Maria*. Will you please hold the line?"

Brassington laid the receiver on its side. Slowly she

33

walked across the living room to the steaming bathroom door. Her nose wrinkled. Gales of strong-smelling pine scent were wafting through the flat.

"You sister is calling." Brassington looking straight in front of her to avoid the sight of a naked woman. The woman must have tipped at least half a bottle of essence into the bath, judging by the smell.

"Is she actually holding on or is it just that crackling business?"

"The latter, Madame."

"Okay. Go back and hold on. I'll get dry."

Brassington returned at a leisurely pace to the writing desk. From past experience she knew that a ship-to-shore call could take anything up to an hour before both parties were actually on the line and talking. Then, as often as not, the line would continue to emit a series of crackles and long intervals of humming before a nearly unrecognizable voice could be heard at the other end.

Such telephone calls were a ridiculous waste of time and money. Yet Mrs. Kerem persisted in trying to speak to her sister wherever she happened to be, and regardless of the time—every morning of her life, on waking. Of course, it wasn't Brassington's place to help either twin save money. Madame Kerem had it to spare, naturally, and so did Lady Drew, who probably made more through her dress designs and jeweled accessories than did her talented husband. Brassington adored Philip Drew in any of his plays, but what actor, even one who'd been knighted, could ever earn enough to compare with the ancestral wealth and go-getting enterprise of his wife?

Brassington looked at her watch and guessed the time aboard the *Maria* to be between eleven and twelve.

Doe Drew appeared at her side, reeking of pine. She had draped herself in a deep-purple bath towel, her corn-silk-blond hair piled on top of her head and secured by a couple of pins. She was without a trace of makeup, her